To Mary,
A wonderful friend.
God's Blessings

One Step To Murder

Auntie Rejoice Murder Mysteries

Much Love
Sade A...

Sade Akisanya

Bloomington, IN   authorHOUSE™   Milton Keynes, UK

AuthorHouse™
1663 Liberty Drive, Suite 200
Bloomington, IN 47403
www.authorhouse.com
Phone: 1-800-839-8640

AuthorHouse™ UK Ltd.
500 Avebury Boulevard
Central Milton Keynes, MK9 2BE
www.authorhouse.co.uk
Phone: 08001974150

First published by AuthorHouse   3/23/2006

ISBN: 1-4259-0878-0 (sc)

Printed in the United States of America
Bloomington, Indiana

This book is printed on acid-free paper.

"I am the Immaculate Conception"
- Lourdes, 1858

In Memory of Peter and Modupe Akisanya

ONE

Rejoice Akintola was regarded an oddball by neighbours in a village full of weirdos.

The early morning was her favourite period. At this time of day she felt like a young bird taking flight.

It was 5.15 a.m. and as usual Rejoice, a cardigan thrown over her slim shoulders to ward off the cold, was on her way to her teaching job at St Mary's Catholic school, with its blue uniform and white edging, the only school in the village.

On either side of the road, as she walked, trees and shrubs twisted and danced in the early morning breeze throwing eerie shadows across her path. This was to become an evil omen for what was to come. Walking allowed her time for reflection.

A black leather bag dangled from her left shoulder. The bag, bulging from side to side containing teaching notes and books on her three main classes, history, literature and biology, hung from her shoulder like the abdomen of a pregnant black goat.

Rejoice loved her pupils and loved the school. St Mary's was such a happy school to work, for staff and pupils. The only fly in the palm oil was Mr Charles Dumbe, the deputy Head, who appeared to hate children.

Rejoice couldn't have walked more than five minutes to the T- Junction where tree- lined Luggard Crescent joined noisy Agege Motor Road, when her eyes caught sight of a glinting clay bowl, a gift to the gods, illuminated by the street lamp, measuring not more than ten inches by eight about two inches deep, on the opposite side of the road, under an oak tree. She looked both ways for approaching vehicles before realising that, at that time of day cars hardly ever turned off main roads into residential streets. She crossed the road and made her way to the clay bowl. It was piled high with foodstuffs. She stood looking down at it. There were pieces of unpeeled and uncooked white yam. The gods obviously ate everything including the hard skin. In the bowl were also two hard-boiled eggs, pieces of cola-nuts, and a white pigeon with bulging eyes, its throat slashed, its head hanging loosely from its tiny body. All these were swimming in blood and palm oil. The teacher stoops down to take a closer look at the contents of the clay bowl. Her eyes popped as she saw clotted blood around a dark object. She was drawn even closer as if propelled by a flesh magnet to the bowl. Something evil, apart from the pigeon, was in the centre of the piled up food, oil, and blood, something dark and fleshy. She looked closer still, then let out a huge gasp. Breath stuck in her throat, her eyes widened unbelieving. She looked again blinking, to make sure her eyes weren't playing tricks on her. The gruesome object in the middle of the bowl embedded in food and gore, was a fleshy heart. Her scientific instinct told her it looked human. Was it a human heart? She asked herself and rose to her feet from the squatting position then bent down again, not knowing what to do, her kneel- length skirt touching the untamed sandy sidewalk.

If it was human, it meant one poor soul, usually a child, pregnant or breastfeeding woman had recently been killed in the village. Her eyes roamed the street. It was dark, eerie and lonely except for the occasional passing cars on Agege Motor Road.

When her eyes settled back on the bowl again she felt an urgent urge to pick up the heart for further examination, perhaps she could take it to her friend, a pathologist at the General Hospital for analysis for DNA testing. The clay bowl was an offering to the gods, she thought, similar bowls but not so gory, were often seen at road junctions, crossroads or reputed mythical open places where the gods could access them. Perhaps the gods couldn't see in the dark or round corners, she concluded. Her mind raced to the past.

In the old days human offerings were deemed necessary to placate the gods. Today, the practice of human sacrifice was unacceptable and illegal but not completely eradicated. Almost everyone, in time gone by, could relate stories of witchdoctors kidnapping and killing innocent women and children as offerings to the gods, in the erroneous believe it gave them and their clients potent power. There were many and varied gods. There were the gods of iron, thunder, the sea, trees, clay, and many more ancestral gods. Perhaps the ungodly aspect of this was that, villagers who proclaimed themselves Christians did not follow The Christ but often worshiped these false gods.

In Aina village it was taboo to scrutinise or touch a bowl of offering for fear of bringing down a curse of misfortune or even death on one's head. Rejoice recognised it at once. This here was a bowl of sacrifice, an offering to the gods. She paused for a moment of reflection. Suddenly a funny sensation overcame her. She felt a pair of eyes watching her every move but saw no one. It was that instance when internal alarm bell began to ring loudly telling of lurking danger. She couldn't explain it, there was no other soul about. Her head felt double its size, as a cold breeze swept over her, her breathing became rapid. She pulled her cardigan tightly round her. There was always a chill in the air in Aina village in early morning, today was no exception as in the rest of Lagos State. It allowed for a progressively and unbearably hot day. By early evening the sun's energy would be flagging and it would turn cool and tolerable again. But Rejoice knew it wasn't that cold to warrant the chill she felt.

Every cell in her body urged her to flee the scene and set off for school, that's what any sensible person would do, she thought. There was a possibility that the jujuman, she had no doubt it was the witchdoctor, who placed the clay bowl there was still lurking in the background. Her mind raced to the one person in the village who could go and had gone this far, using human parts as offerings to the gods. That person was Pa Jibiti, the village's evil jujuman and herbalist and his two satanic sons. Suspicion was rife in the village that Jibiti and his sons made human sacrifices. But the village's Police Inspector in charge was under Pa Jibiti's thumb. No one would testify against him for fear of retribution. I will expose his wrong- doings, God willing, Rejoice thought. If Pa Jibiti and his sons were left to continue in their murderous ways, she and every woman in the village were unsafe and any one of them could be his next victim.

Rejoice shrugged her shoulders and told herself she was being paranoid. She rose from her stooping position, opened her handbag, brought out an A-4 cellophane bag containing some papers, and a white cotton handkerchief.

She removed the papers and returned them to her bag. She folded the cloth into four and wrapped it round the fingers of her right hand, then used it to pick up the heart which radiated warmth through the cloth, a confirmation that it was recently removed from its host. The blood clot around it appeared fresh. She concluded the murder of its host must have been committed within the midnight hours. As she picked up the heart, a terrible squealing noise rented the air. She jumped up with fright, dropping the heart back into the bowl. Her own heart thumping, she took a quick glance around her. No one to be seen. As she gulped air to steady her nerve, a silhouetted object filtered through the branches of the oak tree across her view.

Through half closed eyes, she glanced up and saw a white bird perched on the tree branch almost directly overhead, looking like a decoration on a Christmas tree.

The bird seemed to be swaying with the movement of the breeze. It would be regarded as very beautiful were it not for the unexpected supernatural quality of the occasion. The bird flapped its wings and started descending for a few seconds, that seemed like hours, Rejoice thought it was going to attack her. The shoulder- length plaited hair at the back of her neck pricked, as if ten thousand volts electric shock had just ran through her. The bird suddenly stopped a few feet away from her face. Suspending itself in mid-air the bird starred at the slim figure of the teacher for few seconds as if challenging her to a duel, then soared into the darkened sky and disappeared.

Rejoice crossed herself and recited the Hail Mary then bent down again to pick the flesh. She wrapped the heart in the handkerchief then wrapped it again in the sheets of papers she'd torn from an exercise book, to stop drips of blood and oil into her books. She dropped the parcel in the cellophane before tucking it into her overflowing bag. During the morning she would find time to take it to the Lagos General Hospital and have it confirmed as human. She was not really sure if and how she could prove Pa Jibiti and his murderous sons guilty of the murder of the heart's host but she would try. She decided she had to try, someone had to care, she thought. She reminded herself that there was danger in taking the heart to school. She had to be very careful not to let anyone in school discoverer what's in her possession, or she would be accused of taking part in an un-Christian and abominable ritual.

An accusation of witchcraft was levelled against the deputy Headmaster for much less. Mr Dumbe had sent a pupil to fetch something from his cabinet in the staff room. The boy had seen a clay bowl with a smearing of palm oil. That was enough for the rumour to take root and germinate. Mr Dumbe was a wizard, period! Nothing had been proven but the mud had stuck.

As she walked with trepidation to school, Rejoice was unsure what she dreaded more, the heart being discovered in her bag and the accusation of taking part in satanic ritual or discovering that the heart in her possession might be confirmed as human, brutally hacked out of a woman's or child's body.

Two

No matter how early she arrived at school Rejoice found the Headmaster, Mr. Jaiye always beat her to it. She thought Mr Jaiye was a kind and humble man unlike his deputy, Charles Dumbe who despised the sight of children.

As Rejoice pushed open one half of the wooden double doors that led into the main corridor of the school, the first person she saw walking away, his back to her, was none other than the Headmaster himself. She panicked, froze and nearly fainted. On her way to school she had let her imagination ran away with her, thinking all sorts of heart thumping calamities. Suppose the heart she'd picked up fell out of her bag in front of the school assembly at 7:45 a. m. Suppose fellow teachers searching her bag to borrow a pen, as she'd done herself, found the raw flesh? Suppose a pupil ran into and knocked her over, tipping the contents of her bag out? Suppose- - . Seeing Mr Jaiye brought it all flooding back.

The last time she felt such panic was when she was informed by her aunt, at a young age, that her parents were killed in a motor accident, that her aunt was not really her mother. She panicked then, not knowing where she fits in, in the scheme of things. She'd always regarded her father's sister as her real mother. It was a shock then; it would be a shock now for a good Christian girl like her to be regarded as a ritual murderer. The brain is a funny instrument, it could lift you up by thinking positively yet, send you into a misery pit by harping on past bad memories, if you let it, she thought. Rejoice didn't want Mr Jaiye to see her this way, all sweaty and panicky, relinquishing her usual regal poise.

As she tried to escape into the hiding place of the nearest classroom off the corridor, the bag strap slipped from her shoulder and the bag fell to the floor with a loud thud. Her heart stopped when the Headmaster turned 180 degrees to see where the loud noise was coming from. His face lighted up as he saw her. Rejoice was his best and favourite teacher.

"Rejoice! Good morning!" he beamed, stopping still, waiting for her to catch up with him. Her eyes glazed downwards to the floor. The cellophane was open, the macabre parcel in her bag with a splash of blood had spilled onto the shinning polished wooden floor. Her mouth fell open; her eyes fixed themselves on the contents of her bag on the floor. Rejoice swiftly replaced the heart into the cellophane and stuffed it back into her bag. As she did so she heard, rather than saw the Headmaster's footsteps walking towards her. As he drew nearer, perplexed at her silence, he called again. "Rejoice! Are you O.K?" She felt beads of sweat covering her brow and wondered whether he would believe what she'd just been through. She decided not to chance it, and to keep her own counsel until she got the pathology report. She quickly placed both feet on top of the bloody spot on the ground before looking up with a broad smile. "Morning Headmaster. I'm all right, just out of breath!" After they exchanged greetings, the Head was soon on his way, while Rejoice entered the nearest classroom on her right, to recover. She took a few deep breaths, relieved the room was empty. She gave the Headmaster a few minutes to disappear into his office, before emerging from her hiding place with an old cloth duster to wipe the blood on the ground, binning the bloody cloth. Then she walked quietly to her room further up the same corridor, a few doors from the Headmaster's office. There, she sank into her chair, resting the bag gingerly against a table leg on the uncarpeted floor. To calm herself, as she always did at times of stress, she quietly recited the Hail Mary. Slowly all the tension left her and she began planning for her first lesson.

Through the window of the classroom Rejoice Akintola could be seen chalking up dates on the blackboard for her history class. Pausing between writing to mull over the right time to escape from school and go to pathology department at the General Hospital to hand over her discovery. She must do this before the heart started decomposing in the progressing heat wave.

'1914 – Lord Luggard, a British man, divided Nigeria into three main regions, representing the three main tribes, Yoruba, Ibo, and Hausa tribes. 1960 – Nigeria's Independence from Britain- - Chief Obafemi Awolowo, Azikwe, Sultana of Sokoto – great men who fought hard for freedom'

She suddenly paused, her chalk in mid air, as the classroom door burst open and a seven year old boy, Ayo Dipe, ran bare footed into the room crying.

"Auntie Rejoice! Auntie Rejoice!" he sobbed. (At St. Mary's it was the custom to address every female teacher as Auntie, followed by their first names, so as not to differentiate between married and single women, removing the stigma villagers attached to spinsterhood).

"What's the matter Ayo? You're too early for class-" the teacher began but was interrupted by the child.

"Yes Auntie Rejoice. I try to wake my mother but she won't answer. I try getting ready for school. Called my mother but she don't wake up, Auntie Rejoice! She don't answer me! A knife is in her chest Auntie Rejoice! Blood, blood, all over the mat!" the boy panted between sobs. This was a new phenomenon for Rejoice. It's not everyday a pupil rushed to her screaming murder. But Rejoice was an optimist, believing every problem had a solution. This surely would be no different, she thought.

"Calm down Ayo. Every problem has a solution. Let's go see the Headmaster"

Auntie Rejoice placed the chalk on her desk and clapped the chalk dust from her fingers. She walked the child to the office of Mr Jaiye. His yellow door was shut. Mr Jaiye was sitting at his desk breakfasting before settling down to a long and busy morning.

Auntie Rejoice tapped gently on the door bearing a plaque in big black lettering.

'Mr Jaiye BSc. (Hons.) MSc. MA., Headmaster'. The voice of Mr Jaiye boomed out.

"Enter!" Mr Jaiye, looking smart in a light blue short sleeved shirt and navy cotton trousers, was sitting at his wooden desk, a flask of coffee on the desk by his right hand, a plate of moyinmoyin (bean cake) in front of him. He was sipping the hot coffee from the flask cover.

"You meet me well. Come and join me in this meal?" Mr Jaiye said. He was a generous man normally but a little reluctant to share his meal, prepared by his young wife, also a teacher in the same school. Moyinmoyin was one of his most favourite foods. 'Meet me well' is a customary saying among the Yorubas of Nigeria, inviting strangers or friends to partake in their meals. Only this time Mr Jaiye didn't mean it but would have consented if they'd joined him. It was the custom after all, to share what you possessed. The major problem with this philanthropic tradition was with the never-do-well, bloodsucking, parasitic relatives who abused this wonderful custom. It seemed genetically programmed into their brains to pay visits at meal times and descend on working relatives, bringing stories of monetary woes, a day after pay-days.

Rejoice wasn't hungry, she never breakfasted. But Ayo's mouth was already watering at the sight and smell of the food. Custom demanded the adult spoke not the child, unless specifically addressed.

"No thank you sir. I bring Ayo to see you-" replied Auntie Rejoice.

"He's a bit early for school isn't he? How's your mother?" the Headmaster cut in, chewing his food loudly.

"He said he couldn't wake his mother. It sounds as if-" Auntie Rejoice left the boy and moved closer to Mr Jaiye whispering "It sounds as if the mother is dead sir. Ayo said there's a knife in her chest. I think we need to help him, call the police perhaps? There's no other adult in the house. The mother had a six week old baby-"

"Mama Ayo? The same Mama Ayo? Your mother? Dead?" Mr Jaiye appeared shocked, forgetting the uncertainty of the little boy. The Head temporarily stopped chewing, his brow furrowed, his eyes saucer-wide in disbelieve.

The Headmaster's apparent intimate knowledge of the deceased surprised Auntie Rejoice. No one in the school, except her, knew the boy's mother enough to be that shocked or saddened by her death. Ayo was one of the pupils she mentored. Pupils in the school were divided into groups. Every teacher (except Charles Dumbe who refused) was mentor to a group. The Headmaster got involved only if teachers drew his attention to a particular problem pupil. Ayo had never been a problem.

"You knew Mama Ayo well sir?" Auntie Rejoice said. The Headmaster glanced over their heads to look out of the window to the sunflower plants dancing in the breeze, and the darkened sky, avoiding eye contact with his teacher. For a moment the thought crossed Auntie Rejoice's mind that the Head might be hiding more than a close acquaintance with Mama Ayo. Is there more than he let on?

Words were zooming round in Auntie Rejoice's head but she wouldn't allow bad thoughts to germinate in her mind. After all Mr Jaiye was a good man, a kind gentle soul who wouldn't hurt a fly. Unlike Mr Dumbe who was typical of the less intelligent but educated types. Puffed up and pompous, they went around boasting 'Do you know who I am?' whenever they couldn't get their way. Auntie Rejoice thought engineers were the worse, always adding 'Engr' or something like that, after their names. Most people thought it was a sign of flawed thinking or inferiority complex. The Headmaster cleared his throat and chose his words carefully before speaking.

"We all knew Mama Ayo. Boy!" Mr Jaiye said awkwardly then silence. He left his food, walked round his desk to stand in front of the boy, before speaking again. Ayo's eyes fixed themselves on the Head's shinning brown leather shoes.

"Where's your new baby sister?" Mr Jaiye said suddenly, making the boy jump.

"Baby boy sir. The baby sleep beside my mama" Ayo replied timidly.

Why did he say baby girl instead of baby boy? Was he trying too hard to mislead his teacher? Auntie Rejoice thought quietly.

"Dear me! Shall I go sir? My only problem is I have an eight o'clock class-" Auntie Rejoice said, weighing up what to do. The Headmaster gave a solution.

"I'll get someone to take your class, don't worry about that. Take him home. Such a pity-" said the Headmaster. No sooner had he said this than Rejoice remembered the flesh in her handbag. She was happy to be leaving the school, it would mean going to the General Hospital without giving a reason for her absence. But going to the child's home would delay the heart in her bag reaching pathology department. She wondered how long it took for flesh to start decomposing in the heat. She decided she would go to Ayo's house after she'd deposited the flesh in her bag at the hospital. She tried to give the Head an excuse to take Ayo home later.

"I'll take Ayo home a little later on, after-" she was interrupted by the Head.

"No, take him now, don't worry. I'll take care of your classes. Take him home, Ayo is one of the brightest boys in school and among the best behaved. Let me know the result." Mr Jaiye said, turning away from the window he walked back to his desk and continued his breakfast. Nothing puts Mr Jaiye off his food, yet he remained as thin as a tree branch. For a Headmaster of a small village school he was a cultured man. He got his first degree in English at the University of Lagos and his subsequent degrees in chemistry and psychology at Abeokuta in Ogun State. He'd been Headmaster of St Mary's for the last five years and had seen the school progressed to be one of the best in Nigeria.

Auntie Rejoice gave and explained to Mr Jaiye her Lesson Plan and what she hoped her pupils would achieve by the end of that day. She'd learned how to do this at the Lagos Teacher Training College, a place she proudly proclaimed to have given her some of the happiest years of her life after leaving Goldsmiths College in London.

Mr Jaiye commended her on her diligent work ethic, as she left his office.

Head swirling with ideas on how to get to the General Hospital as soon as possible, she left the office with Ayo by her side.

As they emerged from the Headmaster's office they ran into his deputy, Mr Charles Dumbe, his beer-belly leading his feet, was walking towards them. He beckoned them with a thick sausage- like finger to approach him. They were about ten feet away when he barked in his rough sandy voice, "I see you've been to see the Head. What have you done now, naughty boy! You-"

"I, I-" Ayo sniffed, unable to bring out the words, for fear of saying the wrong thing and being punished. Regarding Ayo through narrow black eyes, Dumbe's breath grew rapid with hatred. He had always disliked what he called goody- goody people. The two people now facing him included. His fellow teachers were beyond bullying so he took it out on the pupils.

"Stop sniffling! You are not a baby, boy!" Dumbe spat. He'd never cared to mentor any of the pupils. His colleagues often wondered why he'd chosen to work with young people. His arrogance annoyed Auntie Rejoice. "Can't you see the boy's upset?" she said.

"What has he got to be upset about? The boy is lazy-" replied Dumbe.

"He's not sure what happened to his mother. Mama Ayo won't wake up, if you know what that means-"

"Poo! Women are lazy! A kick in the backside usually works!" Charles Dumbe cut in.

"You are so- - so- the boy is upset. The mother has a knife in-" she was interrupted again.

"So, are you calling the police?" Dumbe asked, laughing loudly, an attitude Auntie Rejoice regarded as odd in the circumstances.

"I don't know yet." She replied without expanding on her statement.

"I must go out!" Dumbe announced as he rushed out to his car, opened the door and got into the driver's seat. They watched as he drove out of the school's gate.

Rejoice too was on her way to see the dead body of, apparently, a brutally murdered woman, with Ayo clinging on to her hand tightly.

THREE

Ayo Dipe's house was only half a mile away from St. Mary's and he always walked to school. He was one of the lucky ones who lived nearer the school. Some children walked four miles on foot and still managed to be punctual for school assembly.

Auntie Rejoice and Ayo walked through the rickety school gates where Pa Hamed, a stick in hand, to give him a threatening demeanour against naughty pupils, stood guard overseeing who went in and who came out. He greeted Auntie Rejoice with "Welcome Auntie" for the second time within minutes and she responded by nodding her head and muttering 'E karo o' (good-morning).

Auntie Rejoice was not in possession of a car. She sold her last car years ago, hated driving in Lagos traffic, she and Ayo started off on foot.

For people who walked everywhere it took them no time at all. It was still early and dark but villagers were already waking up to their tasks, sweeping the yards, bathing small children by waterless taps, ferrying vegetables and fruits to the markets or catching buses to their offices in the city centre. Behind the walls of most houses smoke could be seen rising from wood or coal fires as breakfast was being prepared. Rejoice never ceases to be amazed at the courage of Nigerians to cope with the Herculean task of eking out existence from hard labour, in spite of the government's indifference to their sufferings.

Auntie Rejoice and her ward tottered along untamed bush roads, watching and picking their path carefully so as not to step on a sleepy snake. Though it was unusual for sensible snakes to make early appearance, you just never know. They walked pass men with hoes slung over their shoulders on the way to cultivate their small farms. They passed Ma Kudirat's 'Allah de' food buka (canteen) where labourers were beginning to gather for their breakfast. There were shops selling melt-in- the- mouth home made sweets, great temptation to pupils. The smell of hot fresh bread, meat stew, monyinmoyin and dodo (fried plantain) waffling in the air reminded Ayo of his empty stomach. The smell of alluring food combined in mid- air with the disgusting odour of stagnant water in dirty gutters and the pong of sheep's and goats' deposit in nearby bush. Like any child, Ayo's sense of smell picked up only food aroma. Next to Ma Kudirat's buka were mineral bukas, displaying all soft drinks at prices much higher than the open market prices at Agege Motor Road or even at the supermarket on Ikeja Road. Prices of goods were higher nearer the school, especially at month end when salaries were paid. Workers were always at the mercy of traders. Prices went up at a sniff of pay award talks, and higher still by four hundred percent rise or more, after actual pay awards. Traders erroneously believed teachers were extremely well paid.

The 'God Sees All' bicycle repair shop took a bigger space than his custom seemed to demand. The most fashionable and best-kept shop in the area was that of Ma Taiwo, the dressmaker with her three apprentices, who considered herself a friend of Auntie Rejoice, which conferred a higher status on the dressmaker. Ma Taiwo was already opening up her shop for business when Auntie Rejoice and her ward walked by. Both ladies exchanged greetings. Auntie Rejoice would occasionally be cornered into a chat but not this time. "I'll see you later" she waved and continued on her way. "Come in for five minutes! I've got ice-cold palmwine in the fridge! " The dressmaker shouted at the teacher's back. Auntie Rejoice turned her head back over a shoulder, "Too early for that! I shall see you later." she replied. Ma Taiwo was always in the middle of a family crisis. This time, her husband had just taken a new girlfriend and her eldest son was about to make an official marriage proposal to one of his many girlfriends, to the dismay of his mother who preferred an older girl from a wealthy family. Ma Taiwo had a lot to talk about.

A few paces away from the shops were some Hausa mallams, from the north wearing long white robes, their mouths red from chewing cola nuts, who had brought their wares south to sell, sat within long bushes minding their goats and sheep. Auntie Rejoice glanced at the animals, scattered widely, chewing on long grasses. 'Nature's own lawnmowers' she thought as she and the boy walked by them. It was a little light relief for a heavy heart. She knew, from the boy's description that his mother was dead and was dreading seeing the body. Auntie Rejoice had a phobia about seeing dead bodies. She often asked herself why? She had no answer.

As they trekked through high and low bushes the boy was asked questions and he talked about his mother and the events of the past twenty-four hours.

The previous day, Ayo had said, he'd stayed at school to finish his homework as usual.

"It was easier to work at school. Always too much work to do at home, plates to wash, water to fetch from the well-." The boy began.

"Same as other poor pupils who can't afford servants!" his teacher interrupted. They walked in silence for a few minutes before the boy continued his narration.

On getting home from school, he found his mother lying on the mat in her room, her new baby by her side. This was uncharacteristic because his mother was always busy preparing diner over the wood fire stove in the yard, on arriving home. He went up to his mother, squatted beside the mat and tapped her gently

"Mama are you all right?" Ayo had enquired of his mother. Mama Ayo opened her eyes slightly. She tried a smile but seemed too tired or too depressed to strain herself. "Do you want me to prepare anything for you?" Ayo asked. His mother blinked twice but said nothing. She stretched out a tired hand and stroke his forehead then closed her eyes. She never opened them again.

Ayo said he saw no outward signs of ill health in his mother, he assumed his mother needed rest, so he left her to sleep. There was no money in the house, so he ransacked the cupboards for food and found pieces of biscuits and stale bread, which he dished out to his brothers. The children had gone to bed hungry. The recall brought a well of tears to his eyes. Auntie Rejoice gave him a pat of consolation on the back.

"What happened to your father? We never hear or see anything of him." Said Auntie Rejoice. The boy sighed heavily, wiping tears from his cheeks with the sleeve of his shirt before speaking.

"My father left us when my mama had another baby boy" the boy said matter- of- factly.

"Why? Most African men want boys not a house full of girls!" Auntie Rejoice said, smiling, knowing that couldn't be the real reason Papa Ayo left home. Ayo shook his head. The memory brought a wry smile to his lips.

"Not my papa. Mama has five boys and me. We be six boys now, too much for papa. Our papa always want one baby girl. He was always weird. He didn't like football. How weird is that?" Ayo screwed up his small nose in disgust. His teacher looked at him and smiled, only a boy could think in that way.

"Where are your brothers now?" the teacher asked.

"They are in the backyard getting ready for going to lesson (pre school). They're too young to know what's happening. Papa just left. One day we woke up to prepare for school, both mama and us were shocked to see he had disappeared. Mama never look for him. I think she was expecting it. Anyway we manage without him. He tilts the soil and plants the crops I do that now with my mama-" Ayo said proudly as if it's a confirmation of his adulthood.

"It's a good thing the school pays your fees." Said Auntie Rejoice. They walked on silently for a few more minutes until Auntie Rejoice broke the silence.

"Did you see anyone else last night?"

"I heard footsteps in the dark. I heard footsteps then whispers. Then nothing. Silence" the boy said, gesticulating with his hands.

"Ayo, listen carefully. Was it your father's voice you heard last night?"

"I don know. I don see his face. I'm sorry Auntie Rejoice." Ayo said.

"Don't worry I'll sort it out. Another question. You remember the last day your father left home?" The boy nodded his head in confirmation.

"Right. Did your mama and papa fight?" Auntie Rejoice persisted gently.

"Yes. That night before, papa was shouting so much. I think he slapped her. She was crying but I was too afraid to get up and help her" Ayo looked straight ahead into the distance, his face a picture of sorrow, his mind full of regret. Perhaps he should have defended his mother. Perhaps he should have been man enough to face his father on her behalf. Perhaps- perhaps-.

Auntie Rejoice thought she better gently teased the boy's memory back to the present.

"How was your geography lesson today? Are you enjoying it?" she said.

"Mr Phillips went to Italy, to Sicily-" the boy began, but the teacher cut in.

"Oh yes! He went with St. Joseph's pilgrimage. Did he enjoy it?" Auntie Rejoice had no interest in Mr Phillip's trip, but felt she had to divert the boy's mind from blood and death. The boy's face lighted up.

"Mr Phillips went round seeing the Byzantine decorations in churches-" the boy said.

"That's a big word to remember, I'm impressed!" the teacher cut in. The boy beamed. "He made us say it many times before we got it! He went to Syracuse and Palermo. Palermo is the capital of Sicily. Do you know that?" Ayo asked.

The teacher feigned distant memory. "Let me see- I think so" she said.

"It is! He went to see the Ruggero Basilica in Cefalu. I don't know what that means. He said Sicily was invaded by many cultures in past centuries to make it what it is now. I enjoyed the lesson very much. Thank you Auntie Rejoice. One day me too will travel the world like you and Mr. Phillips and see all those things for myself."

"I have no doubt you will Ayo. You are a clever boy, remembering all those Italian names! Continue your story about what happened last night and early this morning" she said goading him to talk through what must have been a frightening experience. The muscles of Ayo's face tightened again, as his mind reeled backwards.

"After we ate the bread and biscuits the baby started crying, I mixed ogi (corn powder) with hot water then gave it to the baby. After the baby ate I returned him to his bed beside mama on the mat. We all went to bed at about midnight. About two in the morning, whispering voices then footsteps in the darkness waked me up. I raise my head and look round. I see the figure of a man but don't see the face. It was too dark, NEPA (Nigerian Electricity Power Authority) has taken the light as usual. I heard the name of Pa Jibiti. As I slept on the mat in the next room, I looked across through the open doorway to mama, but saw nothing in the darkness. My brothers slept on beside me-" He paused to swallow and gulped in air.

"Then what happened?" Auntie Rejoice encouraged him to continue talking knowing it was painful for him. Auntie Rejoice had learned, as part of her training, about the talking cure doctors used to cure depressed people.

"I went back to sleep till the small clock that mama gave me for my birthday, beside my mat rang the alarm at four o'clock in the morning. I got up in the dark, walk round to the backyard and had a shower then woke my brothers. I lighted the oil lamps then went to mama. Usually she would be the one to wake me. It was then I saw the knife in her chest and the red liquid on the mat. I spoke to her and shook her but no answer. The baby was fast asleep, I didn't want to wake him. It was then I thought of you, Auntie Rejoice." When the boy stopped talking Auntie Rejoice patted him on the back again in a show of solidarity.

"You brave boy! I'm glad you came to me. Now tell me whose voice you heard. Was it your mother's voice calling Pa Jibiti or someone talking about Pa Jibiti?"

"I don't know Auntie Rejoice. I'm sorry I cannot tell who was talking or if they were calling Pa Jibiti or not." The boy replied, tears falling down his face onto his school shirt.

Old man Pa Jibiti paraded himself as a witchdoctor and traditional healer claiming the power of prophesying the future and performing magical cures. But the only traditional thing about him was his white wrapper typically worn by priests and priestesses during idol worshipping ceremonies. As for healing, the only people claiming a cure from mental affliction by Pa Jibiti were his two oldest sons, who remained as psychotic as a couple of rats in a cheese shop. The old wizard professed to have cured his senior wife of goitre. But only a blind man could fail to see the huge swelling in her neck. Jibiti's power of prediction was limited to seeing into the pockets of gullible clients among whom were politicians and teachers, so-called pillars of society. Jibiti could tell from clients' appearance who was in the money, and charged accordingly.

"We need to find your father to let him know-" Rejoice began, but stopped talking abruptly, starring ahead of them as if she'd seen something that shocked her to the core. Grabbing the boy by the shoulder she pointed a trembling right index finger in front of her.

"Look! Look! Is that not your mother!" Auntie Rejoice said, her voice thin and fearful. The boy jerked his head and gasped as if she'd just cursed his mother, remaining shocked into silence.

"It's your mother, isn't it Ayo?" the teacher repeated to a bewildered child. Ayo followed her finger with tear-laden eyes but seemed blinded with shock.

"It's the mother you couldn't wake, isn't it!" Auntie Rejoice repeated, herself between believe and disbelieve. How could the boy get it so wrong? She thought. Perhaps a genuine mistake, thinking his mother was dead when she was only asleep.

The boy was tongue- tied and clammy as he glanced up to read his teacher's face for assurance. "Did you hear me Ayo?" she said quietly. Ayo's head was swishing with unaltered words that refused to be spoken.

Was it not true that he'd seen his mother earlier this morning, lying on her back, her open eyes unseeing, her ankles crossed and her well formed toes pointing to the sky and the world beyond? Did he not see her with a knife embedded in her chest? Was he dreaming when he saw her and the baby? Did he or didn't he see thick blood around where the blade of the knife met her beautiful dark chocolate skin? Did he make it all up in his head? Was this the beginning of what they call madness? He felt sick unable to speak.

"Ayo?" the gentle voice of Auntie Rejoice woke him from his reverie. "Come on, Let's catch her up!" The teacher was elated now, joyful that all was well with the child again.

"Are you all right?" She glanced down to see fear in his eyes. Her heart missed a beat and started pounding like a talking drum. The boy had been through hell already, and it was not even 6. 30 a.m.

"Yes, Auntie Rejoice." The boy slowly found his voice, but still unsure of his teacher or himself.

FOUR

Auntie Rejoice hurried behind to catch up with the woman they called Mama Ayo while the boy's trotle turned into a small jog as he held his teacher's hand. They both struggled to catch up. It seemed their quickened steps were no match for Mama Ayo. It appeared her feet were no longer touching the ground as she hurried off. Mama Ayo appeared to be floating in mid- air. It reminded Auntie Rejoice of the stories she heard in her youth. Said in whispers, by elderly men and women that ghosts never walked on their feet like humans did. Ghosts floated in mid- air because their feet were not made of flesh at all but airbags disguised to fool humans that they too live as humans in the other world. Of course ghosts fooled no one, especially not wise and wizened elders.

The faster Auntie Rejoice walked and Ayo jogged the faster Mama Ayo floated.

The physical exercise and sheer exhilaration that Mama Ayo was alive, brought past memories flooding into Auntie Rejoice's head. Her past life swaying in front of her. Walking was always a good introspective exercise for her. She loved the aroma of early morning Nigerian air, a mixture of wild elements and unpretentious heap of nature. Her mind slowly rewound itself backwards to her youth, to her past life where love and happiness reigned, until that unforgettable sad day when she was told the tragic way her parents perished. Memories like pebbles on a beach, which one to pick? Her teenage years were hard, she worked like a slave for her Aunt Rose. For a moment she let the river of her past life washed over her mind's eye.

My dearest father, a man of overwhelming kindness and honesty would be proud of me now. I remember in my youth, my aunt relating stories about my father to me. One afternoon, father gave a lift home from school to our neighbour's son, Joe, in his big posh car. A beggar boy, not more than six years old, thrust a dirty outstretched hand through the car window, begging for alms. Joe was very unhappy that beggar boy almost touched Joe's cheeks. Joe shouted 'leave me, go away, dirty boy!' My father rebuked Joe, saying 'Imagine yourself in the poor boy's shoes, Joe. Always give a helping hand to the poor.' My darling father withdrew a ten-pound note (that was when Nigeria used the same currency as England) from his pocket and handed it to the boy beggar who beamed from ear to ear, and disappeared back into the crowd of beggars. Those were the days when notes were worth more than the paper they were printed on. My mother, sitting beside dad, just smiled and said 'Joe you don't know how lucky you are.'

Hearing that from my aunt, I never forget how lucky I've been, despite the harshness of my father's sister who moved into our house to take care of me, treating me as I grew up, more like a slave than her niece. At nineteen I put the Atlantic Ocean between us as I left for England to study.

My aunt and I later became good friends after my graduation and return home from London.

Auntie Rejoice shook the past from her head as she felt a cool breeze lifting up her African print cotton skirt. But the past would not go away. Memories are funny things, they popped up when you least expect them. The cool breeze along the Marina where she'd had a lot of joyful skipping flashed through her mind. A smile creased her lips at the memory of her experience at the CMS Bookshop near the Marina. She was on a queue waiting to pay for the purchase of a book, when she suddenly felt a hard rod poking her bottom. She turned round to face a toothless wretched looking elderly man, wearing a dog-ear hat and a very dirty agbada and shorts. His feet bare and white from dirt. His eyes were closed seemly in joyful experience. She moved forward away from the old man, he too stepped forward, closing the gap between them, sticking to her like a postage stamp on an envelop. She regarded him angrily and placed the book between her and the dirty old man. He felt the hardness of the book, opened his eyes, and gave her a toothless grin. She was so frightened she returned the book to the shelf and left the bookshop. When she glanced back she saw the old man moving behind the next schoolgirl. This was before she knew about sexual predators and paedophiles. She's never forgotten that toothless man.

A long time ago Aina village was called the 'universal ideal village' by the colonial officer in charge of that patch of Lagos Protectorate. It was beautifully rural but peaceful. There was no need of a police station and there was none, disputes were settled by the Oba (King). Now the village boasts easy access to Lagos Island through Eko Bridge and its sister bridges, a small dispensary for treatment of minor illnesses, a post office, its newly refurbished Oba's palace, and of course St. Mary's school, built of tin plates in the eighteen century, expanded in the sixties into a modern red bricked building, which stood proudly at the edge of the village like a giant protective edifice. Two big hospitals were now easily reachable.

Auntie Rejoice glanced down at Ayo. Poor mite, she thought, we orphans should stick together. Wait a minute, Ayo is not a real orphan in any sense, not like me! My mother and father died when I was ten months old, leaving me in the harsh hands of my father's sister.

How can he be an orphan? Ayo's mother is in front of us.

FIVE

Auntie Rejoice and her pupil were on their way to Ayo's house to find out if his mum was really dead. But Auntie Rejoice just saw Mama Ayo walking fast ahead of them. The teacher's joyous relief was too obvious to her little pupil who was in a state of shocked disbelieve. Ayo suspended believe to follow his teacher behind the woman thought to be his mother.

The teacher's footsteps quickened and the boy tried hard to keep up. But it seemed the faster they walked the more Mama Ayo picked up speed. As Mama Ayo turned the corner to her home the teacher and her pupil followed. Turning the same corner Auntie Rejoice found Mama Ayo had disappeared into thin air. They were only two minutes from Ayo's house.

"She's gone!" said Auntie Rejoice aloud more to herself than to the boy. The boy looked into her eyes. "Who?" Ayo said.

"Your mother, your mother had disappeared, just like that!" she said, clicking her fingers in astonishment. The boy decided to express the anxiety he'd felt all along.

"I never saw her. Auntie Rejoice I never saw my Mama!"

Auntie Rejoice swallowed hard. She felt her brain swollen twice its size, her head too small to contain it. She tried to put a lid on the panic rising within her chest.

They've arrived in Ireti Street. As they stood outside the house Ayo took his teacher's hand and squeezed it hard for assurance. She stroke his little hand with the thumb of her right hand, her own heart racing. Auntie Rejoice turned to the apprehensive boy.

"Look Ayo, don't worry about anything. I'll sort it out. Now, here's your house where's your mum?"

"In there on the mat on the floor" Ayo pointed to the room at the back of the small brick house.

"Now be strong. You have been very brave I want you to continue to be brave. If you need to talk any time just come to me. You know where I live so come into my house any time. Promise?"

"Promise." Ayo replied, nodding his head, a faint smile parting his lips.

"Wait here, let me go see what's in there" said Auntie Rejoice whose own heart was pounding so fast but she tried not to hide her fear. She was half expecting Mama

Ayo to be sitting up on the mat, or going about the business of caring for her baby. But then the boy was sure of his mother's death. Ayo was old enough to know death when he saw it. Auntie Rejoice was unsure of her own expectation. Of one thing she was certain. Her heart was fluttering like a butterfly. She dipped her hand into the pocket of her skirt and squeezed the golden rosary beads she always carried, a small white Bible rests in her handbag.

The house stood at the corner of Ireti Street off Agege Motor Road in Mushin, Lagos State. The narrow short street looked clean and almost deserted now in the prevailing darkness. Palm and cashew trees slowly danced in the cool breeze blowing inland from the rivers surrounding the city.

Auntie Rejoice could see that great effort had gone into building and caring for the house. The outside walls were painted a light grey colour and stood in the middle of a grassland with fruits trees dotted here and there round the front and back yards.

The door was unlocked. Doors were usually left open in Nigeria.

Pushing the brown wooden door open Auntie Rejoice came to a large space which she took to be the sitting-room with moderately sparse furniture. There were two long wooden benches placed side by side along one wall, a small round stool stood at the end of each bench, three straight backed chairs and a small wooden table. On the table was a pretty silver ashtray. This surprised Auntie Rejoice. She knew that majority of Nigerians did not smoke. Most considered it a dirty habit. You had to look hard to find an ashtray in a Nigerian home. She lifted and examined it. Though wiped clean, there were traces of ash on it. She replaced it back to the table. A couple of what she assumed were clothes cupboards stood shoulder to shoulder covering another wall of the room. On opposite wall was a big photograph of a locomotive. Auntie Rejoice assumed that Papa Ayo, must at one time, worked for the now defunct locomotive company who went out of business a few years back. That would explain why Papa Ayo was at home (before he legged it) tilling the soil instead of at work.

Auntie Rejoice didn't resist temptation. She opened the cupboards. Hanging in there were women's clothes in two different sizes. She wondered for a moment whether Mama Ayo's weight fluctuated like a yo-yo, like most women's, then closed the cupboards. What a clean room, she thought. A green door led from the sitting- room out onto the backyard. From where she stood Auntie Rejoice could see behind the house into the backyard with its fruits and vegetable patches of land, which provides yams, beans, and other food stuffs, which Mama Ayo sold in the market, to provide for herself and her children.

A brick stove with remnants of dead burnt wood sat just beyond the window in the backyard. The sitting-room led into a large sparse bedroom, Mama Ayo's room, no doubt. This room led into a smaller room which appeared to be the children's room. An open space full of cardboard boxes concluded the rooms.

There were eight wooden windows in the house, one on opposite sides in each room.

A red flower patterned cloth curtain separated the sitting area from the bedrooms.

As she gingerly pulled the curtain aside, her heart stopped. The oil lamp Ayo lighted before going to school was still burning eclipsed by rays of early morning sunlight streaming in through the windows.

She heard the tiny voice first before she saw the body. The baby lay in a pool of blood whimpering like a dying cat.

Auntie Rejoice took a sharp breath in. Afraid of disturbing any evidence, her eyes roamed round the room. She saw five rolled- up sleeping mats leaning against a wall in the children's room. A wooden bench, piled with baby clothes sat below one of the windows. Her eyes came down to rest on the woman on the floor lying on a mat, the whimpering baby by her side. Auntie Rejoice assumed the baby must have cried so hard he was now too tired, having just enough strength to whimper. She bent down and gently picked him up. He stopped whimpering. She removed his blood stained clothes and wrapped him up in one of his mother's clean wrappers she took from a pile on the bench. Auntie Rejoice took the baby outside to his brother and handed him to Ayo to look after.

"I have to call the police but hold the baby while I look round-" she said to the boy.

"Is mama going to be all right?" Ayo asked, his little face anxious with fear of the unknown.

"I'll bring you a chair to sit. Then I'll explain everything. We must hurry up before the sun gets hotter. We don't want the body to start- never mind, wait here" Auntie Rejoice returned to the house and came out with a chair.

"Sit down. My dear Ayo, I'm sorry to say your mama is dead." A pain stabbed her in the chest as she broke the news to the boy. But she felt there was no other way than to say it as it was. His answer surprised her.

"Is she with Jesus?" Ayo asked then burst into tears. He'd heard that good people were with Jesus when they die.

"Yes your mother is with Jesus. He will take good care of her, don't cry, don't you worry" Auntie Rejoice muttered as she turned her back to the boy to wipe away her own tears of sorrow. The sharp pain she felt was not just for Ayo but for the memory of her own childhood. Her own mother had died when she was barely older than this baby.

Ayo seemed troubled as if there were still questions running round his head yet unspoken. After a pause he added "Do you think my mama will go to heaven? "

Auntie Rejoice's eyes filled with tears again. "I have no doubt at all your mother is in heaven. She was a very good woman, everybody says so."

Auntie Rejoice thought of reading a verse, from the little white Bible in her bag, on the promise of heaven by Jesus. But then she changed her mind, this was not the time. In any case she hated showing off her Bible knowledge lest people thought of her as preachy, which she was not. Auntie Rejoice just loved reading the Bible stories.

The boy seemed satisfied with her explanation. He wiped his eyes with the tissues Auntie Rejoice handed him. She returned to the house as the other children were entering the house from the backyard.

"Have you eaten, children?" she said.

"No, and we're hungry" unafraid of the strange lady, they smiled in unison. Auntie Rejoice took out her wallet and gave them some Naira notes to buy breakfast on their way to morning lesson. "Bring some food for your brother before you go to lesson" she shouted after them. They failed to notice that it was unusual for a sleeping woman to have a kitchen knife plunging into her chest. Auntie Rejoice wondered about children's ability at total self absorption. Though she loved children, she decided long time ago that motherhood was not her cup of tea.

She thought it better to let them act as normally as was possible. The children said goodbye to their elder brother who was holding the baby outside, and left, promising to return in minutes with his food. There were many bukas selling meals at every corner of the village. The grey smoke rising to the sky every few yards testified to this, they didn't have to walk far.

Suddenly without warning the next door neighbour, a man called Pa Seyi Shitu, a man of hardly any means at all, in flowing white robe, barged into the room where Auntie Rejoice was. He was tall but bent over like an old man of seventy even though he was still in his forties. His deep brown eyes appeared black from years of smoking cheap cigarettes and drinking gallons of ogogoro (illicit gin) a day. His dead brother owned the house he occupied next door to Mama Ayo's house. They had always been good neighbours to each other.

Pa Seyi gave a piercing scream when he saw Auntie Rejoice bending over the dead woman. Villagers rushed to the house and prodded Ayo into telling them what had happened. Some villagers started screaming, others crying. Pa Seyi, his hands cradling his small balding, oblong head ran out then back into the house, not knowing what to do. Auntie Rejoice eventually cornered and calmed him. He glanced up at her as she spoke to him, his eyes blazing with hatred,

"What you doing here? You have no right in this house! You are only the school teacher! Na you kill her! Na you kill her!" he screamed.

The crowd heard, stood and watched in awe. When Pa Seyi stopped screaming, tongues got liberated.

"Do you really think the teacher killed her?" "She did. What else was she doing with her so early in the morning?" "Why? women do kill you know" "Let's lynch her-" "Not yet. We must find out what the oracle says before we take action against her. Meet in my house tomorrow noon." that, Auntie Rejoice recognised as the voice of the self proclaimed village leader, Pa Jibiti, the jujuman and witchdoctor, an evil wizard. His voice and head always stood out in a crowd. His hair was bright red with matching long thin beard, which parents used to threaten their children when they misbehaved, 'the devil will get you! Pa Jibiti is coming!' mothers screamed.

Everyone agreed it was absolutely un- African to possess a red head, except Pa Jibiti's three wives and his fourteen children, who thought him the best thing since discovering moyinmoyin. The truth was Pa Jibiti suffered malnutrition until he discovered the moneymaking scheme of witchcraft, divination, and fortune telling. Round his neck on a black rope, hung the bleached head skull of an alligator and another of a rat's head. The animals sat menacingly on his wiry bare chest, believed by some villagers to be potent juju. If Pa Jibiti rubbed the skulls in anger, villagers believed, it would incur a misfortune or death on the victim, He was wearing his traditional white long piece of cloth wound round his thin frame like a mummy, with its tapering end slung over his left shoulder. Auntie Rejoice looked out of the window again and saw a fly landing on Pa Jibiti's right arm. He glanced at it for a second, muttered some words as he picked it up and swallowed the fly.

Pa Jibiti was said to possess evil power. His wrists and hands were bedecked in black rings and bangles. His first born, a man in his forties, called Jayle, was built like an elephant. Jayle had the appearance of a depressed lion, whose many failed attempts at eating his mother-in-law had resulted in a twisted facial expression. Wearing more black rings and bangles than his father, Jayle was jumping up and down now, shouting, "Teacher go back to school! Teacher go teach! Stop killing! We go finish yoo too!" Jayle was reputed to be wilder and wickeder than his father. Pa Jibiti stole loving glances at his manic son and smiled proudly. There's nothing like the pride of a father, even if the son deserved to be in a lock- up ward.

Auntie Rejoice couldn't help hearing their voices discussing her and Mama Ayo's predicament. She ignored them and busied herself observing what she regarded as a crime scene in case the scene was disturbed in her absence, while the voices outside continued discussing her fate.

"She can't have! She's the schoolteacher! She's the daughter of Mama Rejoice in number one Luggard Crescent, near the school, before Ma and Pa Akintola gave up the ghost. Remember the Chief of Customs and Matron at the teaching hospital?" said a voice. "Anyway teachers don't kill! Teachers are the pillars of-"

"Teachers want progress. Right? You do what you have to do to gain promotion. Don't you agree?" said another voice. "And the way to progress, some people believe, not me, is to sacrifice a human being. A boy child or better still a breast feeding woman!"

"Is that what you do? Because I've never seen or known anyone who sacrificed a human being before- "

"Didn't you hear me say I don't do it myself but I've heard people say that? What sort of person are you? Are you deaf? In any case are you not Mama Iyanu's daughter. Wasn't she accused of-"

"Listen, if you libel my mother I will sue you. Better know what you're saying, be sure of your facts" "What will you sue me with, peanuts?" "We should teach her a lesson" "Beat her up! Show her what real death is"

People came from far and near to view the near naked dead body of a breast- feeding woman lying in her own pool of blood. Auntie Rejoice peeped into the crowd from her vantage point inside the house. When the crowd swelled to near a hundred, she decided, she would preserve the dignity of the dead. She took a wrapper and covered Mama Ayo's body from prying eyes. This simple act of kindness invoked hissing sounds from villagers with noses thrust into the windows of the dead woman's house.

"Afraid of the dead, are we? What's wrong with paying respect?" an elderly lady nosy- packer spat out. Among the crowd she noticed, were a few media men and women. Two photographers snapped her through the open window, only God knows why?

The argument continued to rage outside

She was a little afraid of the lynch mob but with a strong faith in Jesus she felt He would protect her. She left the room with her chin up, her heart beating so fast she could taste it. Clutching her rosary beads she walked back to Ayo now surrounded by villagers. As she emerged from the house her eyes caught sight of cowry beads and bowls of black soap and palm oil, sprinkled round the compound. She had no doubt it was a juju ritual to frighten her. But she would hold firm. God has been good to her. He would not fail her now. Some people blame God for their misfortunes, not her. She believed, as now in the face of hostility, that God has given everyone a choice. She herself could, right now, walk away. She would not, but she had that choice. She silently began reciting the Hail Mary before she emerged from the house.

Seeing her, a silent calm descended on the crowd. The silence was broken by the witchdoctor's scream.

"I be dee elder in this village, dee only head in dee village. You get no right to intafeer in dis case. Ayo must first and foremost come tee me first! You be only a schoolteacher, what do yoo kno of life? You go suffer foo yoor foolissness!" said Pa Jibiti, his face spoke detestation. The crowd gasped. Pa Jibiti then turned to the baying crowd who feared more than respected him. The witchdoctor rubbed the skeletal animal heads on his chest. The crowd gasped again, knowing Auntie Rejoice faced a serious threat to her life. On her part Auntie Rejoice was determined to dig deep into Pa Jibiti's evil ways. She'd heard, through the grapevine, that Pa Jibiti held midnight satanic celebrations, during which the occasional child or woman was sacrificed.

With one hand holding and feeding himself pieces of dodo his brothers had brought him, Ayo held the baby in his other arm.

"Ayo since there's no phone around and the school is nearer here than the Police Station I have to go back to school and make a phone call to the police. Will you be all right till I come back?"

"I'm all right here, Pa Seyi is around." the boy replied chewing on his food.

"OK, I'll be back soon but the police may be here before me. Don't let anyone go into your house except the police. It's very important OK?"

"OK." Auntie Rejoice turned to Pa Seyi who was standing beside the boy, "Is it all right to leave the children with you?" Pa Seyi couldn't believe she had to ask. Pa Seyi had a hateful habit of cupping his genitals when he was nervous or elated. He smiled now as his right hand went to cup his pants as if weighing up a piece of meat on a butcher's slab. This was the first time Auntie Rejoice had seen a close- up of such disgusting habit from a grown man. It took all of her determination not to empty the contents of her stomach onto his feet, and shout at him to remove his hand from his crotch. She wondered why a grown man would play with himself in public.

"The children be safe. Go wow!" he replied.

"Why do I need to go wow?" Auntie Rejoice said with a puzzling frown. Ayo came to her aid. "He said 'go now'" the boy explained and burst into a roaring laugher. It was then it dawned on Auntie Rejoice that Pa Seyi could not pronounce the letter 'N' He always substituted 'W' for 'N' to the hilarity of the whole village. By now everyone in the village knew and accepted Pa Seyi's affliction except those meeting him for the first time, like Auntie Rejoice. She signalled to Ayo to stop laughing and departed. In a very short time she became familiar with Pa Seyi's speech pattern.

Six

Auntie Rejoice left Mama Ayo's house and walked back to school. She went straight to the Headmaster's office and related the whole story to him.

"Poor boy. Is he all right?" said Mr Jaiye, his eyes moist but, being a man he restrained himself from shedding tears.

"He's remarkably fine but then children are very flexible are they not? I came back to use the phone to call the police. I don't know anyone who has a phone in the village. May I-"

"Of course you can use the phone! I'll go out-" Mr Jaiye didn't finish his sentence before Auntie Rejoice cuts in.

"No! Please stay. I want you to advise me in case I say the wrong thing."

"OK, I'll stay, make a sign if you need my help."

Auntie Rejoice walked to the black phone on a side table under a window, beside Mr. Jaiye's desk and picked it up. She dialled 999 and was put in touch with the nearest police station.

"I want to report a murder-" Auntie Rejoice began, she was interrupted by the excited voice of a male police officer on the line.

"A murder? You got the murderer with you? Bring him to the station. We'll take it from there" the voice said.

Auntie Rejoice was flabbergasted and angry. She decided not to take such comment from someone she regarded as incompetent, guilty of dereliction of duty. In a stern teacher's voice she rebuked the officer.

"How can I have the murderer with me? I don't know who the murderer is. If you send your son to school do we ask you to supply the teacher? You do your job and I'll do mine" She replied angrily. The police officer wasn't amused at being told off.

"You are being rude madam-" he said.

"Are you coming to see the victim or not?" she fumed.

"Well, give me the address then. I'll inform my Inspector"

She gave the address of Mama Ayo's house. Putting down the phone, she turned to the Headmaster.

"I have no confidence in the Police. He wants me to bring the criminal to the station!

If you report a robbery they want you to bring the robber to the police station!"

"I don't know why we pay tax! Only God is protecting us in this country not the government" Mr Jaiye put in.

"As yet, no government in Nigeria has ever put this right. No leader wants to be remembered for putting his people before himself. We need good police service and a decent ambulance system. I better go back to Mama Ayo's house to wait for them" said Auntie Rejoice, walking towards the door.

"Yes. Remember what I said. Take as much time off as you need. I'll get other teachers to cover your classes" said Mr Jaiye.

"Thank you Mr Jaiye. I'll try not to take too long. Although I like Ayo very much I do miss my other pupils when I'm away from them." With this Auntie Rejoice left the school and returned to Mama Ayo's house.

She arrived just as the light blue police jeep was parking on the grassland, in front of the house.

"Hello! You made it here. Thank yo-" Auntie Rejoice began, with a welcoming smile. She thought she might have been too harsh on the police. Just then the Inspector, looking puffed up and pompous interrupted her in a loud voice that the whole village must have heard.

"I'm Inspector Gberaga, in charge of City Police. You are the trouble- maker who called us in?" he roared, as he hooked his hands on the wide leather belt holding up his trousers over his beer- belly.

"True, I called you in but I'm no trouble- maker. My name is Rejoice Akintola, I'm a teacher at St Mary's. In fact I was speaking from the Headmaster's office when I called your station-" The Inspector interrupted her rudely again, she thought.

"Your Headmaster must be a tolerant man! One of these rubbish men called New Men! New my arse! They need a good canning! Now where's the body? I can't stand here all day chatting! Lead the way!" said the Inspector, taking a step forward away from his jeep.

Auntie Rejoice thought there was no answer to that. She led him and two ordinary (and hungry- looking) police constables wearing oversized caps, to where Mama Ayo's body still lay undisturbed, her own fear of the dead put aside. Auntie Rejoice removed the wrapper with which she had covered the dead body. She noticed the shock and fear in the Inspector's eyes. The junior officers were almost at the point of fainting. She hoped they wouldn't, she had little energy left as it was. Auntie Rejoice thought she knew exactly what the Inspector was thinking. He probably thought it might be a ritual killing, deserving of a curse on whoever digs deeper into it.

After a few minutes of walking round the body, shaking his head and muttering 'hummm' the Inspector had made up his mind not to do anything, not to dirty his hands. Not to carry and be tinged with a curse that was surely waiting for any meddler. No, not him. He was not ready to die yet, if ever. He had numerous children and even more mistresses to support. Life was sweet, life was good for him. With the money he raked in, in bribes alone, he never needed to touch his monthly salaries. Compared to the walnuts in backhand he got from 'see you later oga' his salaries were peanuts. Apart from his mud house in a far away village outside Lagos, the Inspector built a palace in Agege town and a house in Yaba, and in negotiation for a deal for a house by the beach. All these from swaggering round Aina village, from ten in the morning to four o'clock if that.

He would find a way to pronounce final judgement there and then. He cleared his throat as if about to declare war on a group of loiterers, before speaking.

"What makes you think this is murder?" the Inspector asked, after a long pause.

"Because there's a knife in her heart" Auntie Rejoice said with a straight face, unbelieving that anyone, let alone a police officer, could ask such an obvious question. The Inspector looked at her then shook his head, as if to say. Stupid girl.

"Where is her husband?" he asked, after another long pause

"He left her some weeks ago, so the older boy told me" Auntie Rejoice said.

"So husband's not around? She was a loose woman and careless with it! Did she have any money problem?" said the Inspector, pulling down his uniform jacket, which had ascended his chest, over his protruding abdomen.

"All women here have money problem. She just had a baby six weeks ago-"

"Ah! Ah aa aa! Husband just left her for another woman, baby blues- I think this is suicide. In fact I'm sure that this is suicide. As a matter of fact, my experience told me it's suicide. Suicide is only one step from murder, you know. In fact suicide IS murder. Only it is murder of oneself by oneself. It shouldn't be allowed! If I have my way, all those committing suicide will be charged with murder. Murder is murder after all-" said the Inspector pausing, then smiling at the wisdom of his own words. He continued, self- adoration written all over his broad face.

"Yes murder should be equal under the law whether it be someone's or one's own murder, the punishment should be the same- hang them!" the Inspector concluded, with a self satisfied grimace.

"In the case of self murder who would you charge to court Inspector?" said Auntie Rejoice, anger sipping into her voice. The constables standing behind their Inspector smiled at the cleverness of the young woman.

"There lies a classic escape from justice! People will do anything to escape justice! A thing we are trying to abolish. Is there a suicide note?" Inspector Gberaga said, removing his cap to scratch his balding head.

"She couldn't read nor write. That's why she took the education of her children very seriously" said Auntie Rejoice.

"So she should. It is the duty of every Nigerian parent to educate her child. In that wise she is no exception. But too much education-" he was cut off.

"Sorry to interrupt Inspector. But what are you going to do about the dead woman?" Auntie Rejoice was getting impatient as the sun was coming down in the sky. It would take no time at all for the body to start rotting. The Inspector took offence to being interrupted

"I was just going to say something important before you rudely interrupt. And if I may say so, you're a good example of the point I'm trying to make. Too much education spoils women. It rots women's brain! They want it all! That's why they are crying they can't get husbands! Who wants a wife with a brain as big as gorilla? A know-it- all? A wife that will let you down in front of your friends? When you say one she says two? They want men to wear skirts on top of their trousers! Effeminate men, that's what I call them! They call it feminism! Feminism, paugh! Everybody knows, you are feminist when you can't get a husband! Look at them, their faces like donkeys! Look at you, you are pretty, very pretty. I know you can get any man you want. But I'm sure you don't go for any man. You put conditionalities, 'am right or 'am right?" Auntie Rejoice's furrowed face concentrated his mind. He coughed and paused a moment from his ranting.

"As to what I'm going to do about this poor lady. The answer is nothing. I'm sure even more now that I've talked to you. This woman died of a broken heart. She took her own life. Inability to read and write I know, is no basis for killing oneself. But not withstanding-"

"You can't say that! You can't stand there and say you're doing nothing to find her killer! You can't! This woman was murdered. It must be investigated by the police, by you!" Auntie Rejoice protested to no avail. The Inspector took out a white handkerchief from the pocket of his trousers and wiped his sweaty head, placed the handkerchief back into his pocket, then replaced his cap to his head in preparation for departing. He took a step towards the door but was arrested by Auntie Rejoice's voice.

"You are not going are you?" The Inspector turned round to face her.

"Of course. There's nothing more for me and my men to do here. Are you related to the dead woman?"

the Inspector said, looking directly into Auntie Rejoice's light brown eyes.

"No, no relation at all-" she began

"Then why do you worry your pretty little head? Why do you care so much what happens to her, after all she could no longer feel?"

"Because someone has to care Inspector. Someone must take the trouble-" she was interrupted again.

"Let me give you one good advice. Give her a good burial, if you have money to burn, and find some relatives to look after the kids. Look, you are a beautiful lady. Find yourself a good man to marry you. Bye for now" the Inspector turned to go again.

"Wait! Who is going to take the body to the hospital?" Auntie Rejoice said. She would like the dead woman to be properly examined, a proper post mortem carried out, and perhaps washed and dressed.

"What for? She's beyond medical help now!" the Inspector laughed. Auntie Rejoice thought it was beyond a joke. This here was no laughing matter. She couldn't believe she would be left with the dead body. She had fear of the dead, which she couldn't explain. After all the dead was dead. The body was just a shell, harmless.

She's got a dead body on her hands with no experience of ministering to the dead. She'd always been scared of dead bodies. She never knew why? After all, the dead just lie there, unable to do anything. Why was she afraid. Now she had to face her demon.

"I think a post mortem is necessary, don't you? Will you help me take her in your jeep to the General Hospital mortuary-?" Auntie Rejoice said pleadingly. The Inspector jumped backwards with disgust, as if he'd suddenly seen a snake beneath his feet.

"You want me to take a dead body in my allocated police jeep? Are you crazy? This jeep carries the living not the dead. When it becomes a hearse I'll inform you! The best thing you can do is find a taxi that will ferry the corpse for you. That is if you are stubborn enough not to want to bury her in her backyard. Do you know how many people are buried without ceremony every day? Some of them probably murdered? Let me know if you need any further help from the police. Good-day" With that the Inspector departed the house leaving Auntie Rejoice alone with her thoughts. She looked out into the streets and saw that most of the crowd had gone. They had come to gloat, hoping for a clash of giants, between Auntie Rejoice and Pa Jibiti. They've had their fill until the verdict. They themselves were too afraid of Pa Jibiti to be actively involved. A few men and women remained, starring into the house through the open windows. Auntie Rejoice turned back into the room to concentrate her mind on the problem of what to do with the dead woman lying on the mat.

As the police jeep started off coughing and blowing dark fumes, the children were arriving from their lessons. They rushed into the death room before anyone had a chance to stop them.

"Mama! Mama!" they chanted happily. "Mama sleeping!" the youngest one shouted. Auntie Rejoice took them out and spoke to their neighbour Pa Seyi who agreed to take them to his home and care for them until alternative arrangement could be made. Auntie Rejoice took out her pause and handed Pa Seyi some Naira notes, more than enough to cover their care for a few days.

Auntie Rejoice glanced over her shoulders and saw the police jeep had stalled and refused to start when the driver removed his foot from the accelerator, for the break pedal. The Inspector got down and summons people to push the jeep back into Mama Ayo's front yard.

"Heh! You! Teacher, come here!" Inspector Gberaga beckoned to Auntie Rejoice. She hesitated before joining him by the side of the jeep.

"You put a curse on my car! It is because I refuse to carry the dead woman, heh?" said the Inspector in all seriousness. Auntie Rejoice was not sure whether to laugh or spit on him. She did neither. She silently recited the

Hail Mary until her anger subsided, before facing the Inspector.

"I wish you no ill, Inspector. I don't believe in curses-" she said.

"Well, you should. There are evil things on Earth-" the Inspector was interrupted.

"Yes, and there is One above all others. You should have more faith Inspector. Goodbye, I do have a body to ferry to the mortuary" she turned her back on him and walked away. He sent for a local mechanic who revived the car, but Inspector Gberaga refused to pay his charges and threw himself heavily on the back seat.

"I am on official government duty. You must be ashamed of yourself asking me for money. Driver let's go!" the Inspector said, banging the roof of the jeep. Knowing he might land in a police cell if he persisted, the mechanic counted his loss and left.

Auntie Rejoice saw Ayo and his brothers settled then, went out to hail a taxi to ferry the body of Mama Ayo to the General Hospital mortuary on Lagos Island. Every taxi driver she hailed refused to carry a dead body saying : 'It would bring ten years bad luck.' 'It's a curse on me' 'It's not good for business' 'If I want to carry the dead I'll go work for funeral parlours'

Eventually Auntie Rejoice saw the sign first, blazoned over the top of the windscreen in black letters on a yellow background.

'When God is with Me Who Can Be Against Me?'

Looking round the village a visitor could be forgiven for thinking the whole village was a religious community. Almost every public vehicle or shop carried a religious quotation or sayings from the Bible. But it was just the fashion. Most villagers called themselves Christians but very few were true believers.

The cab was an old one, driven by an elderly taxi driver. The driver agreed to ferry the body of Mama Ayo to the mortuary. He turned his car round and parked it with the back passenger door, almost touching Mama Ayo's front door to prevent prying eyes.

The taxi driver helped Auntie Rejoice in lifting Mama Ayo off the mat. Where her body had lain they saw marks of bloody footprints belonging to an adult. Not only had someone been in the house the previous night but, that someone had left his or her footprints in blood. This is a police job. They have all the equipment for forensic, Auntie Rejoice thought sadly. After placing the body in the cab she returned to the room to roll the mat to one side with her foot, careful not to disturb the footprints. She would come back later to examine and hide the mat.

The driver and Auntie Rejoice deposited Mama Ayo's lifeless body in the back of the taxi forcing the body into a sitting position. An upright position would fool the public into thinking she was a normal passenger, be it a sleepy one. It was not so easy to do, the body was beginning to stiffen up.

Auntie Rejoice sat in front with the driver, her heart thumping, her head spinning with words of doubts. Suppose the body fell out of the car in the traffic's bumper to bumper or someone actually recognise the passenger as dead? Suppose there was an accident and the dead was called on to witness? Suppose- -

What then? All these frightening thoughts were running round Auntie Rejoice's head, as the car crawled to the mortuary at the General, a place so decrepit that would be barred to both the dead and the living, under a more caring government.

As traffic halted and proceeded at a snail's pace hawkers with toothbrushes, bananas and oranges, fresh bread and cold drinks approached the car. Children came very close to Auntie Rejoice, pressing their noses on the glass windows, urging and calling her and the dead's attention to their wares for sale. She dared not look them in the eye in case they read the fear in her own eyes.

When the taxi finally stopped at the General she got out and searched for the sign pointing to the mortuary.

She saw and followed the blue arrow proclaiming in big peeling paint, 'Mortuary and Reception'. An attendant appeared from nowhere and kindly took over, wheeling a trolley out to collect Mama Ayo's body. Auntie Rejoice checked in the body and gave a short history of how she became involved in the whole saga. She was handed a piece of paper receipt to be submitted for collection of the body. She wondered if the Coroner would be involved. She supposed he would ask for non- existent police report and that would be that.

Now that the body was off her hands Auntie Rejoice had a moment to think, Mama Ayo's death could be construed as suicide, she thought. If only she could believe a woman could possess such a strength to plunge a kitchen knife that far into her own heart. But she couldn't. It was murder whatever anyone said. Suddenly she remembered the flesh in her handbag. She paid the taxi driver, more money than he demanded, and thanked him for his help. Then she made her way to Pathology to see her doctor friend. She explained how she found the bowl of offering, then deposited the heart for examination.

Auntie Rejoice left the General Hospital feeling drained, also feeling one part of a very difficult problem had been solved, but there were several more to resolve.

She hurried back to Pa Seyi's house to check the children were fine. They were all sitting outside, in front of Pa Seyi's house. The older ones were happily scraping off skin from sweet potatoes with tablespoons. Auntie Rejoice thought how good of Pa Seyi, not to let the children use knives, in case they cut themselves. One of these days he would make a good wife for somebody. The youngest boy was playing with a home-made toy car made of empty tins of milk and wires. Auntie Rejoice decided she would go hide the bloody mat, lock Mama Ayo's house and handed the keys to Ayo, in case the children wanted access to their belongings, with Ayo trailing behind her. As Auntie Rejoice came nearer, she saw drops of blood trailing into the house. She stopped, trying to remember if the blood drops were there earlier and she'd failed to notice. If new, it meant the villagers had started celebrating the wake for the dead, by killing chickens and goats, but who could afford to buy these animals among poor villagers. Was the trail of blood that of Mama Ayo? Auntie Rejoice shuddered and decided to look into it. She entered the house and mixed three bottles of baby food showing Ayo how to warm them up later. Glancing round the rooms, looking under chairs and cupboards, her eyes landed on a red cloth peeping from behind the only wardrobe in the children's room, which she'd failed to see in the rush to get Mama Ayo's body to the mortuary. Auntie Rejoice eyed Ayo standing behind her. He looked petrified, his chest began rising and falling as if he was having an attack of asthma. She hadn't seen him like that before and it almost frightened her. The feeling that he might be sick or overwhelmed with sadness was disturbing for her. She patted his head with her right hand. "Are you all right?" She asked. He nodded his head, unable to speak, as if he was expecting a big secret to be uncovered, exposing him as a fraud, a liar. She bent down and pulled out the cloth. She gasped with shock. In her hands was a blood soaked white shirt. The shirt was small in size and couldn't fit an adult male. She took the shirt to the entrance door for a better view in good light. The shirt had blue edgings. It was St. Mary's school shirt. Her heart was thumping now. At once she felt a headache, her eyes were throbbing, she felt a stroke was coming on. She didn't like the thought forming in her head. Her racing mind was thinking the unthinkable. She shut her eyes and recited the Hail Mary to control her nerves before turning to Ayo. "Is this your uniform?" The boy lowered his eyes to the bare cement floor. He nodded his head. Dear God don't let it be him. Not a killer! She prayed silently.

"Why has it got blood on it? Did you put this behind the cupboard? Did you kill your mother? It pain me to ask that but I need to know what happened here Ayo" she said calmly.

"I put it there but I kill no one Auntie Rejoice! I kill no one!" the boy was having an attack of asthma again, his chest rising and falling with rapid alacrity. Fear griped Auntie Rejoice. She didn't want any harm coming to the boy. She liked him too much to cause him harm. What she knew already was enough for villagers to stone him to death, his tender age was no deterrent. Villagers often took up arms against criminals they felt brought shame on their village, because there was no effective policing.

"How did blood get on your uniform?"

"My mama washed it for me. She want to iron it. She tell me so. I kill no one-" the boy muttered, eyes wide open with fear, his words made no sense to her. He was making no sense.

Auntie Rejoice became overwhelmed with pity and tucked the shirt back behind the cupboard. "Don't touch the shirt. I'm sorry Ayo. I'm so sorry" She felt remorseful but a thin line of doubt lingered.

She locked the house and handed the key to Ayo. She turned to the boy and asked if their parents had any relatives she could notify about their mother's death.

"There's uncle Bita, Mama's brother. He lives in Yaba" Ayo replied. Yaba was only a few miles down the road.

"We'll go there first thing in the morning" Auntie Rejoice said.

It was late when Auntie Rejoice got home to her house in Luggard Crescent. As she turned the key in the lock, her housemaid was waiting to greet her.

"I cooked rice and stew for you. You are working too hard-" said Misi, the maid

"I don't feel hungry I'll have a bath then a glass of ice cold palm wine"

After a cooling cold shower Auntie Rejoice took a glass of cold sweet palm wine to her bedroom. Lying in bed with the television on at the foot of the bed, the sound turned off, she ruminated about the day. Why would anyone want to kill a breastfeeding woman? A woman known as good and kind? Did she have a secret life? A hidden life from her family and friends?

'The police came and went, nothing doing. They could tell that Mama Ayo was murdered. It's so plain to see. Auntie Rejoice was convinced Inspector Gberaga knew Mama Ayo's death was murder. He must have considered it a ritual murder. Untouchable! The poor children. Poor, poor children. Well if they won't investigate I have to do it myself.' She said out loud. She walked to the window overlooking a public park and peeped through the lace curtains into the street. She saw the dim outline of a black clad, shadowy figure across the park, glaring at her window. He was all in black, black long sleeved shirt, black trousers, black sunshade (for goodness sake! sunshade at that time of night! Auntie Rejoice thought.). Auntie Rejoice racked her brain for a few minutes, standing there unseen. Even though the night was as black as the devil's bottom, a faint stream of light from the park, fell through the trees in front of the figure. Someone she was certain, was watching her.

She turned back and walked to the bedside table, grabbed the Bible on the table, lay on her bed, placed the Bible on her chest and waited for sleep.

SEVEN

During the next day, Auntie Rejoice thought hard about the implication of Ayo in his mother's death. She knew Ayo appeared thin and stragly, his hair cropped to his head, with big inviting brown eyes. But he was a very strong boy. The day she decided to change her furniture round in class proved beyond doubt his strength. She was huffing and puffing trying to shift the desk on her own. None of the pupils got up to help. Ayo sprang up from his seat and said to her, 'Leave it, I can do it for you, Auntie Rejoice' He lifted the desk all by himself to the other side of the room, without so much as a pant. Everyone clapped him for his bravery. Auntie Rejoice stood open- mouth in admiration of the boy's strength and kindness. With two hands, he would have no difficulty plunging a knife into a sleeping adult. Auntie Rejoice knew that Ayo was a child but, should she be blinded by his age? After all, she had heard of child murderers in America, in England and even in France, the country she couldn't get enough of. She had always said to her friends that, France was a country of her emotions, Britain, a country of her head and heart.

Nigeria, of course was the country of the whole of Auntie Rejoice's body, it gave her birth. It also gave her heartache Even in those countries she admired, children had been known to kill. These were children who had everything on a plate. These advanced countries always put their children first and had laws against mistreatment of minors, as children were called.

Auntie Rejoice thought African leaders would do well to think about giving these same benefits to their own people. At this particular moment there were more child soldiers than child benefits in Africa. Auntie Rejoice shuddered about what she'd read in a United Nations pamphlet, about organisations working in twenty eight countries where armed conflicts put children on war frontlines. Two million children were sent to their death, by evil adults who wouldn't use their own children in armed combats. The article said six million other children were left psychologically damaged, injured or permanently disabled. Auntie Rejoice pondered the fact that, she hadn't seen or heard of people marching on the streets of New York, Berlin, Paris, London, or even Lagos, on behalf of these children, to give them their childhood back.

Although Auntie Rejoice knew there were few bad children in the world, the purity of children was without parallel. She was aware of the intense goodness in Ayo and his ability to empathise with those suffering. It was after all, her duty to protect him and look after him. And she would do her best for him.

On the spur of the moment, Auntie Rejoice decided she would go spy on Pa Jibiti's midnight cult ceremony, from which women villagers were barred. The thought excited and frightened her. That night, she wore a black long dress and a black hat. It would make it easier to merge into the darkness surrounding Pa Jibiti's non- electrified mud compound. She knew her mission was a dangerous one. But she needed to discover for herself if what they say about him was true. It would have a bearing on Mama Ayo's murder. It was said that he, as chief priest of his own cult, made human sacrifices. Sacrificing women and children to the god of clay at midnight celebrations. She conceded this particular night might not be the one for human sacrifice, but it would give her an insight into this evil man's ways. All the same, it was a dangerous game, watching the forbidden, especially forbidden to women. If caught, it would be instant death for her. But the urge was strong and powerful. Power lay in knowing your enemy's weaknesses. Pa Jibiti, the witchdoctor, took no prisoners. There was need for caution.

At ten minutes to midnight she jumped into a waiting cab, which rolled down the small hill to Agege Motor road, then to Aina. At that time of night the roads were clear of traffic. The journey took no time at all. At her command, the driver dropped her five minutes walk to Pa Jibiti's compound. The taxi driver shook his head and asked,

"You want me to wait for you Madam?" she said no. "Will you be all right, Madam?" she replied in the affirmative, paid him and walked away. The driver shook his head again and muttered 'Odd woman, but nice', and drove off.

She had heard from the grapevine that Pa Jibiti's satanic ceremony proceeded from his compound to the nearby crossroad, where human sacrifice usually took place, then turned a loop on itself and returned to Pa Jibiti's compound where concluding rites took place.

She walked quietly but quickly to a huge guaver tree just outside the wall separating Pa Jibiti's compound from an isolated public pathway. Her slim body fitting easily behind the tree trunk, hiding her from view of people emerging from Pa Jibiti's gate. She stayed behind the tree for what was a few minutes that, seemed an eternity. It was few seconds to midnight. Suddenly she heard a loud rhythmical sound, lub- dub, lub- dub, lub- dub. The sound seemed nearer with each breath. Her head doubled in size with fright. Lub- dub, lub- dub, lub- dub. Her sweat pores began to overdrive. She felt sweat droplets in her back, her dress was getting soaked. Lub- dub, lub- dub, lub- dub. Her eyes roamed round but saw nothing. As she listened to the rhythm of the sound carefully, she realised the sound was coming from within her. A realisation that the sound was her heartbeat brought a smile of relief to her lips. Don't be soft, get a hold of yourself. She told herself.

A sudden loud sound of bell ringing alerted her to real danger. The ceremony was about to begin. Another loud bangs on a drum followed. Voices raised in singing praises to the chief priest, Pa Jibiti and his god of clay.

Auntie Rejoice raised herself on her toes and peeped into the compound from behind the tree, and saw two naked boys, not more than five years old. The boys were covered in white chalk from head to toes. They led the procession, dancing acrobatically to the beating drums. They were followed by a teenaged virgin, not more than twelve or thirteen, wearing nothing but a very short white pleated skirt, and white coral beads round her neck, waist and ankles. Her head was completely shaved and shining. The girl carried a big white clay pot oozing flames, on her head. Her hands were tied together behind her back, perhaps to prevent her from tampering with the pot or as a sign of domination by Pa Jibiti, or both.

Auntie Rejoice knew instantly the little girl was a sacrificial lamb. Six elderly women and a teenaged girl called Ruby, all in white wrappers danced in circles around the girl, while Pa Jibiti, also wrapped in white, danced tro and fro before the dancers. His face was joyful, like a dog salivating over its supper. The group proceeded ecstatically out of the compound to the crossroad.

Auntie Rejoice followed the procession, by jumping from behind one tree to the next. Suddenly, it seemed Pa Jibiti sensed hostile presence. His dancing came to an abrupt end. The dancers stopped dancing, the drummers stopped beating their drums. He turned, starring in Auntie Rejoice's direction. She froze. The many ways she could be killed raced through her mind. Then as suddenly as he stopped Pa Jibiti proceeded dancing again, the drummers began drumming and the dancers danced as if tomorrow would never come.

Auntie Rejoice sighed in relief. She recited the Hail Mary to settle her thumping heart. Saying the Hail Mary was always like swallowing a couple of sedative tablets. It gave her instant calm and peace.

At the crossroad the flaming pot was removed from the girl by one of the elderly dancing ladies and placed on the ground at the crossroad. It seemed villagers knew that part of the village was a no- go area as from midnight.

There was not a single person or car in sight, except cult members.

Auntie Rejoice watched as Pa Jibiti withdrew a knife from inside his wrapper. He stuck the sharp point of the knife into and made a small incision in the girl's left chest, below the breast. The girl's agonising scream rented the air. The chief priest drained the blood into a small cup, put it to his lips and drank it. The girl crashed to the ground, but was at once pulled to her feet by the dancing women.

At once Pa Jibiti seemed energised and danced as if possessed. When he slowed to a halt, the procession made a loop and returned back to Pa Jibiti's compound for the concluding rites. Auntie Rejoice decided there probably would be no sacrifice that night.

She thought she'd seen enough and made for home.

EIGHT

The thought of becoming a detective weighed heavily on Auntie Rejoice's mind, keeping her turning and tossing on her bed at night. But what else could she do? Her parents legacy was to always right a wrong, and fight for justice. Her Catholic upbringing only emphasised those rules of love.

By the time the alarm sounded, waking her up, she was tired and ready to have a good night's sleep She struggled to her feet and got ready for school without so much as a look at the meal her maid had prepared her for breakfast.

On her way to school she glimpsed Ma Taiwo fanning a coal fire on which was a smoke-blackened kettle. Auntie Rejoice quickened her steps so as not to disturbed the shop owner, nor be disturbed herself.

Too late, Ma Taiwo had seen her, and gave a shriek of delight. Auntie Rejoice slowed her pace and walked to the dress shop. Ma Taiwo refused to acknowledge that, the teacher was in a hurry.

"Hey teacher! Nice and early as usual! Come and eat, I've just put the kettle on for coffee. I brought some eggs for omelette. It won't take a minute to be ready. Come and sit down! You work too hard! Sit!" Ma Taiwo said pulling out one of the wooden benches from under a sewing table and resting it against the open door of the shop.

"I won't stay long, I have a class at eight-" the teacher said.

"Eight o'clock! You are very odd indeed!" Ma Taiwo shrieked, "But it's not even six o'clock yet! It is just two minutes walk away to your school. Sit!" Ma Taiwo was known for her irrationality. She sometimes behaved as if she'd been nibbled on the bottom by an ant, goading her to shriek out her sentences or act like a roaming actor in need of a script. She seemed to have all the time in world for Auntie Rejoice. The passing of time seemed to have no bearing on Ma Taiwo, the clicking of time was for others. But time was always in short supply for the teacher. Auntie Rejoice sometimes humoured the dressmaker, not because she wanted to chat or listen to gossip about yet another happening in the Taiwo's household, but Auntie Rejoice felt pity for the sewing mistress. The usual topic of conversation was Ma Taiwo's husband and his cheating ways. Auntie Rejoice had long suspected that, no one paid much attention to Ma Taiwo but herself alone. The teacher saw herself as a substitute psychotherapist to the sewing mistress.

"I will have coffee but no omelette please-" Auntie Rejoice said, sitting herself down on the bench which was holding one half of the shop door open. Her eyes roamed the inside of the shop. Light was coming from one naked white bulb in the centre of the white painted ceiling. There were ready- made long dresses waiting for owners' collection. An unfinished skirt, with wonky hem, hung loosely from a wooden hanger which hung from a small nail in the wall. Four short- skirted badly cut dresses hung on hangers on a trolley. Two elderly sewing machines sat on two separate high but narrow tables, under these were red plastic chairs. Another table larger and wider than the others had a bigger machine with assorted sewing spools of threads. Also on this table was four designer catalogues, piled on top of each other. The top catalogue was left open at a page showing emaciated, mini-skirted girls displaying the latest fashion styles in Europe. None of the dress styles bear any resemblance to the dresses in Ma Taiwo's store. It was a known fact in the village that, sewing mistresses were incapable of cutting patterns to catalogues specifications, nor sewing to clients' choices from the catalogues. Even then, Ma Taiwo and most sewing mistresses always insisted on clients choosing patterns from the books. Everyone knew catalogues were just there for show, even then both sewing mistress and client always went through the ritual of looking and choosing. An A-4 exercise book, a biro on top of it, sat beside the catalogues.

Auntie Rejoice's eyes strayed to the painting of the Blessed Mary looking up to her crucified son on the Cross, on a wall. Then she saw a small black velvet pouch tied with black rope, hooked on a nail, hanging from the top of the doorway of the shop. Ma Taiwo had explained that, this was a special juju for luck. At first sighting this small bag, Auntie Rejoice had asked the dressmaker if Jesus wasn't enough for her. Ma Taiwo had replied that her husband gave it to her, that she hadn't really noticed any change in her fortune since hanging the black magic pouch. The sewing mistress's voice interrupted her roaming eyes.

"You need to feed yourself. Look at you, you are thin. Yes, you are very beautiful but thin all the same! You get away with your thinness only because you are beautiful. Because the first thing men see when they look at you is not your thinness. They look at you and think, 'what a beautiful girl!' that's what they think first. Some of them who like good meat on their women will say, 'she's beautiful it is true but a shame she is also too thin!' I promise you men think like that. It is the way of men to think in that fashion, most of them anyway!" Ma Taiwo said, as she examined the soot covered kettle simmering over the coal fire. Seeing that the coffee was brewed, she poured the boiling liquid into two large china cups. She pierced two holes in a tin of sweetened condensed milk and poured over the coffee and stirred it. Ma Taiwo handed a cup to her guest. Auntie Rejoice took the cup, sipped then put the cup on the bench between Ma Taiwo and herself, mirroring her friend's action. Auntie Rejoice wondered why Ma Taiwo was sweeping and cleaning the shop by herself when she had a young son of sixteen and three apprentices to help her. The boy, Demo, was the laziest pupil Auntie Rejoice ever laid eyes on. He was always the last to arrive at school assembly and the last to submit any homework set by his teachers. He had been warned several times that he faced expulsion, but Auntie Rejoice always intervened, giving him another chance. Even she, now admitted the boy was a waste of hers and every teacher's time.

"Why are you sweeping the shop and environs yourself where is Demo and your girls? You have so many jobs to do, you must allocate some to your boy and apprentices" Auntie Rejoice said.

Ma Taiwo sighed as if the weight of the world was on her shoulders, rose from the bench then sat down again before speaking.

"What can I do when he won't do anything I tell him? I was going to ask about his exam. Have you seen his marks? Did he pass?" said Ma Taiwo, swallowing hard.

"I can tell you his overall result. He didn't do well at all. He was one pupil we all knew would not do well. He didn't disappoint! I'm sorry to tell you that." Said the teacher.

"So what sort of mark are we talking about?" Ma Taiwo insisted. Auntie Rejoice shifted in her seat. She hated breaking sad news to people.

"He got no more than five percent of total. I'm sorry-"

"What can anyone do with five percent mark? What? Where would he get a job with that percentage?" Ma Taiwo sprang to her feet with agitation which subsided as quickly as it arose.

"These things are sent to test us. Don't worry, he's young he'll find something. He's lucky to have you!" Auntie Rejoice consoled, but Ma Taiwo's mind had already turned to village gossip.

"I know he is. So what happened with Ayo yesterday? Did you help him?" said Ma Taiwo, pushing her son's failure to one side.

"It's a long story. Someone killed his mother and the police don't want to know-"

"You know this is Aina village! Inspector Gberaga is impotent in all ways, believe me-" said Ma Taiwo. She was interrupted by the astonished teacher.

"How do you know he's impotent in real life? You haven't, have you?

"He's a man, not so? He's very small below, you know! I have idea about men with beer belly! When the belly is too big, it squeezes their manhood, if you know what I mean-" the sewing mistress's face broadened with a knowing smile.

"Here we go, make me laugh. What is your idea?" said Auntie Rejoice, looking at her host suspiciously.

"I come to think men with beer belly have small penis. The belly must push it inwards, like the weight of the whole world on a single hand!" Both women burst into laughter. Auntie Rejoice controlled herself enough to tell her host off.

"What nonsense you talk and so early in the morning too! You should be ashamed of yourself! "

"I know you be the most beautiful in this village, but if I say so, men still find me attractive! I'm not bad looking. 'Am I?" said the dressmaker, fishing for compliment.

"No, you are quite attractive. You dress well. You are not too thin nor too fat, just right. But you are married!"

"That's what you think. What is my husband doing for past five years? Running after other women, that's what he does! Young man like my husband, well he no that young, having one wife and several mistresses. I tell you, I'm not enough for him. He still go after useless girls in short skirts and too much make- up! I get my fun where I can get it too! Listen you must put on weight-" Ma Taiwo advised.

"I don't care. I'm not looking for a husband this early in the morning! In fact I'm not looking for a husband at all-" said Auntie Rejoice.

"I know you had a bad marriage-"

"Ha! That was in my youth. I was very young, too young to know better-"

"Well, you thought you were in love, yes you were in love. But he loved your wealth more. Haruna wanted your money, everybody saw that. The young always think they know better, I did, you did. Now we know there are types of men you don't marry! What about your boyfriend, Peter Rotimi?"

"Peter Rotimi is my colleague not my boyfriend, never my boyfriend! The sea would dry before I call him my boyfriend. No I have no boyfriend. My God and my work are my boyfriends! Peter is not the kind of man serious women should go with. He's only fit for careless girls who are enticed with nice cars and a few Naira notes! I'm not interested in marriage-" Auntie Rejoice said earnestly.

"Don't talk like that! An angel of the Lord may be passing and taking your wish with him. That's what the elders say, always wish yourself well, because you never know! So you don't want a husband? You want to be a detective? I don't think we have woman detectives in this part of the world. I mean independent woman detectives. Plenty of them in the Police Force! Why don't you leave teaching and go into the Force? " Ma Taiwo suggested kindly.

"I don't want to be a detective and I don't want to be a policewoman, thank you. I just want to give Mama Ayo justice. I think I know who killed her. I need to- I must prove it. I just can't let the murderer walk away free. The Inspector may not care for human life, we have to show that we the citizens care for each other. I'm a teacher, but I have to see justice done. I just can't sit and accept it's all right to commit a crime and let the culprits go free. Suppose Mama Ayo was your daughter, would you be happy I'm doing this?"

"Of course I will be happy someone cared. But be careful. Those men in the village are dangerous and Pa Jibiti, his boys, and Pa Seyi are the most dangerous. You know Pa Jibiti was twice accused of ritual killings last year? That missing child last year? His headless body found by the lake, pots of juju artefacts surrounding it? One of Pa Jibiti's special rings was found by the body- " Ma Taiwo was interrupted by the teacher, who had heard it all by word of mouth from pupils' parents and also read the articles in newspapers.

"The ring was found and returned to him. Pa Jibiti took the ring without so much as to ask where it was found? I remember. How can I forget? It was the talk of Lagos! And he got away with it because no one challenged him. He is just a bully, you know. He uses juju as a powerful controlling force. His main weapon is fear, people fear the unknown. Power of fear is used not just by people like Pa Jibiti but also false prophets. Instead of putting their faith in the Lord, they put their faith in juju, false prophets, and witchdoctors like Pa Jibiti. The real truth is, there is no power like the power of the Almighty. Surely if these people have any believe in God, they'll know If God created Satan, that God has greater power over His creation, the Devil! Is that not so?" Said Auntie Rejoice, warming to the topic.

Ma Taiwo frowned and mulled it over in her mind before replying.

"You are right. I never think it like that before. Of course if I believe that God makes everything, why can I not also believe that faith in anything or anyone else is denying God. But what of clever people who say we come from explosion of stars?"

"You mean scientists who laugh in the face of God? What I find incredible are the pseudo intellectuals proclaiming the Story of the Creation to be far fetched but blindly embrace recently concocted story of human being rising from the explosion of stars because some men said so! They proclaim there's no proof of God's existence just as they can't produce proof of making us from stars. It's a contradiction. Isn't it?"

"When you get education beyond the necessary, it blinds you to real wisdom. Anyway most people in those countries only follow those they think are their betters." Ma Taiwo said, but her mind was back on her own problems, "I must talk to you about–"

"I must go." Said Auntie Rejoice. Ma Taiwo screwed up her nose. "You can't. It's still not light yet. Stay a little longer, You should get another car, you know?" Auntie Rejoice nodded but was not really listening. Suddenly the name of Pa Seyi caught her attention.

"What did you say?"

"I was asking about that stupid man everyone call Pa Seyi. Why they call him that I no know! He's only a young man, old before his time! It's de way he lead life, you know. Doing evil things is ageing–" said Ma Taiwo. Auntie Rejoice was becoming impatient.

"What's the point you're making?" she said

"I'm saying I saw Pa Seyi earlier this morning about five o'clock as I left home. Very funny, he was smoking his head off as usual. He looked as if he got something on his mind. He looked troubled, and no wonder, fathering the fatherless! Do you know, he fathered that dead woman's child?" said Ma Taiwo

"He was the father of Mama Ayo's baby?" Auntie Rejoice asked, showing no surprise at all. Ma Taiwo was only confirming the suspicion she'd had all along.

"Of course! Everyone knew that, well, people in the know-" said the sewing mistress.

"You mean people who go round gossiping, instead of being productive!" the teacher corrected, jokingly.

"Gossip is good for the soul! You should do it sometimes my friend!"

"I must be on my way or I'll be here till evening. One more thing. Can you do me a favour?" said the teacher conspiratorially.

"Of course, anything" Ma Taiwo replied eagerly.

"It's about Mama Ayo. Will you sew a burial dress for her? It'll be a kind gesture to the dead?" said Auntie Rejoice, holding back the tears threatening to flood her blouse.

"For you, I will sew a beautiful white dress for Mama Ayo"

"Thank you, my friend. I will give you money for the material and labour tomorrow"

Auntie Rejoice looked up to the sky. A beautiful yellowish ball of brightness was emerging behind the darkness. Auntie Rejoice rose from the bench and was on her way to school.

She walked through the short cut, a narrow footpath, a sea of green, away from the growing traffic. She felt warm and contended. A feeling that was miles away from her earlier thoughts when she left home that morning.

She felt a warm glow for Africa, Nigeria in particular. It is only in Nigeria that anyone could stop at an acquaintance's shop and be made not only welcomed, but free to empty one's mind of misery and depression, and felt better for it. Only in Nigeria could one use a neighbour or even strangers as psychiatrists and not be laughed at. Only in Nigeria could anyone walks into a private party and be fed and watered while the hosts ask each other 'Who is that? Feed him anyway.' Auntie Rejoice smiled to herself as thoughts kept flooding her mind. It angered her to hear about fraudulent Nigerians. They spoil the good name of a beautiful country and kind- hearted people. These people have no shame and deserve all the punishment they get. Auntie Rejoice shook her head, it angered her to read of the unpatriotic antics of some of her fellow men and women, at home and abroad.

She thought they gave fuel to enemies of Africa, who are only too happy making money from Africa's misery, while crucifying the Continent that bestowed wealth on them. Some people, especially rich Europeans who lived on the sweat of Africans, too easily jumped on the bandwagon, quoting these ruffians as examples of Nigerians. What a pity, she thought.

As she came to a point where the grass was tall and thick, the smell of goats' sweat gave them away. She saw goats and a few sheep here and there, mowing the grass, their masters sat, in circles around a small wood fire, eating breakfast from tin bowls. Neither the animals nor the malams gave her a second look. The animals were used to the presence of humans. They did not blink as she walked pass them but continued in their quest of riding the land of unwanted weeds.

Auntie Rejoice sighed with contentment. This is the land of her forefathers in which they were all proud. This is a country that has never known hunger. Not because there are no poor people, there are, but because people share their wealth. The rich give to their poor relatives. There was widespread believe that people are their brothers' keepers. A land that is blessed, with abundant wealth. Although oil is promoted as a major export, there are so many other riches yet untouched, tin, diamond, and the old friend, groundnuts and much more. Yes Auntie

Rejoice reflected, she preferred to be here in Nigeria, Lagos in particular. She had never regretted returning to Lagos after completing her studies in England, much as she liked the British.

And the men! Of all the scallywags in the world, she met and married the worst. The less said about that the better. She thought.

When she looked up and saw the gates of the school, reality kicked in.

Nine

Isa Haruna was the boy who saw the young Rejoice across the classroom and determined she would be his bride, come what may. Since he was a little boy in the little village of Zarun in Northern Nigeria, Isa had dreamt of going to the big city, relocating to Lagos. He'd seen pictures of the big city and hoped to go make his fortune. Since he lacked any money making attributes, he would marry a girl who possessed wealth and would allow him escape the drudgery of his family's poverty. He was a bright but lazy boy who would rather play football than read books his mother snatched from unsuspecting homes. She managed to send him to a free missionary school nearby where he learned to read and write.

Haruna was dubbed a miracle baby by his mother. His mother, known as Moma, had eight babies of which seven died before the age of four. Haruna survived the lack of medical amenities, poor, crammed mud housing conditions and various childhood diseases, including smallpox and malaria from mosquito bites. The incredible hunger for living afforded him a huge slice of love in his mother's heart. She brought him to Lagos in search of better opportunities and found him a new school. In Lagos Isa blossomed. He showed good prospect in his schoolwork, assiduously doing his homework, gaining good grades in exams. He was very athletic with a passion for football. At the age of fourteen, the coach of The Junior Sparrow Football Club visited the school and selected him for the club. Two years later Isa was kicked out for absenteeism and insubordination. He returned to his old school, for university entrance examinations. He proved that little had changed, he remains lazy and insolent. His attention span was very short, his boredom threshold, low. But he persevered long enough to gain a scholarship to the University of Newyoker and got a pass degree in media studies. Isa became the first member of his family to attend any school, the only member able to read and write in any language, Yoruba or English. English had long been made the common language by the British, a prerequisite for employment. In Rejoice's junior school, for example, no child was allowed to speak his own tongue, or any other language except English. Misguided parents were still giving priority to speaking English at home, producing children who regard their mother tongue inferior.

Isa saw Rejoice, who was reading Biology, across the lecture hall, during a class in citizenship for first year students. He left his seat in the fifth row to sit diagonally behind her. Mid- way through the lecture a friend sitting beside Rejoice nudged her in the ribs with her elbow, whispering and nodding towards Isa,

"You know that boy?" Rejoice glanced backward then shook her head from side to side.

"He's been starring at you all the time! He fancies you!" They both glanced back then giggled. Isa smiled at them, hoping he'd made an impression on the girl that would become his wife. Rejoice glanced back again to regard the boy's face. She turned back, thinking he was no picture book Romeo.

He had a plain face with tiny scattered cavities in the facial skin. This was bad news, a sure sign that the boy had suffered smallpox at a young age. A flood of pity descended on Rejoice. She wondered the sort of life he'd had. Life must have been hard with the disease, surviving it was a triumph of his spirit. The disease should have been eradicated in Nigeria by now. It was no surprise to see such damaged faces in towns.

It must have been horrible to carry such a blemish on your face knowing you were an object of derision. Pity for the boy overwhelmed Rejoice. She suddenly noticed the lecturer's lips moving, knowing she should be paying attention, but her mind kept returning to that face and the poor boy behind it. She was admonishing herself for not concentrating when a hand, holding a packet of sweets, thrust itself into her face. It was the boy, stretching a hand forward to offer them sweets, as a way of introducing himself.

"My name is Isa, Isa Haruna. Please to meet you. I know who you are, no need to introduce!" They all smiled. The Akintola family was very well known in the country and very popular, due to the many newsworthy raids on illegal smugglers, organised and usually led by Chief Akintola. The family fame was inherited by his only child, Rejoice. The media still reminisced on the good old days of the fearless Chief Akintola.

After the lecture Isa trailed after Rejoice and her friend, Yinka, like a puppy lusting after food. Yinka introduced herself and her friend anyway, Isa did the same.

"I know you from hearing about your late parents. I heard you were coming to this university, it made me think it must be good, so here I am. I'm quite please to meet you. Will you like to come to the students' bar for a drink, tonight?" he beamed.

Rejoice wasn't as taken with the young man as he was with her, and going to a bar wasn't her favourite pastime. She had visited the students bar only once in the whole year. "I don't like the smoking. Smoke gets in my eyes and irritate them. If you see them water you'd think I was crying! We can go to another place, though it's a little expensive. There the smokers are separated like naughty children, banished to the back of the room. Not a good solution but better than smoke blowing into your eyes when you don't smoke!" said Rejoice.

"I agree with you. I don't smoke too but bar owners are slower here than in New York to ban it outright. It's such a dirty habit isn't it? I'd like to take you to a nice place but I can't afford it. I'm on a scholarship you see. My parents can't even afford to send me pocket money-" Isa was seeking sympathy. It worked in his favour.

"I'll pay for the outing to my father's old club. It's the senior service club. My father was the president. He had his own room, so I was told. They gave me honorary membership." Rejoice said, smiling, not knowing that was exactly what Isa was hoping for.

"Well, thank you. Hope I can reciprocate when I start work!" he laughed, knowing he had no intention of seeking employment, ever.

Like everyone in the country, Isa and his family had heard a lot about Rejoice Akintola's family. He'd seen photos of the late Chief of Customs and his wife in newspaper articles and on television documentaries. It was no surprise he set his eyes on her.

Haruna was determined to use his charm in wooing Rejoice and he succeeded. Rejoice grew to love the boy with craters in his face.

The couple knew their union would raise eyebrows, if not doomed.

Rejoice grew up hearing stories of tribal division and greedy politicians from her aunt Rose. Since Nigeria's division into three unequal regions by the British, the three main tribes, Yoruba, Ibo, and Hausa had harboured a slight suspicion of each other, so Aunt Rose said. The implication was that, the departing colonialists were handing the country to a largely uneducated easily malleable group of Northerners as bribe, in exchange for pillaging the country. The Northerners in their defence, at that time, rejected the name- calling, regarding their detractors as over- educated arrogant thugs. The fire of resentment was fuel, as always, by greedy self- seeking opportunistic politicians, bereft of good ideologies, whose only way to self- glory was to promote disunity among the three main tribes. While the people fight among themselves, the politicians dipped their long arms into the country's Treasury, pillaging the country. Very few politicians wished their fellow citizens well. Fewer still, wanted the betterment of their country in a world of growing globalisation. Yet advanced technical skills are abundant in the country, waiting for a helping hand. Rejoice wasn't sure if all these were true. She was young and, like all young people wondered what all that corruption, and stealing people's money got to do with her. Adulthood was a long time yet. And like the youth of any age, she thought growing old was for somebody else. But she grew up and fully saw and understood her old Aunt Rose's gripe, all those years ago! Now, to Rejoice, it seemed like yesterday as it always does in maturity.

Both Rejoice and Isa knew all these as well as the history of their country and had heard their different peoples spoke of tribal rivalries. Yet Rejoice was joyful in her love of a boy who loved money above all.

Isa took Rejoice on long walks along the beautiful Marina. They walked handed in hand along the Atlantic ocean talking about their bright future.

"I will build you a palace-" Isa said one evening.

"With what?" Rejoice asked, ever so pragmatic.

"Don't worry I will do it. I will get the money, with your help." He concluded without revealing how much financial help he needed from her. She would be a lady of leisure when he came into his money, money made legitimately in a business to be decided, he promised. Nigeria was full of opportunities for risk takers. Nigeria was like America, anyone could make it, he said. He forgot to add that, Nigeria was an ancient country, full of traditions of its three main tribes with thousands of years of history yet undiscovered by the world. As they strolled, the cooling air from the ocean caressed them like a warm blanket on a cold night. The night lights from surrounding shops and buildings made it a romantic night out.

With his arms around her, Haruna found it easy to pluck promises from mid- air,

"I know we've agreed to marry but I need to meet your parents-" she said suddenly, detaching herself from his arms. He had been reluctant to introduce her to his humble home.

Now it was impossible to resist the request. A day or two later, Haruna took Rejoice to his house, behind Mushin market, opposite the dried fish stalls, in Lagos, where his mother had to give her son a chance in life.

Haruna knew his bride- to- be would run a mile than settle in such poverty. The house was very cheap and rented out in rooms. The Haruna family took two adjacent rooms. Pollution hung in the air with the odour of meat, fresh and dried fish from the market. The compound became impassable during rainy season. The tenants had to negotiate two permanent wooden planks that served as footbridge from the entrance of the house to the main street. These inconveniences did not deter Rejoice. She ignored Haruna's poverty and went ahead with the marriage.

His mother couldn't believe the apple of her eyes was dating Akintola's only daughter, the inheritor of a large fortune. Moma celebrated the reflected glory on her own family. No longer would people look down on her and her family as insignificant to Lagos society but she, a penniless nonentity, would be rubbing shoulders with the makers of history, the cream of Lagos society, those who mattered in the country.

After the marriage Haruna refused to seek employment. He had no idea what he wanted to do with his life. But he knew what he didn't want to do. He didn't want to work. He didn't want to be neither a market hawker like his mother nor a layabout herbs seller like his father who'd refused moving south. He knew his father made hardly any money to feed his family from that job. He decided on the job of a house- husband, but hated housework.

The marriage was annulled six months later. Auntie Rejoice had never heard from Haruna since the day of their separation. He just disappeared into thin air.

At one time there was rumour of his death in a motorcycle accident but there'd been no confirmation. His mother no longer lived in Mushin and their former neighbours could shine no light on their whereabouts.

Auntie Rejoice regarded that part of her life closed and never talked about it except when Ma Taiwo brought it up. Everybody had now forgotten that she was ever married, so has she.

Ten

It wasn't long after Auntie Rejoice left the sewing mistress when Ma Taiwo's apprentice, Ruby, appeared, late again for work. The girl was always late. Ma Taiwo had spoken to her about her lateness several times bur to no avail. Ruby stood in front of her boss, arms akimbo justifying her lateness. Ma Taiwo was not pleased at all.

"What time you call this?" asked Ma Taiwo, turning her right wrist round so her palm faced downwards. "It's after six! What time you suppose to start your learning? Five thirty!"

The girl gazed round the floor as if she'd lost a coin, a smile creased her lips, angering Ma Taiwo.

"This is no laughing matter! You learn or not learn. If you don't want to learn, there are boys and girls ready to take your place. Do you know how many people I turned down for training to take you? Do you have explanation or I am to guess what's going on in that big thick head of yours?" Ma Taiwo was angry but her anger never last.

She knew that whatever she said would go into Ruby's ear and immediately emerged through the other ear. The girl, she had decided long time ago, was incapable of being turned into a master sewing mistress like herself. Ma Taiwo knew that, to have good- mannered apprentices, took good home training, a mother and father, who cared enough to tell their children what was right and what was wrong. Ma Taiwo thought her fifteen year old apprentice was raw and common as dust, when she arrived. Ruby didn't know a straight hem from a dropped stitch, and dirt poor. That was the reason she was taken on. Ma Taiwo decided to help the girl get a career. A career that would bring in income to the girl's poverty stricken parents. The last thirteen months had been an endurance test for Ma Taiwo and today was no exception. After this length of time Ruby was still unable to sew in a straight line, nor cut a simple skirt on her own. Many villagers thought this was not surprising, as the apprentices spent most of their time running errands for their mistress. Away from the shop and Ma Taiwo's hearing, Ruby boasted to everyone she was an accomplished dressmaker, who would soon come into the shop's ownership.

There was not a day went by when Ma Taiwo didn't contemplate sacking Ruby. Every time Ma Taiwo determined today was the day to show Ruby the door, the apprentice would do a kind act and all sins would be forgiven again till the next time.

Ruby was an odd teenager who shouldered a big responsibility. Her trainer, Ma Taiwo, had no inkling of her apprentice's high status in the underworld.

When Ruby was not at work she was usually in 'house of clay', a small bamboo hut in the compound of the family house.

The fifteen-year-old girl was proclaimed high priestess at the age of two when her parents dedicated her life to the god of clay. She became chief celebrant at the god of clay annual street festival, with her face and the faces of her parents covered in white clay and beaded masks to protect their identities, as they danced round the village.

As chief priestess, it fell on Ruby to lead her family and cult devotees in daily worship of her god in the 'house of clay' built specially for her. Pa Jibiti, of course, remained chief priest at all ceremonies including the grand midnight celebrations.

At aged twelve Ruby sailed through her rite of passage, which climaxed in a 3a.m. 'deflowering' by Pa Jibiti on the altar of the god of clay at the crossroad, while his wives and worshipers clapped and danced joyfully, welcoming her to adulthood.

After her daily apprenticeship, Ruby would go home to a meal of white foods, white rice, or white yams and white meat like chicken or fish. Her satanic demeanour meant she was forbidden to eat anything off white in colour. The day she ate anything colourful like meat, would be the day she left this world for a hellish existence in the after- world. She grew up with this warning ringing in her ears. A life dedicated to the god of clay was a life of white foods and dresses. Yet her soul was as black as the darkest night.

Ruby's system of beliefs was beaten into her from birth. Pa Jibiti, who held sway on idol worshipers in the village, awarded her the high status of chief priestess the minute she emerged from her mother's womb.

It was obvious to Ma Taiwo that Ruby was an odd young girl. There was something about the girl not quite normal. But the sewing mistress couldn't lay a hand on what was peculiar about Ruby. If only Ma Taiwo knew! After work every girl went home to rest and play but not Ruby. The evening marked a beginning of another day for her. She presided at the day's cult ritual with her father assisting.

The ceremony began when Ruby's father, Pa Ayu grabbed a white pigeon from a collection in one of many birds' bamboo baskets in their backyards. He tied its legs together to prevent it flying away. Dancing in a semi circle to and fro, reciting incantations appealing to the god of clay he would beg the god to curse or showered misfortune on a neighbour or some annoying person. A client might have requested a death on a member of his own family (For a quick inheritance, for example) or on someone at work. It was left to Ruby, the high priestess, to carry out the final sanction and decide if the victim would live or die, or how long the curse would last. A request for a curse of death, in an accident or sudden unexplained illness leading to death, cost a large sum of money and or a cow or two. In the old days money played no part in the equation, curses were exchanged for animals or human slaves, later killed in sacrificial ritual.

While Pa Ayu danced, Ruby prepared herself with the help of her elderly mother, in a side room, washing her hands and feet in dedicated water and special black soap. She would wait for her limbs to dry, before smearing her whole body, including her face, with white clay. The mother then wrapped a long white sheet round the girl's torso up to but below her breasts. A white gele is wound round her head to cover every strand of hair. A ring of red palm oil drawn round both ankles signified a chain to her god. Ruby, a black clay pot on her head, and her mother now emerged from the side room to the sound of Pa Ayu's chanting. The white pigeon, held by Pa Ayu, became a body sponge held in mid air, to dry- wash the girl without touching her skin. Incantations, more intense chanting and dancing continued till near midnight, when the pigeon is dropped into the black pot with some palm oil. At this point Ruby appeared possessed by the spirit of clay. Her body shook and shivered as she chanted loudly and pledged to be faithful to the god of clay. More dancing and singing.

If there was a human sacrifice, Ruby and her group would proceed to Pa Jibiti's compound where the ceremony continue at the crossroad.

But the small in- house ceremony at the 'house of clay' usually ended by a closing pronouncement from Ruby.

"We are ready. The god is ready to listen. Speak names of your enemies and the god will consider your request. Speak! he says! Speak!"

One by one worshippers would come forward, and whisper names into the clay pot.

One name on Ruby's lips at every ceremony was that of Ma Taiwo, the sewing mistress, her boss. If the god of clay was any good, and Ruby believed it was, soon she, Ruby would snatch the shop from Ma Taiwo.

As a final blessing, the pigeon is taken from the pot and given to glazed-eyed Ruby. She raised the bird to the sky then proceeded to wring its neck with little force, to shouts of 'oie, hear my call' 'see the back of my enemies'. Jubilation and dancing followed.

At exactly 3 a.m. Ruby let out small grunts before proclaiming, "Time! Time to go. Time runs out on my enemies. The job is done. The god is happy." worshipers hugged and toasted each other with ogogoro, then made their way home.

By mid morning Ma Taiwo was tired of staring at the pretty but irritating face of her apprentice, Ruby. She decided to take the rest of the morning off. She deserved it, after all, she'd been in the shop since dawn. She left the shop in the hands of her other sewing apprentices with a warning to keep a good eye out for new customers.

As Ma Taiwo turned the corner of the shop, she saw a wretched dog picking at an old, dirty bone. The dog must be hungry, she thought. Then her mind went back to her own fat, well fed Alascan dogs which she acquired eighteen months previously at exorbitant prices.

A few years ago, the last thing on her mind was owning a dog. She hated the beasts or rather she learned to hate dogs. Before her marriage, she lived in a rented flat at Surulere. One neighbour had a pretty dog. That dog gave dogs a bad name. Ma Taiwo remembered it well. This neighbour loved that dog like her own baby. She took it for walks three times a day. She came home from work at lunch, to feed and play with the beast. Neighbours laughed at her and called her 'oyinbo' (European). The British were thought to love their animals more than they loved Africans.

At Christmas time the dog got new toys, and special bone covered with mouth- watering meat. The dog grew fat and lazy. One day the dog owner came home from work, fed and walked the dog as usual then returned to work. On returning home, late afternoon, her house had been burgled. The dog had sat, like a log of wood, watching buglers broke into the house, carrying off her worldly possessions. Not so much as a bark or whimper passed its wide mouth. Neighbours blamed the owner for feeding it too much meat and imported dog food. A neighbour suggested keeping animals was a bad sign of greed. 'If you have money left over after feeding yourself, you should share it with those who have none' she said.

'Do we have the disease they call anorexia here? No, we have not! This is a disease of too much choices of food to eat. No, we don't have that! We have varied vegetables, different yams and sweet potatoes! Fresh pluck- from-trees food! That's what we have! But some have no money to buy these. Feed the people before feeding dogs!' said another, slapping her thigh to thunderous applause.

Ma Taiwo strolled down to Mushin market and bought some meat, bean flour, fresh prawns and vegetables. She felt the urge to make akara and ogi for her lunch. Akara, she found was an easy and quick dish to prepare. Ma Taiwo would mix the bean flour with water, salt, and prawns then rolled into small balls and deep fried in hot palm oil.

When Ma Taiwo got home her maid was nowhere to be seen.

Ma Taiwo walked to her husband's room and turned the door handle. It was locked with the key from the inside. She knew her husband was home. Since his retirement as a junior administrative clerk, he usually frequented his club in the morning, and returned home late evening for his meal before going out again to one of his mistresses. He was home today, Ma Taiwo thought, doing what exactly? She settled herself in the large kitchen preparing her meal. The akara was frying when she heard the turning of keys in the door. Her husband stood behind her in his dressing robe, a young girl at his back, covering herself with one of Ma Taiwo's wrappers.

Anger bubbled within her to the surface. She left her cooking and matched round the big bulk of her husband's frame to the girl. Pulling the girl forward, she slammed her against the huge fridge beside the kitchen door.

"Take that cloth off your body or I strangle you with it!" Ma Taiwo screamed while her husband scratched his balding head in embarrassment, his head bowed in shame.

The romantic love of yesteryears had long gone, now a distant memory. She and her husband had longed ceased to be rampant lovers. On her part the pain of sexual loss was not as severe now as it was, ten years previously. She had learned to cope with a wayward husband who now openly brought home his latest love, flaunting youth and beauty in her face. When she herself was that girl, other men wanted to take her home. She wept silently.

The girl ran back into the bedroom and emerged again wearing her own attire of a tight, figure hugging trouser suit. "I better leave you and your wife! You told me we have the house to ourselves! Look you! A man who cannot control his own wife! No power in his own house-" said the girl running out of the house, not waiting for Ma Taiwo's wrath. As the girl disappeared into the streets of Lagos, Ma Taiwo ignored her husband and turned to the akara which was now nicely browned. She made ogi, and took the food to her own room, overlooking their small garden and ate her lunch in peaceful isolation.

She was finishing her meal when she heard dragging feet on the stone floor of the kitchen. The maid always dragged her feet, as if her body was too heavy for the feet to lift, yet no one considered her fat.

The maid waddled to Ma Taiwo's room and knocked on the door.

"Why did you leave the house in a mess? You know I come home for lunch sometimes, nothing prepared. Good thing I brought my own food from the market eh?" The maid sank to her knees begging forgiveness.

"Not me madam. Na master say make I go out enjoy myself. Because he bring visitor. No my fault I leave home, madam. Sorry madam, sorry" Ma Taiwo knew that her husband got rid of the maid to entertain his new mistress. After her meal Ma Taiwo returned to the shop hoping to send Ruby to lunch. The other apprentices would be at lunch already.

She knew Ruby probably wouldn't need lunch. The sewing mistress knew what the girl got up to when she's left to man the shop alone. Ruby would be flirting with labourers who came to eat in Ma Kudira's buka next door. Ma Taiwo saw Ruby hurrying back to the shop, chewing. Ma Taiwo's heart sank, I really must look for a serious apprentice. The other two apprentices work at a snail's speed but are diligent. I will ask Auntie Rejoice's advice next time I see her, she thought sadly.

ELEVEN

Ayo returned to school and behaved as if the death of his mother was a fact of life.

It was break time and a couple of teachers were looking out of the staff- room windows watching pupils playing in the playground. They watched Ayo kicking a football around with other pupils.

"Rejoice, come and see your protegee, Ayo. My goodness he's good at the games." Said Auntie Bea, the chemistry teacher, a stern looking woman who tolerated no nonsense from anyone, including her colleagues. Auntie Rejoice rose from her comfortable leather chair to look out of the window, where more teachers now gathered.

Auntie Rejoice watched for a few minutes as Ayo played and laughed, got knocked down and got up from the grassy ground, dusted himself down and resumed play. Auntie Bea sighed heavily before speaking. "You'll think he has no care in the world. To look at him you wouldn't think he'd just lost his mother, do you?"

The question was posed to no one in particular. Auntie Rejoice pondered the question. Children are just wonderful, are they not? Although Ayo was very sad at the loss of his mother he seemed to have made a speedy recovery, Like most children in Africa, Ayo carried a lot of burden on his tiny shoulders that would sink many adults in Europe. Who could imagine walking two or three miles to school, then coming home to house- work, and cooking for his younger siblings? Auntie Rejoice pondered in silence, children of Africa should be celebrated. They work hard at break- neck speed, uncomplaining. Smiling through their tribulations, all- respectful without so much as a whimper. Yet, they grow into adults without an ounce of bitterness.

Auntie Rejoice turned to her colleagues, "Aren't they wonderful?"

Before Auntie Bea could reply, the school- bell shrilled the end of lunch break.

As she walked to her classroom Auntie Rejoice felt a pull on her skirt. She looked down to see Ayo following her to class for the afternoon lesson.

"Auntie Rejoice, Auntie Rejoice, you are a detective, I want to be one too!" Ayo said

"What? I'm no detective, I'm a teacher, you know that! I'm going to teach you English Literature now!"

"I know that! But you are going to detective my mama death. I want to help you find my mama killer. Can I, please, please?" the boy pleaded.

"It is a dangerous game, looking for a killer-" Auntie Rejoice said, but the boy has made up his mind he must help in finding his mother's killer.

"Please Auntie Rejoice, please! I feel I want to do something. I will protect you. Now can I detective with you Auntie Rejoice?" said Ayo, his eyes looking up pleadingly. The teacher ruffled his head and relented.

"OK, Ayo you can help me catch the killer. I will tell you when and what to do when the time comes. You can maybe become my secretary. OK?" The boy gave a big grin and nodded his head vigorously, the teacher was afraid he might dislocate his neck. She too smiled back at him.

"What do sec, setc-" Ayo stammered, the word sticking to his throat. Auntie Rejoice came to his rescue. "Secretary." Ayo exposed even white teeth.

"What do secretary do Auntie Rejoice? What do I do?" The teacher's eyes glanced at the ceiling, as if trying to remember the job secretaries did.

Suddenly a cloud of apprehension descended on Auntie Rejoice. Through the fog she saw Ayo holding up a kitchen knife dripping with blood. His eyes glaring down at his mother with hatred. Auntie Rejoice blinked the scene away. She glanced down and saw the angelic face of a young boy smiling up at her. His question suddenly dawned on her.

"Well, you have to look after me. I will tell you what to do and when the time comes, where to do it! You will remind me of my timetables, make sure I don't forget. It's a big job, and very important. Do you think you can do it? You'd like it?" the teacher's brows wrinkled into a frown.

"Oh yes! Yes! I like that!" the boy yelled with excitement. It gave Auntie Rejoice a chance to ask about Ayo's home situation.

"How's Pa Seyi and your brothers? I see you miss school sometimes, why is that?"

Ayo's face turned pensive and morose. "Pa Seyi go out a lot and tell me to stay in the house and cook and take care of my brothers. He don't care if I go to school. He say when he was my age he was working and taking money home for his father and mother. He said I spend too much money for schooling-" the boy whined,

"But he doesn't pay your school fees. The church gave you a scholarship. Why is he doing that? Does he not want you to have an education?" The teacher found that the anger she felt was sipping into her voice, so started talking softly. Ayo looked up to her again, then squeezed her hand. She patted him on the head, with her free hand.

"Pa Seyi sometimes go out for the day or night. He left us alone most of the time. I think he hate us-" the boy mumbled.

"I don't think he hates you. I think he just needs company and it's not easy to cope with five boys and a baby-"

"But I do all the work when I'm not in school. Anyway, when I am your secretary I will be happy. We will catch my mama killer"

"Yes, we will. Now let's do some work. Your classmates are waiting"

They entered the class and the afternoon lesson began.

TWELVE

Big wide framed Oba (king) Kosun Aina was the legal and traditional ruler of Aina village. A man of quiet disposition, known through out the village as a gentle giant. At six feet five he towered over most of his subjects.

The white-bricked palace stood right in the centre of the village, a few miles from Mama Ayo's house. Typical of this millennium for all things traditional, Oba Kosun received less homage from villagers than his grandfather and father did. He was a much-loved Oba who never interfered in the lives of villagers unless they brought their problems to him, unlike his father and grandfather before him who were absolute rulers. The old Obas' words were law, with the power of life and death. Some traditions, such as giving every first born boy in the village to the Oba as slave, died with the late Oba. The immense family wealth, acquired by forceful ownership of lands, had dissipated with the demise of the last Oba. Although Oba Kosun never interfered in village life, he was aware of happenings in his kingdom. Word reached him with every incident that occurred.

Oba Kosun's family had always claimed Aina village was founded by their ancestors. But there were parallel claims that the village existed from time immemorial, that when the Aina family settled in the village they took the name and slotted themselves into a vacant but hereditary position. Over the years, other ruling families, tracing their own ancestors to the village have emerged and disputed unsuccessfully their entitlement of Obaship.

The present Oba had to fight a long court battle to assert his claim to the throne. The Obaship was worth fighting for.

The Oba's palace extended the length of a whole street surrounded by very high cement walls and four gates, two each on opposite walls. The external surface of the white-washed walls were covered with drawings of regal postures of past Obas and traditional drummers. A portrait of the present Oba, resplendent in colourful flowing robes, expensive gold and coral beads cascading down his crown, round his neck and wrists, was at a centre of a wall. A white flywhisk protruded from his right fist. A pair of golden hand-made sandals graced his feet.

Oba Kosun shared some unpalatable old customs with his ancestors, the inheritance of elderly wives from his predecessors. The inheritance of old decrepit women ensured these women had the care and attention they deserved in old age. It was care of the elderly without state intervention or state funding.

The Oba himself had acquired and got donation of more wives than he could humanly coped with. The wives ranged in various ages, mobility, and abilities. Fifty wives were inherited from the very late Oba Lawal who passed to the great palace in the sky twelve years previously. Of course, Oba Kosun didn't attend his predecesor's funeral. Obas never attended funerals. To do so would be to bring down on his head ancestral curse, bringing misfortune to the village, death to the Oba himself and years of ill health and sorrow to the ruling house. The village would see nothing but trouble through out the reign. No Oba wanted the demise of his own kingdom.

Villagers never had intention of testing out the curse. The tradition had survived through the ages, Obas were forbidden to view the dead body of a preceding Oba. There were rumours of scary ancient ceremonies following an Oba's death. The story was that the dead Oba's heart was cut out, roasted and given to the new Oba to eat. This, according to rumours, meant that the new Oba had truly eaten an Oba therefore entitled to be one himself. No one had ever confirmed or denied these rumours. Perhaps if an Oba knew his pre- Obaship nutrition no one would be willing to become an Oba, but then, men were always greedy for power.

The very first time Auntie Rejoice heard about an Oba eating another Oba's heart, was when she returned to Lagos (after a prolonged absence of studying in London). She was astounded at the story. "Why? It's barbaric!" she remarked to Peter Rotimi, her colleague at St. Mary's, who was relating the story. He frowned at her innocence.

"Are you sure the Queen of England didn't do the same with her predecessor's heart? Are the British public told every secret about her coronation ceremony? You just never know. No one knows what really goes on in the Oba's palace! And don't tell the British public knows what goes on in the Queen's palace either." said Peter.

Auntie Rejoice shrugged her slender shoulders in disgust.

Oba Kosun knew not what his death held but he knew what he had to do after hearing about the murder of Mama Ayo and the important part Auntie Rejoice was playing. He was a good and kind Oba who cherished the good people of his kingdom. He'd heard of Auntie Rejoice's clash with Inspector Gberaga, his refusal to investigate Mama Ayo's death, and her struggle to remove the dead woman's body to the mortuary. Oba Kosun decided to summon Auntie Rejoice to a meeting and give her his patronage.

Auntie Rejoice sat calmly across the empty throne waiting for Oba Kosun to emerge from his private apartments to the throne room, not knowing why she'd been summoned.

Suddenly the sound of loud drumming emanating from the inner sanctum rented the air. Ten middle-aged men wearing colourful dashiki and matching dog- ear hats emerged. The men carried talking- drums under their armpits. They beat the drums rhythmically, singing the praise of Oba Kosun. The drummers were followed by four of the Oba's ministers, resplendent in colourful damask wrappers covering protruding beer- bellies. They in turn were followed by six of the Oba's senior wives (one supporting herself with a walking stick, her legs as thin as the stick), wearing only colourful wrappers tied up high on their chests, their arms and upper torso bare. Three rows of coral beads served as their head- dress. Gold chains and coral beads weighed heavily from their necks, wrists and ankles. Their feet were bare of shoes, their toenails brightly coloured in devil red.

Auntie Rejoice knew it was a sign the Oba was about to emerge, sit on his throne and receive visitors. A few minutes elapsed before the Oba emerged, waving a white flywhisk with golden handle in his right hand, bedecked in gold and rare coral beads, which dangled from his neck and wrists. On his head was a beaded crown of gold and coral beads cascading down his forehead.

All heads bowed and knees buckled, big and small, everyone rolled on their stomachs in homage to the first among the un-equals. He sat regally, legs apart as if expecting a small train to run between his massive gold embroidered trousers. His arms were stretched across the extended arms of his golden chair. He cleared his throat before speaking. "Rise." He addressed the audience who rose from their bellies to sit crossed-legged on the floor, their heads well below the Oba's waist. The Oba looked directly at Auntie Rejoice.

"Welcome, welcome, my daughter. Are you well?" said the Oba, waving his flywhisk at her, a sign permitting commoners to speak. She did a little bowing of the head before replying.

"Kabiyesi (Your Highness). I am well, I thank God. I thank you, Kabiyesi." Said Auntie Rejoice quietly. Kabiyesi smiled shaking his head up and down in appreciation. Auntie Rejoice kept silent until addressed by the Oba as custom demanded. Oba Kosun remained silent for a few seconds before speaking again.

"I heard about your clash with Gberaga. He refused to take up Ma Ayo's murder. I thank you, on behalf of everyone for your effort. Tell me what progress you have made." The Oba shook his whisk at her again. Auntie

Rejoice examined the Oba's golden shoes then found her voice.

"Inspector Gberaga refused to investigate Mama Ayo's death. He said her death was suicide-"

"Suicide? How can a woman with a knife in her heart commit suicide?" The Oba interrupted. Auntie Rejoice's palms turned up to the ceiling, an emotional reflex to a statement beyond believe. The whisk pointed in her direction again.

"I was shocked at his pronouncement too Kabiyesi. But that was what he said and wouldn't shift from that position. I took the body to the General Hospital-" Kabiyesi cut her off again.

"I heard about all your trouble my child. You showed mercy to motherless children and the God of all mercies will have mercy on you too. Where are her children now?"

"Kabiyesi, the children are safe at their neighbour's house, Pa Seyi. They were quite happy to stay with him. I made sure of that, and he was happy to have them. So all are happy in each other's company. Ayo is such a sensible boy, he'll look after his brothers. I've told him to come to me if there's any problem-"

"I heard the boy treats you as his second mother. That is a good thing for them. Children need a kind adult to trust. You are that adult. God will keep you well and give you all you ever desire, my daughter." The whisk pointed again.

"Amen. Thank you Kabiyesi, thank you sir." Said Auntie Rejoice. The Oba's next statement surprised her.

"When I heard about the case of Mama Ayo and your selfless fight to get justice for the dead woman and her children, I put some of my men on the case. I am not without some power, you know. I still have good contacts in the Police and the government. But I cannot interfere in Police or government matters. You know hereditary rulers are not suppose to meddle in such matters. You know that don't you?" the Oba said, waving his whisk at her. Auntie Rejoice thought the whisk was a useful instrument. It served as fly beater and for pointing at people without being rude. It also helped to emphasise a point.

"Yes Kabiyesi." Auntie Rejoice replied, restraining her excitement at having helpers to solve the case. Her enthusiasm was soon quenched.

"Yes, I put my people on the case. Do you know that Gberaga is the son- in -law of our Attorney General? That's how he got the job. Not only that but the Attorney himself possesses only the most elementary schooling. He attended law school at night, got the basic, the very basic education. All examinations he did, he failed nearly all! I have his papers in my possession! He's a donkey head! Ask me how he got his job. Go on ask me! Ask me how he got his job, ask!" the Oba was getting excited, Auntie Rejoice had never had an audience with the Oba before, so she was surprised how child- like he was becoming, while his ministers and wives listened with eyes downcast. She herself was almost infected with his enthusiasm. She smiled and shifted in her seat with the joy of discussing the case with someone, anyone, who was slightly interested in her plight, to bring Mama Ayo's killer to justice. She had no choice but to ask the question the Oba commanded, the whisk was pointing her way.

"Kabiyesi, how did the Attorney General get his job?" she said grinning. It was almost like talking to the sewing mistress, Ma Taiwo at the sewing shop. Gossiping.

"He got the job because he was friends with the Commander of the Armed Forces. I mean, if you are going to have a friend in high places the commander is a good one to have. Because why? He could be the President tomorrow, not by election, of course, but by staging a coup. His word is law until he too is stabbed in the back by a junior officer or politician. In civilised countries, the Army defends the country and protects the citizens. In an undisciplined and backward- looking worlds the Army wants to rule, and threatens the people it is employed to protect. See that? World turned upside down. Until everybody knows and is proud of their own jobs and concentrates on it, the country will not, cannot progress forward. This here, Nigeria, is a great country, Africa is the greatest of all the Continents. The mother of all Continents.

But we have some bad of the bad but also the goodest of the good. When the good and true patriots rule, the world will sit up and be respectful of Africa. That is why America and the rest of world leaders are afraid of African unity. They know, Africa will rise from its slumber and rule the world. That is why America and the others do not support us when we have good governments. But it will come. As sure as I am the Oba of Aina village today, good leaders, who love their people beyond their own self- love, will come. Mark my word.

My ancestors said a hundred years is not for ever, corrupt leaders forget this. If you steal five million dollars, you can't sleep in more than one bed at a time, or eat with more than one mouth. And you can't take the money with you when you die. As sure as the sun will rise in the sky tomorrow we will all die, the millionaire and poverty-stricken. It's six feet for everyone, even the man who owns acres and acres of land. A good man who is poor will live in the memory when he dies. People will forever say of him 'he was poor but good.' No one talks good if you leave no good memory behind. You will forever be remembered as that man who stole the people's money! I ask you Rejoice, what sort of legacy is that to leave your children or for the memory of your mother? What sort of legacy for the world to say to your children's children 'yes we remember your grandfather, he looted the country of money meant for the poor, money for clean water, money to buy drugs for the sick '?

So Inspector Gberaga's actions are to be expected. He didn't come from a good stork but, I know you did, and it showed. I knew your parents well but that's for discussion another day. My soothsayer informed me that, Mama Ayo's killer is closer to home than you may think. She was a wayward woman, you know. Her end was not a surprise." The Oba's statement shocked Auntie Rejoice. She'd understood Mama Ayo to be a decent law abiding woman. Though Auntie Rejoice was in shock, she maintained a calm exterior.

The Oba allowed his words to sink into the teacher's head before continuing. After a long pause the Oba spoke quietly.

"Watch your back my child. If you need help call the palace. I've told my people to put your call through, any time. The wicked ones are planning a hole for you to fall into. But with God's grace it is they who will fall into the hole. Ma Ayo was a fallen woman, but no one deserved to be killed in such a way, with her baby by her side. It was inhuman. Go in peace, my daughter. May the god of our ancestors go with you" the whisk pointed and the

Oba rose from his throne. All prostrated again, with eyes cast down to the floor.

"Thank you Kabiyesi, may you reign for ever" said Auntie Rejoice. She knew the meeting was over. The Kabiyesi turned his back on his audience who ran forward in unison to lead the way back into his apartments. The talking drums started praise songs again while the women danced out of the room. Auntie Rejoice rose feeling a little deflated on the comment of the Oba on a woman she'd regarded as faultless.

Thirteen

Auntie Rejoice sat at her veranda on a high rocking chair, her legs dangling in the air as she rocked herself back and forth, like a little girl. She had the veranda built in memory of her late father who loved to sit in the yard for hours starring into the park opposite, according to her aunt. This place served as a refuge where she sat away from her fusing maid or the pile high school papers on her worktable in the house. Here, the house looked onto a large, beautiful, well-maintained public park. The park had an area of water fountain running into a small lake. Very peaceful to watch. The park was demarcated from private properties by low cement walls interwoven with high –bibed- wires and iron gates. It was a dream come true for lovers of tropical flowers tenderly planted and maintained to very high standards.

She had gone to bed, but every time she shut her eyes she saw the frame of Mama Ayo lying in a pool of blood, her whimpering baby beside her. Eventually at three in the morning Auntie Rejoice rose and went to her veranda.

She sat now rocking herself as she starred into the park, unseeing, thinking about her life and the case of Mama Ayo. Her mind was full of doubts and wonderment at the boldness of her action in taking the case on single-handedness, she, who couldn't bear seeing a dead body without being overwhelmed by fear. There she was, in Mama Ayo's house, stuffing a lifeless body into a taxi with her own hands. What a turn up for the books! What glorious frightening thing for her, of all people to do. The thought of it now brought shivers down her spine. She felt vulnerable, wishing the father she never knew was there to put his arms around her, telling her all would be well. No wonder she couldn't sleep. Some thought her brave, but Rejoice felt it was a stupid thing to have done. But then who would do it for love or money? Was she right, taking the case of the dead woman so much to heart? Shouldn't she have given up the case when Inspector Gberaga refused to proceed with it, pronouncing it a suicide? Was it in fact suicide and was she wasting her time pursuing a dead case? And if she proved it to be murder, then what? The murderer would certainly not thank her nor would Inspector Gberaga. In fact she was sure the murderer or his accomplices would chase after her with murder on their mind, her murder. The Oba has warned her. Was justice worth dying for? The thought of what her late father would do crossed her mind. She stopped rocking herself for a moment and sat upright. Her great father. The kindest and most generous man she never knew. A man who fought dangerous battles for justice and freedom. Her mind went right back to her father's many wise words, related to her by her aunt and his many friends. She remembered when she came home from university at the end of her degree course when she told her aunt she had met the man of her dream.

"Are you sure? Do I know his family?" her father's sister said, the words her own father would have uttered. Auntie Rejoice answered 'yes' to the first question and 'no' to the second. The young Rejoice said she'd known the boy for one year but never paid any attention to him before until they were thrown together during a seminar and found they had so much in common. They'd been inseparable since then. Yes, she said to her aunt, I love this man and want to marry him. The young man, Isa Haruna, was the son of a hawker woman who was ecstatic after knowing about her son's choice for wife.

Auntie Rejoice glanced across the darkened park and ruminated, if her father was here now, what would he say to her? She decided that her father would certainly not give up in the face of danger. Wasn't she told that his mantra was 'go to bed with a clear conscience'? Indeed he did, and so would she.

Her father's words, rang now in her ears as she weighed up the path to follow.

She stood up from the rocking chair and entered the house, comforted by her father's old wisdom, determined it was right to fight on. She felt she, by now had an idea of who that killer might be. But she must find prove to nail the murderer. She returned to bed feeling elated having made her decision. By the time she was ready for sleep, the alarm clock shrieked in her ears to get up.

FOURTEEN

An early riser, Auntie Rejoice said her prayer and read a verse (Romans : 11-14) from the Bible, before leaving the house to do the ten minutes walk to St Mary's where she hoped to feed back her progress to the Headmaster. Although it was 5: 46 a.m. Mr Jaiye was already at his desk, eating moyinmoyin and coffee as usual.

"You meet me well. How was your day? Auntie Joko was good enough to take your classes yesterday. She didn't really have a lot to do so she was quite happy- you look tired. Are you all right-" the Head said anxiously.

"No, I'm not all right. Mama Ayo's death is more complicated than I thought. Her murder-"

"Hey? Can you prove it? It was murder, the evidence? How? Why? By whom? We know how?" Mr Jaiye was about to put a piece of moyinmoyin into his mouth but stopped the fork holding the food in mid air. He stopped eating his favourite dish, which was unheard of. Mr Jaiye put his fork down on a paper napkin and wrapped the rest of the moyinmoyin in the leaves it had been cooked in.

He drained the drops of coffee in the lid and screwed back the lid on the flask. Putting everything aside he repeated his question. "How can you prove this? Why? For what reason was she murdered-"

"I don't know sir. It is a puzzle. The worse thing is I called the police. You were here when I dialled for the police-"

"Yes! Yes! I heard you calling them. What happened? Are they going to investigate and arrest the murderer?" Auntie Rejoice saw that Mr Jaiye was getting more agitated.

"The police came and went. They said the death of Mama Ayo was suicide. Suicide my foot! They did nothing even when I told them it was murder. Inspector Gberaga insisted it must be suicide. There's nothing worse than those with eyes but cannot see" Anger was crawling up Auntie Rejoice's chest.

"You mean they couldn't see it themselves? But why?" the Headmaster said.

"He said the woman has just given birth, it was baby blues. Her husband has left her-"

"The law enforcers are truly fools, are they not? They think it was not murder, why? for what reason?" Mr Jaiye exclaimed. This gave Auntie Rejoice a moment's pause for thought. Her resolve for the truth as she saw it grew stronger.

"The boy told us in the morning there was a knife in his mother's chest. Now I'm not a detective but I could see it was impossible for Mama Ayo to knife herself to death in that way. I just have to get the proof"

"Well whatever you say" the Headmaster concluded. Auntie Rejoice read the Headmaster's mind. He too had doubt about putting herself in danger.

He was thinking of the many people killed and buried in a less obvious murderous way.

Mr Jaiye pulled his flask closer to him, opened it and poured some coffee into the flask cover. Auntie Rejoice knew her time with him was over.

"What do you want to do now? Where is the body? When is the burial?" the Headmaster said.

"I took the body to the General Hospital mortuary for a post mortem examination. The result will be out tomorrow. Today I think I'll try and find one of Mama Ayo's relatives so we can arrange the children's welfare. I promised to go with Ayo to see their uncle at Yaba. Then we can arrange the burial perhaps for two days' time. Sir can you keep a secret?" The Headmaster looked startled.

"Of course I can keep a secret!" he replied, taking a sip of coffee.

"Then I'll tell you. I have proof of the killer. I've kept it safe, somewhere no one would look right in the nose of the killers!" Auntie Rejoice whispered.

"What was it? I won't say a word to anyone" Mr Jaiye promised, like a child promising not to open a Christmas present before breakfast.

"The killer left footprints on the mat. I've kept it in a safe place."

The Headmaster looked even more startled. "Why didn't you give it to the police, to Inspector Gberaga? It might change his mind-"

"Because he would have dismissed it like he did everything else. He was not interested in solving the murder though I know he knew it was murder! Besides he would have exposed me to the murderer" said Auntie Rejoice candidly.

"Be very careful. These are dangerous people. I admire you for your effort for a child and family you are not related to. Doing all these must have cost you a lot of money, taxi fare, mortuary fees, the list goes on. The school will make a contribution to your pocket but don't spend too much. I will call a meeting of the school board and decide how much to pay you. I promise you to cover much of your expenses. Take a week off to clear all the mess. I'll cover your classes with the help of my other staff" Mr Jaiye said as he unwrapped his moyinmoyin.

Auntie Rejoice walked out of the school not knowing what lay ahead.

As she came out of the school gate she saw Ma Taiwo at a distance, waving her in the direction of The Lord The Good Shepherd Shop. The last thing on Auntie Rejoice's mind was gossiping, Ayo has gone ahead to wait at home for his teacher. She waved back to the dressmaker. She decided to stop at the shop if only for a moment. Ma Taiwo thought herself a good friend who unloaded her problems on Auntie Rejoice's shoulders. Ma Taiwo obviously had a problem and needed to talk right now. She tried to run to meet up with Auntie Rejoice, but her run turned into a duck waddle. Her son, Demo, was at St Mary's but not doing well at all. Auntie Rejoice knew this fact was the basis of the sewing mistress' love of the teacher.

"My good friend, come into the shop-" said Ma Taiwo.

"Listen. I don't have time-" said the teacher, tapping her wristwatch.

"I won't keep you long. Listen, My son is no good at school but, do you know, that stupid son of mine, wants to get engaged to that good- for- nothing girl!" said Ma Taiwo. Auntie Rejoice smiled, and thought, of all the tragedies in the world Ma Taiwo was worried about a boy getting engaged to a girl.

"The girl you don't like?" said Auntie Rejoice, trying not to show the irritation she felt.

"That girl, all powder and lipstick and short skirt! He came home last night saying 'Mum, I want you to meet her parents soon' I said 'Is she pregnant?' Thank God she is not. The girl is-" Ma Taiwo was cut short. There was a young lady in the inner shop trying on her new dress. The poor girl was tired of waiting for her dress adjustment she cried out, "Ma are you ready for me? I can't wait any longer!"

"Give me a moment girl! Don't you see I'm talking to an important guest?" replied the dressmaker.

"I can't keep you any longer. Go back to work I'll see you later" Auntie Rejoice said as she went on her way, happy for the distraction..

When Auntie Rejoice arrived in Aina village, Pa Seyi and the children were sitting on the grass outside Mama Ayo's front door eating bread and akara.

Aina village was a picturesque and one of the most beautiful places in the country. Villagers would have strangers believe it was the most beautiful place on earth.

True the village had an inspiring prettiness, that compelled outsiders journeying through the village to stop and wander round its quiet thatch roofed mud and contemporary buildings, its narrow and mostly untared roads, not to mention its preserved annual egungun and new yams festivals. The country- like environment seemed like a page out of the pre nineteen sixties Lagos, intertwined with the new. The aroma of assorted foods, including roasting fresh cashew nuts plucked from the many scattered cashew trees, was tonic to those who did not obtain their nuts from imported tins.

Mama Ayo's children ran to and hugged Auntie Rejoice as soon as they saw her from afar.

"Auntie Rejoice welcome!" the children shouted happily, holding on to their bread. "Auntie Rejoice you meet us well" said Pa Seyi, eating from a tin plate in his hand.

"Did you sleep well?" Auntie Rejoice asked no one in particular.

"We had little room to move about! Sola kicked me in the bottom in the middle of the night and I woke up!" said five year old Yomi while munching his bread with such ferocity Auntie Rejoice thought he might break his jaw.

"It's a smaller room than ours" said Ayo cheerfully, adding. "Can we go back home today?"

"That's why I'm here to arrange a permanent accommodation for you all. Remember we are going to see your uncle Bita this morning?" Auntie Rejoice said. The boy nodded "Yes Auntie, when?"

"Now, as soon as you finish your breakfast"

"I've finished my breakfast!" the reply came like a shot. Auntie Rejoice guessed that Ayo wanted to escape. Escape from what? She wondered.

"OK let's go. We're going to Yaba so we need the Yaba bus from that bus- stop across the road" said Auntie Rejoice pointing to a small crowd waiting by the roadside. There was no particular sign to indicate a bus- stop,

In Lagos, it seemed buses, especially the so called Kombi ones, determined to make maximum amount of money, stopped anywhere and everywhere passengers waved them down. The bus- stop opposite Mama Ayo's house was no exception. There was no sign indicating it was a 'bus stop' either. Those who wanted public transport buses stood by the road and hailed one. Dedicated bus stops were built by local councils but were in short supply. Auntie Rejoice with Ayo's hand tightly clutching her right hand, crossed the street to join the disorderly queue of passengers waiting for the yellow bus. They waited not quite ten minutes when they saw the bus mincing towards then. Above its windscreen big letters proclaimed, 'Blessed Are The Peace Makers!' written in black paint. As the bus creaked to a stop the waiting passengers rushed forward to get on the doorless bus. The young conductor, a boy not more than thirteen or fourteen, holding a short leather whip, jumped down from the bus shouting "Oya, oya, come on, come on! Get on! Don't waste my time! Time is money!."

It was not an unusual sight to see young street children doing adults jobs in Lagos and all over the country. Auntie Rejoice fixed her eyes on the little boy doing adult job, in a country that cared little for its orphans.

Auntie Rejoice pondered their fate, as she stood in the bus holding on to a seat handle.

Lagos was a magnet to a lot of these so young homeless urchins wearing dirty, torn adult male shirts and formally- white- but- now- brown shorts. The children appeared out of nowhere and often finishing up sleeping rough in gutters, garages, and rubbish dumps. Often ending up sexually and physically abused by adults. The lucky ones like this conductor, managed to find work, working all hours and paid peanuts. There was no obvious government's or charitable organisation's initiative to rescue or send these children to school, so the children fended for themselves. Their lives started and ended on the streets with no mourners, forever a wasted generation. Auntie Rejoice wondered if the young conductor could have become a scientist or a doctor. No one would ever know because the world never gave him a chance to find out. What a tragedy for the child. What a drain on the country, Auntie Rejoice sighed.

Passengers, wearing assorted colourful clothing, fought their way into the bus and found that all seats were occupied, the bus was full to capacity, just as the conductor wanted. Auntie Rejoice held on tightly to her bag to avoid pickpockets. Thieves operated in crowded areas especially at bus- stops. Thieves! It never used to be like that. Lagos was a very peaceful city where doors are left open, no one stole or abused people or properties.

After the civil war of 1966/67 things fell apart. Many people immigrated to Lagos bringing home- made and European supplied guns. Life was never the same again.

Auntie Rejoice ruminated on the negative effects of war. War never did anybody any good, no matter how much politicians justified it. The world would be a better place if warring politicians were given swords or guns to fight it out among themselves, without involving their respective soldiers or citizens. She considered other wars and wondered about the agony that befell young men in their prime and the pain of families. Auntie Rejoice thought wars must be abolished.

The civil war changed the value and quality of life that was lost forever. She sighed and watched.

The newly entered passengers, including a pregnant woman, stood shoulder to shoulder. As there was no space for the conductor, he clung precariously with half his body outside the bus, one leg in the doorway of the bus, the other leg floated in mid- air outside the bus without concern for his own safety or other road users.

"I haven't got all day! Enter! Enter! Get your money ready! Money at the ready! I have no change! Correct money ready! I'm coming for the money!" The sound of coins clanging could be heard as people undid their wrappers to bring out their coins.

He squeezed his tiny body between passengers, one hand gripping the tin roof of the bus the other hand collecting money from passengers with shouts of "Hey! You with the yellow dress, your money!" The lady in yellow dress handed him her fare in loose change. The conductor was jovial as he told her,

"You want to put holes in my pocket!" everyone laughed except the woman, who retorted, "You are lucky to get any fares at all, with your loud mouth!" Again people laughed. When the conductor turned to Ayo who was in front of his teacher, and said "Little boy where's your money?" An elderly woman who could probably not afford to feed herself three full meals a day answered, "I'll pay for him" wrongly thinking the boy was on his own unable to afford the bus fare. "He's with me" said Auntie Rejoice who paid for herself and the half fare for Ayo. That was one of the things Auntie Rejoice liked about this country. People are kind hearted when needed to be. Everybody was their brother's keeper. She felt sad that a few apples give the country a bad name here at home and abroad.

When the bus reached Macauly Street, Ayo indicated it was time to get off. They left the bus and walked another ten minutes before reaching uncle Bita's house.

The small house, (more like a hut) was built of tin and was an extension of the main grey bricked house. Auntie Rejoice straight away had a bad feeling about the visit.

"This is it, my uncle Bita's house" Ayo said excitedly pointing to what Auntie Rejoice hoped was a mistake. "Are you sure?" she asked "Yes. I came here many times with mama" They climbed the four stone steps built over an open gutter and stood at the tin door. Auntie Rejoice tapped on the door and waited. When the door opened a man of about forty five stood there barefooted in dirty white shorts chewing a teeth cleaning stick. It was still early morning. But by this time workers had left home for work and hawkers were already hawking their wares in the streets and along motor- ways, leaving the unemployed and the lazy at home. A sign of acute laziness was chewing cleaning sticks at this time of day. Auntie Rejoice was not impressed with uncle Bita at all, but tried not to show it.

Seeing his nephew uncle Bita removed the stick from his mouth, turned his mouth sideways and spat the juice into the gutter before turning full attention to Ayo ignoring the lady beside the boy.

"Ayo? Ayo? What are you doing here?" Bita said, accusingly.

Ayo looked uncomfortable as he shifted from one foot to the other. He had never liked his uncle but always gave uncle Bita his due respect according to Yoruba tradition, respecting anyone older than oneself even if the elder's behaviour seemed lunatic.

"Hem, hem, I'm-" Ayo stammered as he always did when stressed. His teacher came to his aid.

"I am Rejoice Akintola. I'm Ayo's class teacher-" Auntie Rejoice began to explain but was interrupted by uncle Bita.

"What are you doing here? Shouldn't you be at school teaching? No wonder the state of school children are getting worse-" Bita snapped.

Auntie Rejoice couldn't take any more of what she considered useless ranting.

"If you allow me the courtesy of listening to what made us leave school and come looking for you, perhaps you will learn one or two things! Now can we go inside? I don't think what we have to say should be said in public"

"OK, come inside" said uncle Bita, turning to enter the house. Auntie Rejoice and Ayo followed him inside.

What Auntie Rejoice saw, confirmed her unfavourable opinion of uncle Bita.

The shack looked like a small hut outside, but it was a single small room, made even smaller with hordes of cardboxes full to the brim with old ragged clothes, old papers, worn out shoes and cooking utensils. A single bed sat in one corner of the room. At the other corner there was a single hard straight-backed wooden chair. Auntie Rejoice noticed there was only one window in the room and that window looked out into the backyard. Rising above the window was smoke from a firewood stove on top of which was a covered blackened cooking pot. Uncle Bita followed Auntie Rejoice's eyes to the smoke.

"I haven't had breakfast yet. Why do I deserve this visit?" he said, depositing his toothbrush on a small table by a chair. Auntie Rejoice had been deliberately slow to break the bad news of his sister's death. She wasn't sure how he would take it. Having seen his behaviour she was sure he wouldn't be too sad. Uncle Bita seemed a self contained, selfish individual. As we stood here you'd think he'd offer us drinks or breakfast as custom demand but uncle Bita was not the type who cared much for tradition of generosity, Auntie Rejoice was thinking this as she stood in front of the man. She looked him over before deciding how to break the news. Uncle Bita was a thin man with a strong face, the face of a labourer or an athlete. Auntie Rejoice felt his thin figure was hunger related. Not as in a rich country like England, or America where thinness could be due to too much wealth. Wealthy people in those places, it was said, eat less fatty food, only lean meat and fish. But Auntie Rejoice could not imagine uncle Bita had enough to eat let alone be fussy about what he ate. The circumstances in which they found him proved the exact opposite. Auntie Rejoice decided to go straight to the point. That usually was the best way forward.

"Your sister, Mama Ayo is dead-" she said calmly.

"What? You are joking!" uncle Bita said in disbelieve.

"Death is no joke mister Bita Banwo. I assure you I am not joking. Your sister died yesterday-"

"Why didn't someone come to tell me about it? Why wait till nothing can be done? Anyway how do you know she's dead? You are not a doctor!" uncle Bita said angrily.

"Because she's in the General Hospital mortuary. She was murdered-"

"What did you say, murdered? Come on! Who would want to murder my sister, Moji? If you say they kill me, I'll say I maybe deserve it. I know many people who want to see the back of me. Not my sister Moji. She was kind and most generous person I know, everyone says so. Who would want her dead? Impossible-"

"Well she is, isn't she Ayo?" Auntie Rejoice thought she better bring the boy into the conversation least he thought she'd forgotten him.

"Yes. Mama is very dead with a knife in her chest. I went to school to call Auntie Rejoice for help-" the boy said but was cut off by his uncle.

"Why didn't you call Pa Seyi next door? Why run miles to call your teacher, she's no family?"

"I like my teacher more. And I was afraid of being late to school if I stayed home. That is all sir."

Uncle Bita saw that the boy was telling the truth. He nodded as his right hand went to rub his greying head. He seemed to be thinking what to do or say next.

"I hope you are not pushing the children on me to look after? I don't like children, never have. They eat you dry and are forever ungrateful whatever you do. They desert you in your old age when you need them most. Just cast your eyes out and see many examples of what I'm saying. Nigerians are getting sensible now, all that stupidity about you must have children for your old age! Old people now know that's not true but it's too late for them. They're rotting in nursing homes or begging on the streets. Use your wealth on yourself. That's my motto. We've only got one life-"

"Mister Bita can we talk about your sister and leave everything else till later?" Auntie Rejoice cut into uncle

Bita's long self- loving speech. She was right to think Bita was unconcerned about his sister's death. A thought struck Auntie Rejoice. Was uncle Bita a conspirator, or did he master- minded his sister's death? If so, for what reason? She suddenly heard uncle Bita's voice.

"What do you say? All I know is, I can't take any rascals in. Look at this place! It's not fit enough for one person let alone six children and an adult. Don't you agree?"

"I do agree this place is not good for children but-"

"You mean my house is unfit to live in, teacher?" uncle Bita snapped impatiently. Auntie Rejoice never meant to offend but she was always blunt at telling the truth.

"I don't mean-. All I mean is your nephews need you, only for a short time, until a permanent arrangement can be made. You don't have to keep them here. In fact there is more room in their house in Mushin and it's not that far from here as you yourself know. I am a school teacher who needs to teach. And the children are not related to me as you said, but Ayo is a wonderful child as you will see if you get to know him. And his brothers are too." Auntie Rejoice tried to convince uncle Bita to look after the orphans until she could get a permanent carer for them.

"Why can't their father, that useless man look after them?" Bita snapped back

"Because he is useless that is why. Besides no one knows where he is. He has disappeared off the face of the earth."

"Where is the money to feed and clothe them and myself?" uncle Bita continued to search for excuses not to take the children.

"I think you should do what their mother was doing. Cultivate the small farm behind the house and sell the fruits and vegetables in the market-" Auntie Rejoice suggested.

"What? A farmer at my age?" Bita exclaimed.

"I'm sure Pa Seyi next door will help so would Ayo and the kids"

"Seyi is a useless man. You don't know him? That his house belonged to his junior brother, Eddy, who worked in the city as an insurance man. Eddy had a wife and two girls. Because Seyi was always losing his jobs and begging Eddy for money, Eddy invited him to stay with them. The following year we heard that Eddy's house was burnt down with everybody inside except Seyi. He, of course inherited the house as the only living relative of the deceased. If that didn't tell you what type of man he is, nothing would. He is a wizard! He'll kill at the drop of a banana."

"I will also give you an allowance for the children. And the money is strictly for the children. Now will you come with us? We need to arrange the funeral-"

Auntie Rejoice knew that the funeral expenses would fall on her alone. She decided to take up the Headmaster's offer of financial help. She would also ask all the other teachers in the school especially the six female ones to help in a practical way. Nigerians are usually helpful and most would freely give his or her time to a good cause. People are like that, helpful. Mama Ayo must be buried with dignity. Custom demanded that a woman with children, especially one as good as the deceased, be given a good send off. There's the problem of buying a coffin, drinks and food to feed those coming to pay their respect. Visitors won't care where food and drinks came from. They would just want to celebrate Mama Ayo's life. After all, she was regarded very highly in the village. Or so Auntie Rejoice thought. This explained why villagers wanted someone to pay for her death, even if that someone was one of the most respected village teachers. Auntie Rejoice's mind raced back to the witchdoctor, Pa Jibiti. Consultation of the oracle was arranged for later and by the morning Auntie Rejoice's life itself might be in danger. The previous night after drinking her night-cap, Auntie Rejoice prayed and read her Bible (Romans : Chapter 13). 'Let every soul be subjected unto the higher powers. For there is no power but of God. The powers that be are ordained of God' No power of witches nor that of wizards in the village or anywhere else could touch a single hair on her head. She who has the protection of the One who has all powers. After this Auntie Rejoice recited the Hail Mary and slept peacefully. Nothing worried her after that, knowing the Lord Himself was protecting her. Some villagers thought her lack of concern about her own safety was a sign of how powerful her juju was. Only a witch with such power could be a killer, they said.

"I will not go with you but I will meet you at home in Mushin. Go on-" uncle Bita said.

Auntie Rejoice felt if she followed uncle Bita's instruction and leave without him she might not see him again at least, not soon.

"Whatever you need to do we will wait for you. We will all go together, it's better that way unless you want to pay the mortuary bill." She puts the fear of God in him by asking him to dip his hand in his pocket.

"I can't. Where do I get the money? I must tell you now I can't afford to buy a coffin or anything at the moment"

"Don't worry the Lord will provide. I will ask the school to contribute-"

"In that case can I order a new suit for the funeral from my tailor on our way now?" Bita enthused.

"Money is very tight mister Bita. I am squeezed as it is. Are you ready to go?"

"OK. I hope I won't regret this. What is the police doing about the murderer?"

"The police think it is suicide."

"With a knife inside her chest? My sister is, sorry, was not that strong!" Bita shrieked.

They returned to Aina village.

Fifteen

Auntie Rejoice starred out of the window of the bone cracking bus conveying her, Ayo, and uncle Bita back to Aina village, lost in wonder. Her mind roaming from one thing to the other. I wonder how different life would be if mama and papa were alive? I'd probably be wandering the world at their expense! I'm lucky, got a job I love and enough inheritance to chuck it all up if I'm bored. Her eyes caught the meandering sea that surrounds Lagos, in the distance. The sea view, the bridges over it, the miles of greenery was very stunning, she thought. A short distance away, she saw the shabby tin and mud shanty huts, the abode of the poorest of the poor The sun, the sea, and a warm friendly people. Lagos is truly beautiful, she thought. Good infrastructures would bring tourists flocking in. People in colourful dresses and robes went about their daily business in a temperature that could fry an egg.

As the bus crawled by St. Anne's church, Auntie Rejoice saw a line of beggars waiting for worshippers.

Beggars were the bane of church goers.. They sit on the dirty grounds, bowls in hand, waiting for alms. It was said, some of those beggars possess houses, many wives and children in their own villages.

As the bus whinged on like a cat with arthritic hips, Auntie Rejoice sighted the Ebute Metta bridge and colourful Oyingbo Market, across the river on her right. A huge open market selling various commodities from cloths to provisions, biscuits and sweets in wholesale and retail packs.

The Ebute Metta Bridge was the only connection between mainland Lagos and Victoria Island, Built by the British before independence. It now appeared tired, old and worn. Of course, other bridges now take the stress off the ancient bridge.

Auntie Rejoice sighed heavily as the old bus crawled to a bus stop, distracting her thoughts. Crowd rushed forward to get on the bus. A mother carrying a child tied to her back was struggling with the rest. The child appeared half dead. Auntie Rejoice had seen dead babies carried by mothers who thought their children were asleep or perhaps were unable to let go. The passenger sitting next to Auntie Rejoice got off the bus.

A young conductor was screaming his lungs out for no good reason, Auntie Rejoice thought back to what her father would have said to the conductor, 'You don't have to yell or shout, the person you're talking to is not a mile off. Shouting is a sign of appalling manners, of bad home training."

She smiled and glanced at the child on its mother's back again, now sitting next to her. The child's thin, dry-looking legs seemed lifeless. It was obvious to Auntie Rejoice that the child's lower limbs were paralysed. Auntie Rejoice's sharp eyes told her the child had been afflicted with polio. Polio is a disease of the nervous system that leads to wasting of muscles, easily preventable by inoculation, Auntie Rejoice thought what a pity.

Auntie Rejoice could not hold her thoughts to herself any longer.

"Is the baby all right?" she turned to the child's mother. The mother eyed her sadly, paused before replying. "No, he no be all right. He sick. We go Ikeja hospital. He go to do fysiorapy, eziscise for him polio legs. He no sit, he no stand. With fysiorapy he sit small, small now. I thank you" finishing her reply the mother wiped tears from her face with the tail of the cloth she used to wrapped her child. Auntie Rejoice was a little lost for words. She rubbed her neck, searching for comforting words.

"Don't worry, I'm sure the good God will heal. Follow the instructions from your Physiotherapist. Give the child good, fresh food-"

"My husband be farmer, plenty vegetables, no meat! We no get money for meat for the baby-" the mother smiled as she said this. Auntie Rejoice opened her handbag, brought out some Naira notes and handed them to the mother.

"Take this for some meat. Look after yourself too." Auntie Rejoice said as the mother got off the bus to change into another heading for Ikeja. Auntie Rejoice glanced across the seats in front of her. Ayo was fast asleep, his head on uncle Bita's shoulder. She turned her face to the moving window again.

Do ghosts exist? She asked herself. She'd never given it a thought before, until now. She was certain there were things on this Earth mere humans couldn't see or touch. There has to be. There were too many powerful indications to think otherwise. She'd accepted that some things are beyond our understanding and had never disputed that. Was it not Mama Ayo she saw floating in mid- air yesterday? Yes, it was, she nodded her head. Did she not see the woman with her own eyes until the woman vanished into thin air? Yes there are things on Earth beyond human comprehension. But ghosts? If ghosts exist why haven't they made contact with us? Or do ghosts take a vow of silence when they died, sign a contract of non-disclosure of happenings on the other side? Do they mix blood with St. Peter and make promises on their mothers' grave? Surely the existence of these creatures, or things, would have been obvious by now? Wouldn't dead mothers and fathers come back to pacify or sympathise with their loved ones? It was enough for Auntie Rejoice to doubt her own sanity. She couldn't be sure if the stress of work and ferrying the body of a dead woman across Lagos, hadn't a part in her seeing things. She'd let it rest for now.

She was the young girl who grew into a beautiful kind hearted woman. She reflected on life. Auntie Rejoice reflected with fond memory now and smiled to herself as she was been rocked to and fro by the rickety bus.

She had briefly enjoyed her years of sojourn in London, replacing mainland Lagos for Central London. Well, This rickety bus would never dare trail the streets of London. The government would never allow it to foul the roads.

Suddenly her reverie was interrupted. There was commotion in front. The bus slowed to a stop at a dangerous blind corner. The driver walked through the aisle shouting, "Any doctor dey for bus? Doctor dey for bus? Show your face. Doctor-" then he laid eyes on smartly dressed Auntie Rejoice. Pointing a dirty finger to her he screamed, "You be doctor?" She looked at him perplexed. The crowd was blocking her view, it was impossible to see what was happening to a man on the floor near the driver's seat. The driver shouted again. "You! You are doctor?"

"Me?" Auntie Rejoice poked her own chest for emphasis. "Yes you! You yourself! You be doctor?" She shook her head from side to side "I'm not a doctor. I'm a teacher." The driver was not convinced. Waving her up from her seat, he snapped.

"Yer, same difference! Come help the man in front'

"What's wrong with him?" she asked.

"God knows. He don collapse. He maybe no eat today. Him clothes be tear and yeye! He be old man. Full of hunger"

The man on the floor looked old but Auntie Rejoice thought he could not be more than thirty five. Hunger and wretchedness had eaten away at the fabric of his life. She loosened the tight clothing round his neck and put him in the recovery position on his side. She checked his airways. His breathing was a little laboured but otherwise he was really OK. She told the driver this. "Perhaps you can drop him at the Teaching Hospital-"

"What?" The driver shrieked. "I no get money for medicine for People!" The driver climbed onto his tin-made chair and addressed his passengers.

"People! This man is dying of hunger. Old man dying of hunger-" as the driver spoke the dying man was heard to whisper "I be diabetic, tell dem! I be diabetic, food, food-" The illiterate driver listened then continued his speech.

"You hear that? He be dying of hunger. He no get diet to eat. No diet! For those who no know, diet is food. I want those who have food to give him now. Those who no get food to give him money. Now please. I need to move bus before yeye traffic policemen come ask for bribe. Quick with your money!"

As if by magic, someone donated unopened bottle of soft drink, another a loaf of bread. And others threw Naira notes on the sick man, with the driver acting as lookout, keeping an eye on thieves. Auntie Rejoice watched as life slowly returned to the dying man. He gradually pulled out a cloth bag from the pocket of his shorts. When the donation of goods and money ceased, the man slowly rose from the floor and filled the bag with the food and money. He thanked everyone who contributed and left the bus.

Suspicion arose in Auntie Rejoice when the driver shouted after the sick man, "Jimoh, see you later! You eat all, you eat death!" It clicked in her brain that the passengers had been had. It was all a scam, a plot to collect money from gullible, kind hearted people. It worked. The driver and the sick man were partners in crime. Auntie Rejoice decided there was nothing she could do. If she told the crowd, the driver would be lynched. The fifteen Naira she donated she put down to a lesson in watchfulness.

No one taught you how to cope with such behaviour at school, even a good school like St. Mary's. She too had been bad once. In her own junior school, she hadn't been this thoughtful girl that she was now. Sister Maglena was her principal. Auntie Rejoice closed her eyes momentarily to shut off Sister Maglena's face from the passing cars. Harsh and acid- tongued Sister Maglena gave students hours of tongue-lashings.

"I know why Sister Maglena is so bitter! She wanted to take over God's slot! She asked God to move over but He declined!" One student concluded.

Rejoice shuddered, remembering the harsh she made of another student's hair cut and the tongue-lashing Sister gave the poor girl.

One very hot day, the students were restless after classes. Abiba, one of her classmates, feeling bored, said she would be glad of a volunteer to cut her hair. No one volunteered. Feeling sorry for Abiba, Rejoice volunteered to cut her hair. Day pupils and boarders gathered round Abiba, sitting on the cement demarcation between classroom and playing field. Rejoice stood over her client, with scissors in hand. Rejoice had never cut anyone's hair in her life. Bravely she plunged the scissors into Abiba's hair. After a few seconds it was obvious to her and everyone present that the scissors were not obeying Rejoice's hands. Auntie Rejoice tidied the head as much as she could then give up, which led to an explosion of laughter.

"What have you done to my hair? Why is everyone laughing?" Abiba said, calmly at first. "I have a small mirror in my bag. You should see yourself! You look like Pinocchio!" said a classmate. Laughter! Laughter! She handed Abiba the mirror. One look in the mirror and Abiba yelled out, "You have ruined my head! You have destroyed my face! Oh, my head, my face!" screech of laughter followed.

Sister Maglena heard the commotion, came out of her office, and walked to the gathering. As the girls saw her approaching, one by one they legged it. For a small crowd still rolling with laughter, their backs to Sister, it was too late to run.

"What is all this commotion? Who is making all this noise? Day students you should be home by now. Your parents will be wondering if you stopped at boys' homes. Go! Now what is the cause of all the noise? Rejoice tell me"

Rejoice narrated the story.

At the end of her story, Abiba cried, "I look so bad Sister, everyone is calling me Pinocchio!"

Sister turned round to Abiba and in a stern voice said, "Is that why you are making all this foolish noise! Did you not look like Pinocchio before the hair cut? Stop the noise or I'll punish you if I hear another word. Now everyone disperse!" Happy memories, Rejoice smiled.

Sixteen

Auntie Rejoice sat in the rickety old bus. Turning her head to the left she starred across the river to Lafiaji district of Lagos, on the island, where she was born.

Her mind raced back to her parents' marriage at St. Mathias' and Michael's Catholic Church in Lafiaji. Her own schooling began at the school of the same church, age three, chaperoned by her aunt. Closed to her parents former residence in Ikoyi. She remembered Ikoyi, regarded as a no- go area to the locals during British colonisation, now a free- for- all residential area. At that time, however, the only Nigerians seen around Ikoyi were servants and gardeners or low calibre civil servants on errands for their masters. Exceptions to the rule were very senior Nigerian civil servants regarded worthy, though not quite equal to Europeans.

The apartheid was almost as distinct as it was in the old South Africa. The segregation of the races was complete with sport clubs exclusively for Europeans, with Nigerians serving cold beers. This largely went almost unnoticed except by the few like Obafemi Awolowo and his co- fighters for freedom.

The Lafiaji of her youth was mostly populated by Roman Catholics, who worshiped at St. Michael's or the nearby Holy Cross Cathedral, the seat of the Archbishop of Lagos. Rejoice remembered resenting worshipers who displayed wealth in gold and diamond necklaces and silver shoes, flaunting their wealth in the face of poverty. A smile brushed her lips.

Seventeen

It was late morning when Auntie Rejoice, Ayo and uncle Bita arrived at Mama Ayo's house. Ayo's brothers including the baby were out of sight. Auntie Rejoice's heart missed a beat. What could have happened to them? From her experience, she knew quiet children were either up to mischief, eating, ill, or some evil had befallen them. Which was it? There were children kidnappers about, she'd heard. Men and women who roamed the streets, looking for children out of sight of their relatives. Children were easily enticed with promises of money or food. These are the ages of gullibility, she thought, all that talk of children needing parents! Children need a good supply of food and safe surroundings. Give them these and they're anyone's. She hoped Pa Seyi had not been careless with them. These children were the sweetest and gentlest anyone could wish to have around, Auntie Rejoice loved them all. She would adopt them except she really couldn't abide with the noise and whinging for this or that, the demand they make on you! And the fighting! One brother screaming, another punching! No, not for her. But she would help with their upbringing, as far as they want her to do so. Maybe their father would emerge from his hiding place, show his face and accept his responsibilities. Then, she'd take a back seat, unless of course, father and children wanted her involvement in their lives.

There was such a lull everywhere it was uncanny. Even the village appeared to contain less people.

Auntie Rejoice kept her thought to herself so as not to alarm uncle Bita and Ayo.

She hurried into Pa Seyi's house, only to find him sucking on the baby's bottle, singing and pacing the floor trying to rock a wide- awake baby to sleep in his arms. The baby's eyes fixed themselves in the direction of sunrays seeping into the house through the curtains, ignoring him. When she approached him, Pa Seyi's finger went to his lips, motioning her to be quiet not to wake the baby. Auntie Rejoice peeped into the baby's face. His saucer-like eyes starred back at her. Men! You'll think he could differentiate a sleepy baby from a playful one. She mused to herself.

"This baby is not ready for sleep. Give him to me" taking the baby from him she put him over her shoulder. Her heart was thumping as she whispered

"Where are the other children? " she waited as Pa Seyi drained the last of the baby's milk, saw the horror in Auntie Rejoice's face before banging the bottle on a wooden table.

"I drink it because the baby refused it. I don't want to waste it-" he justified himself, as one hand went to fondle his genitals. Auntie Rejoice's stomach turned in disgust . She swallowed to ward off the sickness she felt.

"Where are the rest of the children?" she repeated. Pa Seyi looked as if he'd just lost a Naira note. He shrugged his shoulders, "I no know. I dey see them this morning then I sleep. Dis baby no let me sleep at noght. I close my eyes for one minute, dis baby know at once. He dey cry, cry and cry more till my eyes open. And I sleep no more. Dis na the trouble. He no let me sleep! Dee children hit the mat they sleep! They no hear small brother cry at all at all. Only me, only me do all for dis baby. I tell you, I no know how long I cain do dis. I no sleep well. When dee baby dey sleep, me too closed my eyes. I tink that be dee time the children disappear. No my fault. I no know where they be-" he said, lowering his eyes.

Auntie Rejoice's heart sank further into her chest, she must try to wad off the feeling of panic fast rising to the surface. Where could the children have gone? They were not street- wise unlike some local ones. The oldest was only five, the youngest only two, too young to know the ways of the world. Was Pa Seyi treating them unkindly? Have they decided to run away, knowing Ayo would take care of himself? Were they stranded somewhere, unable to find their way home? She ruminated.

The clouds in the sky were rolling grey now, and getting darker by the minute. It looked like a storm was brewing. In the tropics rainstorms were heavy and could be frighteningly violent. Thunder was something else, it had to be experienced to be believed. But then she'd heard Europe was experiencing something similar now, because of pollution.

Poor children, she thought. For a split second she wondered if she'd need the services of Inspector Gberaga again. Her stomach churned as she remembered her collision course with him over Mama Ayo's body.

"We have to search for them." Said Auntie Rejoice out loud to Pa Seyi. As she spoke Ayo who had been listening with his uncle Bita outside, came in and joined in the conversation. "They are in lesson" he said then ran out again.

"They decide go lesson, that na good tin. I tink they be bored wit me" said Pa Seyi, feeling sorry for himself. The teacher sighed. She'd let her imagination ran away with her. Thank God the children were safe. She was pleased the children enjoyed learning. Whoever becomes their guardian won't need to encourage them to learn.

Auntie Rejoice looked behind her, Ayo was out again, she wondered where uncle Bita was.

"Where is uncle Bita? I want him to meet Pa Seyi-" she said out loud to herself.

"He's here with me!" Ayo shouted. Pa Seyi peeped a cursory glance at the boy then set his snake- like eyes on Auntie Rejoice.

"He no go enter here! Bita no go dirty him foot to stepping in my house. He no speak to me after him house burn down. Everyone dey accuse me of burning dee house down. That na ten years ago! Ten years ago! I ask you! Imageene, me kill my own brother and his family because I want dis house? Me? Me, killing my own brother? It be very cruel. I no get over it espesial with people like Bita. Mama Ayo and dee husband help me get over dee depression inside me. They tak me see Jibiti, the jujuman. He chained my hands and legs to big stone, gee me concoction for drink. I dey there until I better. I tink the village now stop tinking I'm brother- killer, till I meet Bita in Oyingbo market two years ago. I said goodday to im. He no answer me. Then he return to face me, put im face to my face. I tink he want make amend, I smile. Then he say dis words in my ears, 'brother killer' I jump and walked away from im. Since then if I see im one way I cross the road to another side-" Pa Seyi paused for breath, but Auntie Rejoice thought she'd heard enough. She didn't know what to believe. Ten years ago Auntie

Rejoice was not interested in village gossip. She was only interested in getting good grades for her pupils.

"Let's go outside to meet uncle Bita. It is not a good thing to keep malice you will agree?" Auntie Rejoice said as she took the first step towards the door. Pa Seyi pulled her by the sleeve. She turned round to look at him then continued walking out.

"Listen to me Auntie Rejoice. The fault is no mine. It is that gigolo's fault. He snub me!" Pa Seyi said pounding his chest. "Me! Me Seyi!" She turned at the door to face him.

"To get peace, everyone concerned must accept some guilt." she said. He glanced at the ground dejectedly and nodded his head as they trooped out of the small house to meet uncle Bita outside.

Uncle Bita was sitting on one of the five stone steps leading to Mama Ayo's front door, his back resting on the locked door. Ayo sat on the stone below his uncle. As his eyes spotted Pa Seyi, uncle Bita turned his grey head away from the offending sight. Auntie Rejoice walked straight to Bita.

"You need to make your peace with him. I heard you two were great friends until the unfortunate death of his brother and family? Is that true?" said Auntie Rejoice.

"True. We be bestest of friends before, before. Yoo see my sister, we be men of equal same feathers. He no get job I no get job. We both dey get junior brother or sister who get better state in life than we. Sometimes we dey come down from our high state to beg them so we fit eat. Yes we get plenty for common together. But I stop at killing! Never I dey kill for my own pocket!" said uncle Bita angrily.

Auntie Rejoice was taken aback. How could one man accused another of murder when he wasn't present at the scene of murder ten years previously? She thought.

"What prove have you to say he killed his brother and family by burning down the house in the middle of the night?" Auntie Rejoice asked.

Even if Pa Seyi was guilty, the police had done nothing, and no one in the village seemed it worthwhile to do a little investigation.

Pa Seyi's recollection of that night was that he was drinking beer with a group of friends he hadn't seen for a while. That could have been easily proven. Almost everyone in the village believed in Pa Seyi's guilt because one person, uncle Bita had started the rumour. Auntie Rejoice was pondering this when uncle Bita got up from Mama Ayo's stone steps, shook the sand from his shorts and shouted to Auntie Rejoice. "OK. we meet. You be right, I no get proof. I wan punish im because of his carelessness. He be careless to see the house burning, he be drunk that night. I dey visiting my sister that night. I don help pouring water on dee fire. But Seyi, im benefit from im brother. He be rolling in dee sand too drunk to know what. It no good, im no good-" uncle Bita said grumpily, he was interrupted by Auntie Rejoice.

"Being drunk is not yet a criminal offence."

"You be right 'course. I go settle my quarrel with im" Bita said, his lips almost parting into a smile.

"Good. Usually it is those who are bitter who suffer. Bitterness eats into the fibre of the embittered person not the offender. It is better to look forward than back. thinking what could have been, is always a waste of time. Come meet Pa Seyi" Seyi walked forward picking his feet as if he was about to step on a lizard, hoping his staunch enemy would meet him half way.

"Yoo much wiser than yoo look. I feel beeter, ten years bitterness don go, don leave my shoulders already! Thank yooo very much" said uncle Bita smiling as they met Pa Seyi, who was still holding the wide- eyed baby in one arm.

"Do you want to be the one to say it or, should I tell him what we've decided?" Auntie Rejoice said to Bita light-heartedly.

"I tell him. Listen Seyi I sorry to cause you sorrow all dis years. Make we be friends again-" Uncle Bita did not have a chance to finish his sentence when Pa Seyi ran to him, hugging his old friend as if he'd been waiting for this. They laughed and hugged. It seemed a feud of ten years was settled in a stroke.

"As you know, uncle Bita will stay with the children until something permanent can be arranged. That could be soon, it could be later-" Auntie Rejoice began.

"What to decide?" Pa Seyi interrupted.

"It will obviously depend on the children. What the children want takes precedence on what anybody else wants. Do you both agree?"

"Yes" they chorused.

"Now I have to leave you. I'm on my way to see the teachers at school. I shall see you tomorrow. Please think of the plan for the funeral. Mama Ayo will be buried in a day or two-"

"Na only Wadenesday today! Is it too soon? I tinking of dee preparation for food and beer and-" said uncle Bita, knowing no penny of his would be added to funeral fund.

"Are you going to go to the market and buy food? Or are you contributing beer and drinks?" Auntie Rejoice put in trying to stir things up.

"I tell yoo already I no get penny to my name. If yoo be take me and shake me upside down, no penny will drop out of my body-" said uncle Bita. Auntie Rejoice felt the heat of annoyance rising in her chest. Who was this rascal of a man who made no contribution either financial or emotional, to his sister's funeral.

"Then you have no say in how and when your sister is buried" she said. "As I was saying I'm going back to school. Have you got the key to the house? I want to look round the rooms again" Pa Seyi nodded and withdrew the key from his pocket. He handed it to Auntie Rejoice.

Auntie Rejoice crossed over to Mama Ayo's house. She grabbed Mama Ayo's blood stained mat from its hiding place and examined it thoroughly, then decided to hide the mat behind one of the wardrobes in the sitting-room where she knew no one would look. She turned back to the rooms. Her eyes weighed up the rooms and its contents. Something was missing from the room, she thought. Her eyes roamed from the tables to the benches and chairs then back again. What was it? For a moment her mind went blank. She couldn't placed the missing object. But knew something was definitely missing from what her eyes previously recognised as part and parcel of the room. Then it clicked. Her mind jolted to a space on the small table by the entrance door. The beautiful silver ashtray had gone from its place, leaving a mark on the wooden table. Someone had taken, or stolen the ashtray. But why? If she was not careful the whole contents of the house would disappear. That's one more thing to investigate. Whoever took the ashtray might possibly know more about Mama

Ayo's death. Auntie Rejoice felt the murderer was closer than she'd thought, the Oba was right. She shut the door behind her, keeping her own counsel. As she emerged from the house she saw the children coming towards her. Her heart lifted. They were returning from lessons. They ran to hug her shouting 'Auntie! Auntie! Auntie Rejoice!' Her smile widened.

"How are you children? Enjoyed your lessons?" They nodded.

Ayo might know about the missing silver ashtray. She led Ayo away from his brothers, out of Pa Seyi's earshot.

"Ayo, has anyone being in your mother's house apart from the children?" Ayo nodded his small head. "Yes, uncle Bita just went in and Pa Seyi went in also" Ayo replied.

"You mean uncle Bita went in while I was inside Pa Seyi's house?"

"Yes. Auntie Rejoice" the boy said.

"But the key was with Pa Seyi. Oh-" the teacher began, then remembered she met the door closed but unlocked.

"He left the door-" Ayo was saying.

"Open" Auntie Rejoice completed his sentence.

Auntie Rejoice paused for a minute then said "That's all right. Are you happy as things are now?"

"Yes, but we like it when you are with us" the boy replied. Auntie Rejoice felt a pull on her heart. The children were not completely happy, she could tell.

"You know I can't live with you. I have to work, don't you?" the boy nodded again then smile.

"Look after your brothers." She returned the key to uncle Bita with the words, "See you in the morning" and left for school.

Auntie Rejoice left them standing outside Mama Ayo's house. She could feel their eyes in the back of her neck as she walked away, wondering what would become of the children.

Eighteen

Ma Taiwo had determined there was no way she would allow Auntie Rejoice to pass in front of her shop again without detaining her teacher friend. Too much was bubbling inside her chest, if she didn't spill it out she was sure she would burst.

She sat outside her shop, waiting, knowing the teacher was bound to pass soon. She had watched her going to and fro only to be dismissed with a wave of the hand promising to see her later. That won't do, she thought. The promises only served to make her more anxious and eager to find out why the teacher she considered a good friend was keeping her in the dark on Mama Ayo's death, the hottest gossip in the village for a while. How she died if not the why of it, was no longer a secret in the village. What was a secret was why she was killed and who did the deed. She, Ma Taiwo, one half of a twin, would get to the bottom of the goings on, if it was the last thing she did. Twins were special creatures according to Yoruba mythology. They brought luck and prosperity if accorded due homage.

In Yorubaland twins are known by special names. Taiwo, 'The first to taste the world' and Kehinde 'The last taster'

The myth was factual as far as Ma Taiwo was concerned. So she behaved as if the whole village owed her a living. Most villagers tolerate her grandiose postures because sooner or later they needed her services, despite the over- charging and crooked workmanship. After all she was the only sewing mistress in the village with a huge signboard proclaiming to be 'London Trained'.

Villagers knew she'd never set foot beyond the Bar Beach, still they humoured her..

She perched on a wooden bench outside her shop while a customer tried on a finished garment inside, attended to by an apprentice. A few minutes of helping the customer on her dress, the apprentice came to Ma Taiwo.

"Madam, the customer said the dress is, too much tight in the arms for her. What do I do?" said the apprentice.

Ma Taiwo was not in the mood for fussy customers. She was waiting for a bit of juicy gossip from Auntie Rejoice on her way back to school, everything else must wait.

Lately married life had been difficult for Ma Taiwo. Her marriage was loose, the elastic ties seemed easily broken. Her son didn't see education in the same light as his mother did. Ma Taiwo's mind was not on her trade. Ma Taiwo heard the apprentice but her brain didn't registered the girl's presence. Her eyes suddenly caught sight of the apprentice still waiting patiently beside her.

"The dress is not tight. It's her! She put on weight since the measurement! Call her out here, the stupid woman!" Ma Taiwo said irritatingly. The apprentice disappeared and reappeared again with the complaining customer wearing the said dress.

"This dress is not too tight, you know!" said Ma Taiwo, pulling on the armbands. The customer frowned and squeezed her lips together, then finding courage to express her displeasure.

"I think it is Ma. It is me who is wearing it not you. I can feel it cutting my arms off underneath-" the customer began but Ma Taiwo cut in with venom.

"Of course it is cutting into your fat arms! You see, when we measured you, your arms were thinner. You have put on a lot of weight since I saw you last. It is no good coming here shouting and complaining! I don't put food in your mouth, do I? In any case you were supposed to collect your dress two weeks ago. Two weeks is a long time to wait. You eat-"

"Ma, can you let it out a little?" the customer said, apprehensively. Anyone who knew her could testify that

Ma Taiwo was prone to quick loss of temper. Snapping at people when they least expected had made customers weary of complaining about Ma Taiwo's work. No matter what style customers choose from the pile of English style catalogues the end results was always the same. Ladies' blouses always had the same round necks and flared waists. Complaining that their dresses bore no significant resemblance to the styles or shapes in the catalogues, only served to ignite Ma Taiwo's exasperation. She believed herself to be the best ladies' dress designer and sewing mistress in Lagos who should not be challenged.

Noticing the customer's twisted miserable face Ma Taiwo relented.

"OK. Give it to the girl. She'll let it out. Collect it tomorrow. But please don't wait another two-" as Ma Taiwo spoke she looked up and saw Auntie Rejoice making her way on foot along the road back to school. Ma Taiwo dismissed the customer and her apprentice instantly, jumping up, she waved frantically to gain the teacher's attention.

"Rej! Rej! Here my friend!" No one could fail to hear that grinding voice or see Ma Taiwo's lumpy arms in the air. Of course Auntie Rejoice couldn't miss her. Auntie Rejoice mulled over their friendship and wondered why Ma Taiwo was so demanding of her time. It was not that their friendship was deep. Both women never really met socially except on occasions when avoidance was practically impossible, such as the school's parents' meeting or sports days.

"Come on in! I was looking out for you! Have you had a bad day? I bet not as bad as mine! What a bad few days I've had! What a bad few days!" When the teacher failed to response Ma Taiwo sensed there was something wrong and changed the topic from herself to the teacher. "You are not sick are you?"

"No, I'm not sick-" replied the teacher wearily.

"Then what is wrong? Is it Ayo? What happened to him?" Ma Taiwo said, in more self- interest than concern for the teacher.

"I'm battling with the death of Mama Ayo" said Auntie Rejoice quietly.

"I hear that already! It's old news! It's all over the village already. That young pretty woman! Mind, the life she led- it wasn't surprising that she'll come to this end. A bad end. Though I feel sorry for the children. Who will look after them now? I heard the husband left home. But that too is not surprising. Which husband will take what she was dishing out! That's why I want to talk to you, I want your opinion. My husband is courting again can you believe it? I caught him red-handed-"

"What? How many girlfriends can a man cope with?" said the teacher, not really interested.

"I've had sleepless nights thinking about it. I'm never going to sleep with him again. I hope he get HIV-"

The teacher had escaped before Ma Taiwo finished her sentence.

Nineteen

A few hours ago the village had seemed empty. It was no surprise. Because the curious, the gossips, and the forced, were all at Pa Jibiti's house for divination to establish Auntie Rejoice's guilt. The witchdoctor had concluded Auntie Rejoice was guilty of Mama Ayo's death.

Villagers congregated at his house at noon. Some villagers had obeyed the call to meeting fearing the consequence of not showing their faces. Curiosity had dragged others along to see how far Pa Jibiti would go in his hunger to discredit Auntie Rejoice and grab complete power over villagers. He viewed Auntie Rejoice as a rival and a challenge to his authority in the village. Here was a woman, a woman for God's sake, who breezed into a dead woman's house without so much as consulting him, the self- styled village elder, or seek his permission before meddling in villagers' affairs. Deep down, he didn't really believe Auntie Rejoice killed Mama Ayo, the teacher's family was one of the most respected in Lagos. As good, upright citizens go, Chief of Customs Pa Akintola and his wife had no parallel. No, Auntie Rejoice couldn't have murdered anyone, she was from the best blood. A better blood could not be found in the whole country, Pa Jibiti thought. But evil doesn't see goodness. And if he could tame Auntie Rejoice, villagers' terror of him would increase many folds.

He was ready to put Auntie Rejoice, though she was not yet present, through this kangaroo court. The verdict was already decided. Instilling fear in villagers was at the root of this divination. If he could do this to someone as good and popular as the schoolteacher he was capable of doing worse to them.

As soon as Auntie Rejoice left the children, Pa Seyi deposited the baby in his home- made cot (a drawer placed at the corner of the kitchen), locked his house and hurried to Pa Jibiti's house for the meeting. Pa Jibiti's house was traditionally built in mud bricks and white washed. The house had six rooms shared by Pa Jibiti's fourteen children and three wives. They all sat crossed- legged on the ground, listening to their father accused the teacher, in her absence, of insolence, disrespect and murder.

Pa Seyi kept himself to the back of the crowd, making appropriate noises of support.

"We neeed kip our village free from crimes lik the murder of our deer departed Mama Ayo. A good woman, a very good woman. We kno how good we hold her in our hearts. We must avenge her killing, bring dee murderer to justice-" At this point someone shouted "Yes! We know who the killer is, the teacher by name of Rejoice, the daughter of Pa Akintola! We go get her!" Pa Seyi strained his neck to peep at the heckler sitting in front of the crowd. It was Jayle, Pa Jibiti's eldest son, no surprise there, he thought.

"Leet us do dis correctly. We bring dee culprit to justice note my word, justice! No less no more. No revenge for past deeds I know some people are not honest.

People use any excuse to punish deer enemies for revenge. Not me! Anyone who is tinking revenge cain go out of this meeting now!" Pa Jibiti shouted.

"Well said!" said a voice, it was Jayle again. Heads turned in his direction then returned to the witchdoctor. "Now we come to dee core of the matter, dee divination. Dee gods will tell us who dee murderer is. Dee gods never lie! Dee gods of our fathers' fathers always foretell dee truth. I have two hens here, both girls. Because dee culprit, dee accused is a woman must not blind us to justice. I have mixed together ingredients taught to me by our forefathers and sanctioned by dee gods. Dis are ingredients used from time immemorial, used over and over to decide who dies and who lives. They never fail, the gods never let us down! Dis things are no longer

188

commonly used in our country. I feel dis is a shame. There is a lot in old cures. And as we kno, notin is as good as dee old-" He paused as a voice cut him off.

"Get on with it baba!" Heads turned again to regard the owner of the voice. It was an unbeliever. Pa Jibiti did not challenge the speaker. He continued his oratory.

"As I was saying notin work like old measures. Now! Yoo kno dee procedure. I am going to geev dis potion to these hens. Dee hens' legs tied to stop 'em running away." The witchdoctor held up a small brown plastic bottle containing dirty looking liquid. Pa Jibiti cleared his throat self importantly and resumed his speech.

"Dis hen here with dee red ribbon round its neck is Auntie Rejoice. Dis other hen with a white ribbon is for truth and honesty. Both hens be given dee potion. If dee red hen die Auntie Rejoice is guilty of murder. On dee other hand, God forbids, if dee white ribbon hen die we are all wrong-"

"You mean you are wrong! Then you will apologise to Auntie Rejoice!" said another voice, again Pa Jibiti ignored the heckler. Silence descended on the crowd as tension rose as they waited anxiously for the result.

The tension in the air, as tick as school's tapioca, could be cut with a knife. If Auntie Rejoice was found guilty there would be a riot in the village. Kangaroo courts were unlawful, but the police kept their distance from Pa Jibiti, too afraid of the power of satan to meddle.

Villagers regarded the school as a way out of poverty for their children. They would not be happy to entertain school closure. Tension grew as both the hens were gathered by Jayle and raised up to the sky in praise of his god. The hens made chicken- like noises, as if they knew the end was near.

Suddenly Pa Jibiti raised his thin voice, shouting incantations. "Baba we orun wa babawa gbe. Baba wa orun sokalewa ba wa gbe ee!" for a few minutes, perhaps to increase the tension. Grabbing the hens from his son he took his seat again. He placed both hens between his legs while Jayle poured the dark liquid down the hens.' throats. They were released to wander round the audience. A few minutes later the hens began coughing, splattering saliva and retching in an attempt to vomit the awful poison, but never did. It was a disturbing sight. Slowly, like watching a film of wall painting, one hen sat down groggily, the other staggered drunkenly among the crowd.

At first it seemed both hens were on the point of death. Closing and opening their eyes, with heads too heavy for their thin necks. Suddenly one hen shut its eyes as if the pain of looking at the baying crowd was beyond it, and fell sideways, dead. The crowd gasped loudly, moved by the cruelty. They hadn't got over that shock when the second chicken followed the same fate.

Some of the people present shook their heads in sorrow and shed tears at the horrific way the hens died. Pa Jibiti leapt to verify which hen was dead, hoping against hope that the right hen survived, confirming Auntie Rejoice's guilt.

The crowd rose to its feet and rushed to surround Pa Jibiti and the dead hens. Suddenly shouts of 'God is great!" 'God has spoken, great is His name!' "Fake! Fake!" rented the air. Pa Jibiti felt the mood of the crowd had turned nasty.

He gathered his family and ushered them into the safety of his house and locked the door against an increasingly hostile crowd. The white hen had died first. Two minutes later the red hen collapsed and died also. Shouts of "Fake! Fake! Fake!" rang out for hours, from a large section of villagers, while others were shocked into silence.

TWENTY

It was lunch time by the time Auntie Rejoice entered the school gate. As usual Hamed, the school guard said 'Welcome Auntie.'

'Thank you. How's your day?" Auntie Rejoice replied.

"We're here. We thank God." he replied, turning both palms upwards to indicate God's will.

In the distance Auntie Rejoice's eyes caught Peter Rotimi in his car. He was starting the engine. She hurried along the school's unpaved sandy footpath, to avoid him and his constant talk of diner dates. Too late he'd seen her. He turned off the car engine, came out of the car to wave her down and hurried to meet her. She managed a cheerfulness she didn't feel.

"Hello Rejoice! Hi there! Are you back at school now?" said Peter smiling from ear to ear. He admired and loved her company but frustrated knowing Auntie Rejoice found his company repelling.

"Yes, thank you. I came in to brief the Headmaster and-"

"I heard you went to Ayo Dipe's house where his mother was found dead? It fell on you to remove her body to the General Hospital mortuary. The Headmaster called a staff meeting to inform us. We have divided your classes between us for the next week or two. You are our hero! We admire what you are doing for this poor family. I mean, we know the boy as much as you. Yet you took it up like a member of their family. In fact you are doing more than his family could ever do. We commend you and of course you are in our prayer-" Peter's gazed at her lovingly, embarrassing Rejoice.

"You or anyone else would have done the same thing, if Ayo came to you first and said his mother was dead. I just happen to be around at the time. There was no other adult in the house as we all know, you would have followed the same action."

"True, but no one would have done as much as carrying the body to the morgue or challenged Inspector Gberaga, the raging beast-" Peter paused.

They both laughed. "That's better! Nice to see you laugh!" said Peter.

"I'm going to see the Headmaster as I said-" Rejoice repeated herself, taking a step forward.

"I know. But before you go, listen! I will contribute ten catoons of beer for Mama Ayo's wake. As well as give money to the Headmaster's collection for the burial. He'd asked us to contribute to a funeral fund and the wake. I also wanted to let you know that my new car is at your disposal. You don't need to be jumping on Kombi buses, those horrible tin- coffins! They are death traps, you know? You may ask what happened to our oil money?" Peter said.

"You know how I feel about that. I agree with all you said but don't have the time to stand and chat-"

"I know. Will you give me your itinerary for the coming days? When and where you need the car?" Peter said.

"I will put my timetable in your letterbox. Thank you very much for your help. Now I'm going to Mr Jaiye, see you later" Auntie Rejoice said, walking away while Peter looked on, uplifted by their conversation.

Mr Jaiye was having his lunch when Auntie Rejoice appeared in his room. There was a spread of dodo and fried fish stew on his table with a flask of cold ice water. "You meet me well. Have a seat and join in the feast-" he said with a wave of his hand indicating the chair in front of his own.

"No thank you sir. I've come to inform you of how far I've gone with Mama Ayo's funeral. I'm going to the

General Hospital as soon as I leave here to give them time of collection, tell them to prepare the body for burial in a day or two. I thought the quicker we do it the better for everyone-" the Headmaster interrupted Auntie Rejoice.

"Especially for the school. We are not a rich parish, we can't afford to spend too much of the school fund on just one family. Teachers earn little as it is. You all, especially you, Rejoice, have done the impossible, you've given not just money but your time and emotion. I thank you on behalf of the boy, his family and the school. Have we heard anything about the runaway father?" said the Head.

"Nothing sir. Absolutely nothing. I thought maybe we should advertise in local papers or on radio. Even if he didn't read or listen to radio maybe someone somewhere will hear or see and inform him-" said Auntie Rejoice.

The Headmaster looked troubled. "You will keep the name of the school out of the newspapers, won't you? The church who owns the school do not like publicity except it be on spiritual matters." The Headmaster said, interrupting his meal.

"No sir, I wasn't thinking of using the school-. That's all right. Can I ask you to thank Peter for me. He has volunteered to ferry me in his car to save me bus fares-"

"Those busses are death traps anyway. I don't know why you use them when you are rich enough to buy a series of them yourself. You have money, you don't depend on teachers' salary to live well. You can buy a car, the best car and get a driver to ferry you around. I've said this before to you, I don't like you on those tin coffins-"

"You say the truth sir but it's the freedom to go and come whenever I want without checking the oil gage or servicing the car or have it breakdown on motorways. Anyway, I hate Lagos traffic-" said Auntie Rejoice.

"OK have it your way. So the funeral is in two days time? We have collected money for the coffin and other things. Do you want to allocate anyone to do anything?" said the Headmaster who stood up and walked to a set of drawers. He pulled out a box containing wads of Naira notes and handed the box to Auntie Rejoice.

"This is the money we collected-" he said, returning to his seat again.

"Can you keep it here sir. Hand the money to staff as they buy coffin, drinks, and other things. Can Auntie Carol see to buying the coffin from that carpenter down the road. He had some coffins on display, maybe one would be suitable. And Peter can take care of the drinks and maybe someone else can see to the food. I will deal with the hospital and other arrangements. Thank you for all your effort sir-"

"No. It is you we must thank. May the blessing of Our Lord be with you." Said the Headmaster, rising with outstretched hand. They shook hands. Auntie Rejoice was about to depart when she turned round to Mr Jaiye again.

"I almost forgot, I have arranged Requiem Mass with Father Mark Lagan-" said Auntie Ayo, wiping sweat off her brow with a handkerchief. The Headmaster cut in.

"I spoke to Father Biodun too. He wanted to know if Mama Ayo was a practising Catholic-"

"Oh, I don't know sir" Auntie Rejoice replied, frowning.

"Don't worry about that. I told him I didn't know. He said it was enough the child was a good boy. I agreed. When Ayo grows up he would look back on the way his mother's funeral was conducted and thank God he went to the best school! Mass will be at two in the afternoon. The church and school will share the cost, plus teachers' donation of course. There's more than enough money to build a house here!" said the Headmaster proudly.

"I will arrange a photographer to attend the ceremonies for photos, to be kept in store for Ayo and his brothers." Said Auntie Rejoice.

"That, Rejoice, is a very good idea! You always have tremendous ideas! You've got a brilliant mind, always thinking ahead! Great for the school! You take from Africa, you take from Europe. Your mind is broad and wide. In the next few years I can see you taking over my job!"

"Oh no! I don't ever want to be the Head sir!" Auntie Rejoice exclaimed quietly.

"Why not? You've got the mind for it and the initiative. You'll make a good, wonderful and likeable Head" said the Headmaster.

"I see all the meetings you attend, all the hassle you take. Life's too short-" said Auntie Rejoice with a smile.

"You soon get used to it. Believe me! Anyway I must finish my meal and get ready for another meeting on Lagos Island!" said Mr Jaiye, stabbing a piece of dodo with a fork.

Auntie Rejoice left the school, her mood lifted. Things were looking up for the funeral. All she needed do now was inform the children about the arrangement. And if they couldn't locate Papa Ayo then, his wife would be buried without his knowledge. No one could afford to keep a body in the mortuary for too long, the cost was too high. Everything demands money in this country. The dead were not exempted. The living continue to pay for their dead.

Twenty-One

Before Auntie Rejoice left the school she called on Peter Rotimi and gave him her programme for the next three days. Rotimi was more than pleased to be her chauffeur, at her beck and call. Yes, of course he would be too happy to drive her round in his swish new car to the General Hospital mortuary now, he pronounced.

The scent of new leather hit her in the nostrils as she opened the car door. She wondered what became of Peter Rotimi's last car, a beautiful shinning black Triumph Sports. What was it with men and cars that make them hankered after every new model as they do with women? If men put the same energy they invest in metals into relationship with their partners life, for them, would be more peaceful, Auntie Rejoice thought as she took a sideways glance at Peter Rotimi. He was secretly pleased with himself. There was a glow of joyous self- satisfaction about his pretty face, happy Rejoice finally graced his car.

At the hospital, having crawled through the traffic jams on Eko Bridge flyover, the parking lot outside the hospital was full. There was a snail- pace line of cars trying to get to the Mariner or away from the Marina or searching for parking spaces, interwoven with the cars were lines of child hawkers with wares on their heads selling fried fish, oranges and bananas, peanuts and mangoes, combs, and sponges, jostling for space between moving vehicles. Outside the hospital walls a line of women traders had set up hot coal pots, roasting plantain, peanuts, cashewnuts, and yams. School children gathered round them buying the food.

"Why don't you drop me here then go find a parking space in that school building. If you can't get a space, maybe go for a drive for ten minutes then come back to pick me up. I'm just going to let them know we are collecting Mama Ayo in two days. Does that sound all right?" Auntie Rejoice said, pointing to the private nursery school opposite the hospital.

"That is an excellent idea. Get down then. I'll go round the block. I may even stop at the Bar Beach for fresh air. Give you fifteen minutes, knowing how slow these people are when the weather is so hot. OK see you." Peter replied cheerfully.

Auntie Rejoice opened the car door gently, trying not to knock a young hawker off, a girl of about six years carrying pawpaw and guava fruits on her head and shouting, "Buy my fresh fruits madam?" Auntie Rejoice's heart went out to her. How could such a young child be hawking fruits to strangers at this time of day when she should be in school, learning.

Auntie Rejoice almost bought some fruits then thought better of it. She wasn't carrying fly- infested, unhygienic food into the mortuary. When in England, she'd heard of ward nurses chewing food as they wrapped up dead bodies. She might get some fruits on her way back.

She opened the door to the mortuary and went straight to the young man at reception. It was not the same cheerful receptionist who had helped her collect Mama Ayo and gave her a receipt.

"Yes? What do you want?" the not- at- all pretty receptionist snapped, looking over her shoulders, Auntie Rejoice turned her head round to see if he was addressing someone else behind her. No, it was her he was speaking to. Then she realised that, his eyes were out of focus. He was crossed- eyed, like a deformed lion. What a rude man, she thought, being ugly was no excuse for rudeness. Kindness always detracts the onlooker from an ugly face, she thought. It takes less energy to be polite, more muscles to frown than to smile or so she'd heard.

"I'm here to let you know we will be collecting Mama Ayo's body in two days-" Auntie Rejoice began to explain but the rude one interrupted her.

"Who is Mama Ayo? I suppose to no her, me no see her, eh? eh?" he barked. Auntie Rejoice didn't know either to laugh or cry, but maintained her cool.

"I brought her body here myself two days ago. I was told the post- mortem would be ready today and we could bury her from now. I was given this." Auntie Rejoice handed the receptionist a piece of paper on which was written the name of the deceased, date of arrival at the mortuary and the name of the person depositing the body. The receptionist examined the paper unconcerned then returned it to Auntie Rejoice. "Enyone can write dis! Enybodee con give dis paper to enybodee else! What you won me do now?" said Crossed-eyed.

"I want you to go into the morgue and look for the body of Mama Ayo. The funeral is very soon." Said Auntie Rejoice, the pitch of her voice rising with anger.

"Wait here." Said the receptionist, walking off in a huff. He opened an inner door and disappeared into it, unseen from the outside. He was gone for what seemed like an eternity but was only a few seconds. When he returned the muscles of his face were tighter than before.

Auntie Rejoice wondered what could have happened. Since Mama Ayo could not be dead twice. There couldn't be anything major wrong, she thought.

"Nobody call Mama Ayo here! Yoo make me go luk for body in vain! Before next time make you be sure where you put body befoo you come speak to we! I get plenty work to do yoo know! How yoo make me go round and round looking for no body! Instead of sending me for useless errand! Now, I hav plenty work for do!" the Crossed- eyed one said haughtily.

"I did bring the body here. Kindly go and look again. The body can't just vanish." The teacher said in annoyance. "Call me your supervisor please." At the mention of supervisor, the Crossed- eyed one visibly shrivelled, his cross-eyes seemed even crosser.

"No supervisor business here!" he smiled, shaking his head. "Madam! I don look and look, and look again. Looking no make the body appear like magic! Your woman no dey here! Not in this here mortuary anyway. Maybe yoo don carry him to Teaching Hospital mortuary? Because of yoor sorrow, yoo be confusing this with our own General! People dey do that yoo know! Sorrow dey do strange tins to people, yoo know! Them leave body somewhere else, they turn up somewhere else to collect body, fools all! Them be fools! " The eyes were looking beyond the teacher again, hideously rat- like to gaze at.

"I can assure you that I'm no fool. I certainly brought a body here. What have you done with it? It couldn't have vanished but-"

"Lady, I dey busy for plenty work. I no get plenty time here to talk and talk, beautiful as yoo be! Yoo dey get dee message? Yoo hear me?" Said the receptionist, smiling suddenly. The smile didn't improve his face.

"What do you want me to do now?" said Auntie Rejoice with exasperation, knowing there was no way she would get any sense out of the receptionist.

"Me tink say you be go away and tink very aard where you put the body. It no be here!" seeing her sad face the receptionist's face cracked into a smile as he added, "I no get joy to see yoo so sad. Sorry I no fit help at all at all."

When Auntie Rejoice emerged from the mortuary into the hot glaring sunlight, there was no waiting car nor any sight of Peter Rotimi. She wondered whether he was lost in the heavy lunch- hour traffic. He might be enjoying the peacefulness of the Bar Beach, a few seconds drive away. While gazing into the horizon in pensive thoughts, she was approached by a girl hawker, not more than five years old, carrying a tray of fried fish on her head for sale.

A pang of pity for this little girl overwhelmed her. The fish appeared stale and inedible playing host to giant flies.

The little girl looked up forlornly at Auntie Rejoice who smiled back at her. Encouraged by Auntie Rejoice's friendliness the girl touched the helm of the teacher's dress.

"Buy my fish Auntie?" It is the custom in Yorubaland never to address anyone older than you, (even by two hours) by their first names. Words like 'Auntie' 'Mama' are usually used. "Buy my fish Auntie?" the girl repeated.

"What is your name?" said Auntie Rejoice. The girl hesitated before speaking, considering if the stranger deserved her trust. Perhaps her mother had warned her not to speak to strangers, Auntie Rejoice thought.

"I am Funmi, Auntie" said the girl in a childlike voice, rocking from one foot to the other.

"Why are you not in school?" said Auntie Rejoice, smiling. The girl lowered her gaze and studied the black leather shoes on the teacher's feet. The question was repeated. The girl smiled, using her right foot to draw lines in the sand.

"My papa no has school fees for me" she said shyly.

"Why are you selling old fish? You should be at home or school-"

"My mother give me fish for sell. Me and my sister go round selling it" a smile brushed her lips, proud to be helping her mother.

"Will you like to go to school?"

"Yes Auntie! I like go to school!" the girl jumped up with excitement, scattering the fish from her tray onto the ground. She screamed with pain, scooping everything up in her hands. She sat on the roadside wiping the fish one by one with her dirty wrapper and replacing them on the tray ready for the next customer. The teacher's stomach lurched in disgust, but she remained silent until the tray was back on the girl's head.

"How much are all the fish in the tray?" the teacher said at last.

"You will buy my fish? You will buy-" the girl's voice rose with excitement.

"How much?" Auntie Rejoice repeated.

"All of them is-" the girl chewed her fingers, gazing up to heavens. Unable to add, she had no idea of the total price. Her eyes roamed left and right and back again calculating loudly but getting her sum wrong. A few seconds later two fingers went into her mouth to concentrate her mind.

Auntie Rejoice released her from her agony. "OK, how much for each fish?" the teacher said helpfully. The child smiled, at least she knew that much. "Ten Naira for one Auntie" she said. "How many fish on your tray?" the teacher asked. The girl chewed on her fingers again. Auntie Rejoice counted the fish then announced, "Eight. That's eighty Naira" She said and dipped her hand into her bag, withdrawing hundred Naira. She handed the money to the girl.

"Here. This will cover everything. Wrap the fish for me" The girl put her tray on the ground and extracted some old newspaper from a second tray under the fish tray. She pilled up and wrapped the fish into the papers handing it to the teacher and they exchanged goodbyes. The girl was joyfully rearranging her trays when Auntie Rejoice glanced up to see Peter Rotimi's car parking beside the tray. He emerged from the car to the sound of blaring horns.

"You are not buying that cholera invested fish, are you?" he said, frowning. Auntie Rejoice smiled and shook her head. She waited until the girl skipped away before speaking. "No, of course not!" She held up the parcel of fish and threw it in a rubbish bin. They both smiled. Auntie Rejoice had almost forgotten the predicament of the missing body.

"Finished the arrangement?" Peter asked.

"You won't believe it. They've lost Mama Ayo's body!" she sighed.

"What? How could they lose a body in a mortuary?"

"Don't ask! Let's go. I think they are blaring their horns for you to get your car moving"

"Where do you want to go next?" Peter said

"If we go back to school, the Headmaster will want to go make a fuss at the mortuary Let's go to see Father Mark or Father Biodun. They can advise us. If a Priest appears at the mortuary it will generate more sympathy. You know our people have great respect for spiritual people, especially those who dedicate their lives to the service of God!" said Rejoice.

"True. Off we go to the priests. Fr. Mark must have been here for over-" Peter began, rubbing his hairless chin.

"Well over fifty years! Father Mark has been in Nigeria longer than I myself have been!" said Auntie Rejoice adding. "He's a loveable man. Very kind and Godly, he even took the trouble to learn Yoruba language, not many of them do. He treats everyone equally-" said Auntie Rejoice.

"If he didn't, he wouldn't have lasted. We did have one or two snooty ones but, they never stay anyway. What do you think happened to Mama Ayo's body?" Peter's mind turned to the mortuary.

"Don't know. What I'm sure of is that the body couldn't have vanished just like that! Perhaps the crossed-eyed receptionist looked in the wrong drawer. I can't imagine anything else-" Auntie Rejoice said.

As he drove Peter kept glancing at the rear view mirror. Something was wrong, but he stayed calm. He was trying his best not to alarm his passenger. He drove on carefully, his heart hammering his ribcage. He saw they were being followed by a dark blue Toyota. The car had trailed them from the General Hospital, had slowed behind Peter and sped when his own foot pressed down on the accelerator. Why? Who could it be? He starred into the mirror at every traffic stop to see if he could catch sight of the driver behind. No, the glare of the sun and the distance were obstacles. He would drive on. At a point he might be tempted to get out of the car to challenge the driver.

"You don't think the body was sold for medical experiment, do you?" Peter said, as a car stopped to allow him joined the snail paced traffic line along Eko Street. It was a woman driver in beautiful native attire. Peter strained his neck to admire her. Typical, thought Auntie Rejoice. He waved his thanks and stole a quick glance at Auntie Rejoice.

She was deep in thought. He wondered what she was thinking. What a pretty profile, he thought. He wished she was meditating on him, but he knew better.

"Do you think body snatchers are operating here in aid of medical research?" she asked, her mood darkening.

His eyes strained to the rear mirror and back again.

"I shouldn't think so. The dead as you know, are well respected here. I can't imagine anyone messing with bodies." Peter said at last.

"I wonder if Father Mark is home now or on visits to parishioners, if so I hope Father Biodun will be home. At least one of them is always in. Here we go. What I'm going to do is park the car at the school and we walk to Priest House-" said Peter.

"It's only a minute's walk-"

"The church had foresight to buy this massive parcel of land. The Priest House itself can be used as two football stadia!"

"Those were the days of free and cheap lands. Now people would kill for a space not bigger than a shoebox!" said Auntie Rejoice. Peter cleared his throat as if he had something important to say, taking a quick glance at Auntie Rejoice he proceeded to express his devotion to her.

"Rejoice, don't take this in the wrong way, but I do care for you and you know it. I love you very much and would like to marry you-"

"Yes, like you care for Mercy? You love Agnes, care for Grace? And Celia, the waitress at Eko hotel? You made Mercy's life miserable. She told me what lies you heaped on her. You have a reputation as a gigolo round here. I'm not desperate for a man or marriage. I'm certainly not desperate to make my life hell by giving in to a man who can't keep his grubby hands off women! 'Any woman will do' is your motto " she teased. His eyes shot across to the mirror again, unaware that Auntie Rejoice was aware of his anxiety. Her words seemed to be time- delay before reaching his ears.

"Now you are exaggerating! Mercy knew the score before we began seeing each other. I told her I love somebody else. She said 'you will learn to love me in time.' Her very words. I never did learn to love her. Women deceive themselves into believing what they want to believe. You'll think after reading all these women magazines telling them about the ways of us men, they would have learnt their lessons? No they haven't. They beg us for marriage, as if we are bank managers giving out loans. But-"

Auntie Rejoice cut in, changing the subject "But nothing. Why do you keep looking in the mirror? Who are you looking at? Don't think I haven't noticed. What's wrong? Tell me Peter." She turned her body round to face him. He cleared his throat nervously before speaking.

"Well, I didn't want to worry you. For the last few miles, we have someone trailing us-" he began. Auntie Rejoice's heart leapt to her throat. She turned her head to gaze through the back window. "Where is the car?" She said, unable to differentiate one vehicle from the other. Peter's hand patted her lap.

"Don't look now. It's the dark blue Toyota. It was behind us at the General. I didn't think anything of it.

But then it kept following us. I tried to lose him but he followed. I know he is definitely following us-"

"But why? What for? Are you in trouble with anyone?" she said. This surprised Peter. "Me, in trouble? I think it's you they're after. I'm sorry to be so blunt."

"Me? Why?" said Auntie Rejoice, her facial muscles twisting into a deep frown.

"Why? You don't have to look further than Mama Ayo's death for the cause. They're after you. I warned you about it. These men are dangerous." Peter said earnestly.

"Well, I have no choice but to continue." She whispered.

"Just be careful. I will drive recklessly now. Hold on to your seat!" Peter said, his foot pressed hard on the accelerator, to blaring horns. He was weaving the car through the traffic as cars and buses cleared out of his way, avoiding collision. Greater risk was called for if he was to save Auntie Rejoice from this maniac. He squeezed his car through tiny spaces between cars, slightly scratching one without stopping. The result was commotion. Drivers got out of their cars, waving their fists in anger at him. He made it. When he glanced in the rear mirror again the dark blue Toyota was nowhere to be seen. Peter and his passenger took deep breaths.

"I wonder what the priests will say about the loss of Mama Ayo's body?" said Peter, ignoring his reckless driving as if it was normal to drive like a maniac.

"I know what any of the Reverend Fathers will say. That we should take him to the hospital straight away. Are you prepared to drive back through that horrible traffic?"

"Of course! I'll drive all day to the moon, if you want me to. If you give so much of yourself why can't I give a little?"

They arrived at the school and parked the car in the staff car park. The two walked round the school gate to the church and Priest House gate, both church and house were on the same huge compound. The Priest House's gatekeeper smiled and greeted them. They returned his greeting with bows of the heads.

One of the Priest House housemaids was already holding the carved wood entrance door open by the time Auntie Rejoice and Peter Rotimi reached the door. From the television monitor in the hall she'd seen the visitors approaching.

"Father Biodun de inside but Father Mark no de. He go visit parishioners who sick. He be here soon. Come inside, I go get Reverend Father Biodun" She showed them into a large room full of large dark wood furniture, dominated by a large desk at a corner. A huge drawing of the Secret Heart, looking down on visitors, was on a wall and that of His mother on opposite wall.

"Sit down please" said the maid indicating chairs with a sweep of her hand. She then disappeared out of the door into another set of doors. Minutes later the Nigerian priest, looking like a younger version of a Hollywood star came through the door to greet them.

Father Biodun appeared lean in the face, his long body firm and athletic. He looked slightly tired but cheerful. He breezed into the sitting- room clapping his hands together as if his visitors were a couple of old mates, which they were.

Hello there Rejoice, hello Peter! To see you in the middle of the day means there's an urgent business-" the Priest said.

"Yes Father. Rejoice has problem with Mama Ayo-" Peter began but Father Biodun cut in. "You mean the mother of the little boy who found his mother dead with a knife in her chest? "

"Yes Father. As you know I deposited the body at the General Hospital mortuary?" Auntie Rejoice said. The Reverend Father nodded his head "Yes, Jaiye told us"

"Right. Well I went back today to inform the hospital we're collecting her body soon. You know, the burial is in two days"

Father Biodun nodded his head again. "At two o'clock" he added.

"Right. The attendant said there is no Mama Ayo's body to be had! They've either misplaced her or she has simply disappeared from the mortuary! I can't believe it Father can you? We thought we'd come to you. I know the Headmaster have too much on his plate and we don't want to disrupt him. I thought you won't mind helping-"

"Of course my child! Shall we go back to the mortuary now? We need to have everything sorted. Are you all right to drive Peter? Then lead the way." Said the Priest responding to Peter's nod.

The Priest and the teachers climbed into Peter Rotimi's car, the Reverend Father Biodun in the passenger's seat in front by the driver and Auntie Rejoice at the back behind the Reverend. The three had known each other for many years since the Church owned the school, though the school was managed by its own Board of Governors chaired by Father Mark, Head of the Church in the village, or Father Biodun. Father Biodun became Deputy four years previously when he transferred from The Holly Cross Cathedral in Lagos.

Father Biodun was a priest of our time, Auntie Rejoice always thought. He was born to a wealthy Muslim family of Lagosians. At the age of seven he ran away to join the Catholic Seminary at Ibadan in Oyo State, some ninety miles from Lagos. When the Seminary contacted his parents, his mother travelled down to dragged him back to Lagos saying 'No child of mine will become a Christian let alone join the priesthood." But what he later called his 'calling' never left him. At eighteen he returned to the Seminary and was baptised. Determined that church life was for him Father Biodun has never looked back.

When the car stopped in front of the General Hospital, the traffic jams had almost reduced to zero. There were parking spaces in front of the hospital, so the car slid into one. Auntie Rejoice followed the arrows as before to the reception area of the mortuary and went directly to the desk. It was a lady wearing too much make-up, at the desk. The sour faced male receptionist was nowhere to be seen.

"Yes, may I help you?" said the lady. Auntie Rejoice couldn't believe the change of tune, the politeness in her tone was a welcome change Auntie Rejoice gave her a wide smile before speaking.

"Yes, I came earlier in regard to a body I deposited two days ago. The man I met on this desk said you don't have the body. That I must have made a mistake-" She withdrew the receipt from her bag and handed it to the receptionist.

"I'm Father Biodun from St. Mary's. Can you check for us if the body, that is Mama Ayo's body, is here. She is to be buried soon." Said the Reverend Father.

"Yes Father, no problem at all. If you wait here I'll see. Is the name on her 'Mama Ayo'? No other name?" said the receptionist smiling.

"Yes, it's Mama Ayo. I wasn't sure what name she called herself. Everyone called her by her first born's name, as is usual in our custom. A sign of respect. I thought it was appropriate. Thanks" said Auntie Rejoice. The receptionist disappeared into the same inner doorway as the Cross- eyed one did earlier, in search of the lost body. While she was gone, a group of four, one man and three weeping women joined the queue behind Auntie Rejoice and the others, at the reception desk.

After a few minutes the receptionist re-emerged smiling turning to Auntie Rejoice she spoke quietly. "Did you say the body was missing earlier?"

"Yes, so I was told." Auntie Rejoice replied.

"Well I can put your mind at rest. Mama Ayo's body has been well taken care of and ready for burial. We have removed the knife in her chest, washed her, and gave her one of the better hospital's white gowns. She looks pretty. You can collect her any time as planed." The receptionist said warmly.

"That is a big load off my mind I can tell you! Thank the Lord. I couldn't concentrate all day. Thank you Father-" said Auntie Rejoice.

"I need to know one thing before you go. Who told you the body was missing? That you made a mistake?" the receptionist asked.

"It was a male receptionist I met here at about two o'clock this afternoon. He had a sharp sour face-" said Auntie Rejoice, now visibly relieved.

"With funny eyes?" the receptionist added cruelly. Auntie Rejoice nodded.

"That would be Akrika! Wait till I get my hands on him!"

"Please don't beat him" the Reverend Father pleaded.

"If you gave him a bribe, a few Naira notes perhaps, he would have got the body out for you somehow! No, I won't beat him physically but I have to report him so he never do it again to other people. Akrika was not suppose to be on the desk. He likes to appear like a big man. He is only the floor cleaner, with no business on the desk. The reason he couldn't find Mama Ayo's body was because he couldn't read or write. But if he gets a bribe, he will rope in someone to search for the body" said the receptionist, adding, "Pretending to be something you are not is a big problem in this country. People showing off money they didn't have, money they borrowed or stole. Things are changing. He will probably get fired."

Auntie Rejoice decided not to beg mercy for Akrika. She thanked the receptionist for her kindness and politeness. The three of them left the mortuary and got into the car for the drive home.

On the way Auntie Rejoice begged the Priest's permission and asked Peter Rotimi to head for Pa Seyi's house, to check on the children. "What a great idea!" Father Biodun beamed.

Something horrible was brewing inside Auntie Rejoice's mind. She felt unable to share her thoughts with the others, not quite yet.

From a distance she heard the Reverend Father's voice intruding into her thoughts..

"It will be nice to see all the children together. I've met Ayo, that wonderful young boy. It's almost a sin to call him a boy. He has so much insight."

"Yes Father. He's a wonderful boy. I need to see how they're getting on, and remind them again of the funeral arrangement."

The car winded its way to Aina village through moderate traffic on Eko Bridge to Surulere then via Agege Motor road to Aina village.

The children were again sitting on the grassland in front of their house playing. Pa Seyi sat at one end of the wooden benches, formerly in Mama Ayo's sitting room, now propped up beside Pa Seyi's front wall. Uncle Bita, naked except for khaki shorts, sat at the other end chewing at something Auntie Rejoice could not fathom. The two men sat with their backs leaning on the wall. The baby was nowhere around. Auntie Rejoice rightly thought the baby must be in his home- made cot, in the kitchen. This was exactly what Auntie Rejoice was hoping for. She wanted an excuse to nose around Pa Seyi's house. They sat in the car, each with his own thoughts until Auntie Rejoice broke the silence.

"It's surprising the children ignore their uncle Bita. They cling more to Pa Seyi. I don't understand it but I will say nothing, so long as they are all happy-"

"You've done your best you are not expected to do any more. They've got their blood relative with them. Let them get on with it. What do you think Peter?" the Priest tried to reassure Auntie Rejoice.

"I quite agree with you Father and I agree with what Rejoice said earlier. As long as the children are happy it doesn't matter who their guardian is."

The car pulled to a stop in front of the house and the children ran to the visitors shouting "Auntie Rejoice! Auntie Rejoice!" They ran and hugged her and the Reverend Father in turn. But when they got to Peter, they stood still not sure what to do. The Priest was less threatening. Peter knew Ayo as a pupil of St. Mary's of course but he was not his main teacher. Auntie Rejoice was.

"Hello children" said Peter uneasily. He was awkward with children in private, though he loved teaching them. He knew that his power over them in the classroom was total. But outside the classroom, children were unpredictable, he always thought.

Auntie Rejoice strolled to Pa Seyi while the priest and Peter chatted to the children.

"May I see the baby?" Pa Seyi nodded and led her into his house to where the baby laid in its wooden cot, at a corner of the room. Auntie Rejoice lifted the drawer and placed it on a chair. Her eyes roamed round the room. When she saw Pa Seyi staring at her, attempting to read her mind, she spoke.

"I haven't really seen round your home before. Can I look round now? Do you mind?"

He shook his head from side to side, relieved she wasn't finding fault with him or the way he treated the children.

"Come, I'll show you round. This is of course the kitchen beside the parlour. This is my room. There are enough rooms here for me-" he spread his hands gleefully showing off the small poky house. Intermittently one hand went to cup his genitals as an indication of his happiness or nervousness, Auntie Rejoice wasn't sure which. An act that always guaranteed to bring the contents of the teacher's stomach sharply into her chest.

"That's enough for a bachelor, is it not?" she said forcing a smile. Auntie Rejoice returned to the kitchen, looking in drawers, opening cupboards. Pa Seyi stood behind her watching her every move.

"Your cooking utensils. The cutlery, the cooking stove. All nice and compact, just right for one person. You now also look after the children. They like you. You never know, we may need to go to court for custody. The Court may want me to make a case for the children to stay with you. At least I can say I've been through your house and I know you well. You are a trustworthy upstanding fellow-" As Auntie Rejoice spoke, a broad smile wrinkled Pa Seyi's already wrinkled face. He smiled his crocodile-like charmless smile,

"Oh! That is why yoo looking round my humble 'ouse? I was a little worried. OK, OK! I get it now!" he said.

"Actually I've seen everything I wanted to see. Thank you, shall we go out? I'll bring the baby. The children give you no trouble I hope?" She picked up the baby from its cot and they joined the others outside.

"No. We all get on." Pa Seyi muttered, trailing behind her.

When they emerged into the open air they found the Priest and Peter in the middle of the children chatting and laughing. Auntie Rejoice informed the children and adults about the funeral programmes. She handed the baby back to Pa Seyi. The trio got into the car and drove back to the church.

TWENTY-TWO

They drove past the church to drop Father Biodun at the Priest House. When the car stopped, the sun was still shinning but had lost its oven-like heat. On the step of The Priest House stood Father Mark looking smart and priestly in his long white priestly robe, his hair, the colour of his robe, white as snow. His face was copper brown and nicely rounded like a loveable uncle who visited at Christmas time bearing gifts. He had a warm smile for the trio and as Auntie Rejoice got near him, his outstretched arms were waiting to embrace her.

"Well done my child. The maid told me about your search. How is it?" he greeted her. His kind words opened locked- in tears. Peter and Father Biodun looked on perplexed and saddened, wondering if they could have done more to prevent her breakdown.

Father Biodun went over and patted her on the back, "Now, now, Rejoice you'll be all right. I think you've taken on far too much. I suggest we collect the body of Mama Ayo from the mortuary and make arrangement for the remaining burial procedures with Peter. You don't have to go to school tomorrow. Take a rest. If that's all right by you? Father? Rejoice? Peter?" He looked at each one of them as he called their names. Each said 'Of course' in response. "Settled. Now I bid you good evening." With that Father Biodun left the group and entered the House to go about his priestly duties. Father Mark suspected there was more to Auntie Rejoice's breakdown. He stroke her plaited head gently and spoke in whisper.

"Now Rejoice what is the matter? Do you want to come inside for a private chat?"

Rejoice paused for a second before shaking her head. It would be slighting Peter to leave him standing alone. He'd moved away from Rejoice to retain her secrecy when talking to the priest.

"I'm all right Father. I saw Mama Ayo yesterday, as I walked Ayo home, when she was supposed to be lying dead in her house. She disappeared into thin air as we ran to catch up with her. It was scary Father. I couldn't tell anyone-." She blurted out. It was like a big weight off her chest, to speak out about these things. She had not realised the weight of the burden she carried. Her shoulders seemed lighter now. The Priest interrupted her.

"In case people thought you mad?"

"Yes Father." A smile creased her lips. She hadn't really smile in two days. It felt good to talk to someone who understands, she thought, the Priests understood.

"You know my child, there are things in the Heavens and Earth that we don't understand. We who possess faith are the lucky ones. Because our minds are open. But please take a little rest, as Father Biodun suggested. A grown man would have collapsed under the weight you've carried so far. Come in and chat to me or Father Biodun any time-"

"Thank you Father. Please give Father my thanks also" she said as they parted.

Peter Rotimi and Auntie Rejoice walked back to the adjoining school gate, where Peter parked the car.

Cars were still in the parking lot, indicating the staff were still at school, though pupils had left for the day. Auntie Rejoice and Peter headed for the staff room.

The room was large and comfortably furnished. A huge refrigerator, sat behind the door, full of personal perishable foodstuffs brought in by staff, because the school electricity was never affected by NEPA. The school had its own electricity generator independent of the national grid. In addition to the overhead fan, two standing fans stood at each end of the large room. On a long work-table were various mugs, cups, and saucers. A metal tray, beside the sink, held an assortment of coffee jars, teabags, powdered milk and three tins of condensed milk. Beside the cups was a stainless steel electric kettle At the far end of the room stood a wide screen television with a video recorder. The floor was covered in red square lino with clusters of easy chairs scattered in groups of threes and fours here and there. It was indeed a very comfortable place for relaxation. But no teacher ever sat long enough to relax.

As Peter pushed the door open to let Rejoice into the staff room,, the teachers put down their coffee mugs and clapped their hands to the yells of 'bravo! Well done Rejoice! Bravo! And Peter too!' Both Rejoice and Peter were startled and overwhelmed with the unexpected warm reception.

"Coffee?" someone offered. "Please" Auntie Rejoice and Peter chorused. Auntie Rejoice planted herself in a chair. Her eyes settled on the piles of cardboard boxes stacked at a corner against a wall. One of the teachers followed her gaze.

"We got the drinks for the wake. Sister Ceecil has bought the coffin, we'll collect it on the way to the mortuary" the news gladdened Auntie Rejoice.

Teachers and priests were united in giving Mama Ayo a good send off.

"That is incredible. You all worked so hard for this motherless child. God's blessing be on everyone!" Auntie

Rejoice said, accepting a cup of coffee from a colleague who spoke for the rest.

"Amen! You've done the most difficult jobs, we'll take it from here. You are staying home tomorrow. That, my friend is Father Biodun's command and I dare say that of Father Mark too! You better not disobey! We are the enforcers!" Auntie Rejoice shook her head from side to side in disbelieve. "No! I enjoy my work-" she began, cheerfully but was interrupted. The whole staff of eleven, seven females and four males, diverted their gaze to Auntie Rejoice.

She was interrupted by a male teacher they called Smilie, who never smiled. They called him 'Smilie' anyway, on account of his protruding two front teeth. "You can't disobey the Priests! It's for your own good. I remember when my mother died. I ran round like a headless chicken, denying myself sleep. On the way to buy the coffin I dozed off while driving through the traffic, ramming into the car in front. My God I'll never forget that day. I could have killed-" He demonstrated the crash by knocking a fist of one hand against the palm of his other hand.

"Thank you Smilie, I think Rejoice got the message." Said another teacher, cutting Smilie off.

"I think you should do what will make you happy. You know what the school feels" the Headmaster, who had remained silent, cut in. Auntie Rejoice sighed heavily before speaking. "All I can say again is, thank you all. I'll pop in for a couple of hours to clear my desk. Just that!" she declared. They nodded and left it at that.

"Good, all settled! We all know what tasks each one of us is doing tomorrow and day after?" he said.

"Yes, we're ready, got our tasks well and truly rehearsed. It will be a funeral the boys will be proud of" said a married female teacher adding "If we have nothing more to discuss I better make a move. I have to stop at the market before going home to cook-"

"You should train your husband to cook-" said Auntie Rejoice jokingly. Theresa wrinkled her nose in sadness "My husband is useless. He won't do anything in the house but if I'm away to see my parents, the idiot cooks himself good meals. You don't know how lucky you single women are-"

"Oh we do and we thank God for His mercy every minute of the day!" another singleton chipped in. The group began to disintegrate and slip away home leaving the Headmaster, Peter and Auntie Rejoice in the room.

"Well, I better go too. I think you should too Peter. The fact is, if we don't go home Mr Jaiye won't go. The first to arrive and the last to leave. A hard working Headmaster you will never see! See you in the morning sir" Auntie

Rejoice said as she walked out of the door. Peter hurried to catch up with her.

"Can I give you a lift home?" he said hesitatingly, feeling he already knew her answer. Auntie Rejoice smiled indulgently as if to a child.

"I live not quite five minutes from here" she said

"I know. Will you come out for a drink tonight? We can go to the Holiday Inn or Eko Hotel or-" Of course he could afford such extravagance. He was single and St. Mary's teachers were paid a little above national average.

Staff were mainly recruited by word of mouth. Mr Jaiye found that his school's popularity went far into every corner of the country.

"I'll go out with you tonight" Auntie Rejoice quickly burst out, before reason put a stop to her foolishness. She felt like letting her hair down, released some of the stress she'd been under a little. She owed herself that, at least.

Peter looked astounded, he was expecting a negative response. The shock of acceptance was almost too much for him. Auntie Rejoice noticed his drawn face and tried to put him at ease. "Or you'd rather I don't see you tonight?" she teased him. He shook his head from side to side

"No, no, I want you to come out with me! Of course I do I'm very glad you consented. Where would you like to go?" he said, his grin getting bigger by the second.

"Anywhere. You chose-" she said.

"In that case I'll collect you at seven o'clock. Don't eat because we'll go for super and drinks"

He dropped her at home and they said their goodbyes, only to reunite at six forty five,

Peter drove to the Beach Hotel on Lagos Island, with its flashing neon lights proclaiming itself 'The best hotel in the country. Home from home'. The Beach Hotel was a majestic extravagant edifice in the middle of the sandy beach itself. As he parked the car in the car lot in front of the hotel Peter turned to Auntie Rejoice, "Here we are! Are you all right?"

Auntie Rejoice turned her head sideways to glance at him. In the soft lights of late evening, Peter seemed quite handsome and debonair, he would one day make a dreadful husband, she paused a little then added, for some unlucky woman.

"Yes, I'm fine, just enjoying the view. Lagos is beautiful at night isn't it?" she said. He nodded as he jumped out of the car, to hold the car door open for her.

"Yes, truly magnificent. It could be heaven on earth. So much beauty concentrated in one place!!" he replied, turning the key inside the anti- theft device in the car.

He led her into the hotel. As they walked in, the sound of Yoruba High Life music rented the air. A life band, stationed at the forecourt of the hotel was playing. Couples danced on the cemented floor. Behind the double glass doors inside the hotel, diners were enjoying their meals. On the left was a spread of buffet diner, on the right, a waiter service.

They stood at the door eyeing both sides of the door until Peter spoke.

"Would you like a buffet?" he said.

Auntie Rejoice shook her head from side to side, "No! I never take buffet meals outside. You never know how long it's been standing there. I normally don't eat out actually-" she said, adding, "I like to know what's on my plate!"

"I do almost all my eating in hotels! I don't like cooking!" Peter said.

"From what I heard it's your girlfriends who do the cooking for you!"

"Well, every unmarried man is at the mercy of rogue women! There are too many women with no self respect!" Peter said. A waiter in green and white uniform, the colours of the Nigerian Flag, approached them. "May I help you sir?" the waiter at once assumed the man to be master.

"Yes you can give us a good table at that side of the room" Peter nodded his head towards the service area. The waiter led them to a window table over- looking the Atlantic ocean and handed them menu sheets.

"Feel free to choose anything you fancy. I'm not counting my pennies.-" Peter said jovially.

The drinks waiter was soon at their elbows waving a drinks- card. Peter turned to Auntie Rejoice, "Wine or hot drinks or beer?"

"Brandy, Napoleon please" she said without hesitation.

"Of course madam! I shall bring you Napoleon brandy in two seconds! And you sir?"

"Bring me ice cold beer please" said Peter. The waiter disappeared and returned with their drinks.

"My colleague here will take your order for food sir" Setting the drinks down on the table the waiter disappeared, leaving them alone.

Auntie Rejoice hadn't been out on a date for a very long time. She sat back now wondering if she had made the right decision in coming out tonight. Her mind was on Mama Ayo and her killer. She felt she knew the killer's identity. But could she trust Peter with her secret? Peter seemed a kind but foolish person, whose only fault laid in pursuing women, an energy sapping quest. She decided not to reveal her secret. He might be too hot-headed when he met the killer. No she couldn't chance it. She sipped her drink again, aware that Peter's lips were moving but, his voice seemed far, far away beyond her hearing. How could she prove the killer's guilt? She'd lapsed into that private world of her own again. She knew what to do, but would it work? Of course it would, it must. She would drop hints and set a trap for the killer, watch and wait. Pity she couldn't expect help from the Police. Her ears caught the tail end of Peter's voice.

"I wonder why she was knifed to dead. Such a violent death. Pity the murderer got away free. Lack of police action-"

"The killer won't get away with it-" Auntie Rejoice said, almost in a whisper.

"What? You don't mean that!" he interrupted. She glared straight into his eyes as if to say 'how dare you doubt me?' She turned her gaze away to glance through the double glass windows overlooking the Ocean into the horizon. Instead of seeing the beautiful blue sky disappearing into the Atlantic Ocean, it was the face of Ayo that starred back at her. A knife dripping with blood in his right hand, he was gazing malevolently at his pleading mother on the mat. Temporarily, her face froze into a look of horror. She blinked the scene away. When she recovered, she saw that Peter hardly noticed her frozen posture. Her eyes surveyed the horizon again. She loved the surroundings and she loved the cool air blowing in from the beach. What a sight, what a stress- free place! If only she could do this more often. Perhaps after the case was solved. Right now her mind was never far away from Mama Ayo's murder.

Maybe she would reconsider staying indoors night after night and venture out a little bit more. A woman on her own in a posh hotel is always viewed a prostitute by idiotic men, Auntie Rejoice thought. This was a good life for those who could afford it.

In no time at all, their glasses were empty of drinks and Peter called for a refill.

As the waiter was leaving their table, their ears pricked to a sharp voice shrilling behind them.

"So this is you? This is why you left me? Peter? This is what you left me for? This is you with a new girlfriend?" Peter and Rejoice turned round at the mention of his name to see whose was the offending voice. Peter gasped loudly as he glimpsed her. The voice belonged to a colourfully dressed lady pouting devil- red lips, with a kilo of green eye-shadow sitting over owl-like eyes. Her very short skirt revealed a pair of K-legs that wouldn't look out of place in an elephant kingdom beauty parade.

She walked round to the front of the couple. Auntie Rejoice emptied her glass and set it back on the table while glaring in disbelieve at the new- comer. The lady (calling her this, was an injustice to ladies) was in her thirties wearing a scanty red skirt and breast- revealing white blouse. A pound of powder hugged her face like a long lost friend one would prefer to remain lost. Her voice was thin and screechy, like grinding stone on stone, either from shouting her words all day or lack of good home training that teaches shouting is what louts do. Ladies never shout. She was loud and obnoxious. It's no wonder Peter left her, thought Auntie Rejoice quietly.

"This is your new girlfriend eh? This is the reason you left me eh? Yes she is pretty but no more than I am, what sort of man are you? Lady, your man is a double dealer! A rogue, a lady killer! Be careful he'll have his way with you then leave you dry! That's his method! Mad Peter, love them and leave them Peter! Mad, mad Peter, womanising Peter! You left me for this bush woman! You-" She snared, pointing at Peter. Auntie Rejoice had had enough. She got up and walked out of the glass door. Peter got up to follow her. The lady saw her chance of maximum embarrassment and grabbed him by the waist. He pushed her away. She fell into a line of plates on a trolley. Peter ran after Auntie Rejoice pleading,

"Please, you must believe me she is a mad woman. I finished with her almost a year ago now but she won't let go. You must give me another chance. At least let me take you home. I beg you, please listen to me. Listen to the voice of reason- mine!"

Other diners looked on with incredulity, and an overwhelming sympathy for Rejoice.

"OK, take me home" replied Auntie Rejoice calmly. It was after all, more or less what she'd expected from the like of Peter Rotimi, a famed skirt chaser. She was only sorry she had not followed her instinct to stay home. But it had been a good attempt for her to wash away the sadness of death, and indulged in a little bit of nonsense talk from Peter Rotimi.

They drove leisurely but in silence along the beach to the Marina. The traffic was light, unlike earlier that afternoon, when the streets were jammed.

When the car sailed to Eko Bridge the traffic took its normal snail's pace. A car, had broken down on the bridge causing the jam, with no hope of a quick tow away. The car driver was staring into the open bonnet in awe, shouting and kicking the car as if it were human. The breakdown was put squarely on the dead car, the driver explained to Peter when Peter parked his own car and went to investigate the delay. The oil tank was empty, the car had not been serviced for months. The driver's excuse was, the car was on loan to him. Peter gave advice, returned to his own car and continued to drive in silence until they reached Auntie Rejoice's front door.

Parking the car in her driveway he switched off the engine, hoping for a few minutes' chatting to close the gulf between them. Auntie Rejoice had no feelings one way or the other for Peter except disappointment and fatigue.

She descended the car then poked her head through the open window.

"Thank you for the drink" she said, walking through her front garden to enter the house. Peter's voice filled the air.

"I am sorry, you know. That girl is crazy, you saw her yourself. I wasn't expecting that to happen-"

"Of course not. Listen Peter, I'm not angry with you. I'm just disappointed that's all. It's what I would have expected to happen but still disappointed it happened. Goodnight see you in the morning" Auntie Rejoice turned and entered her house. Peter drove off home wishing the ground would open and swallow him.

Twenty-Three

After tossing and turning in bed Auntie Rejoice got up at 4 a.m. An invisible force dragged her to the window facing the public park. She gently pulled back the lace curtains to see the park faintly illuminated by a distant street lamp. The government maintained the park in excellent condition, but wasted no money on illumination. The reasoning was that, the park's closing times were in the hours of daylight, five o'clock.

She gazed out into the wide expanse of space. It was quiet and eerily still. There was not a single human being about, she thought. A shiver ran through her when she caught sight of a flicker of movement behind an oak tree. She was sure there was something or someone beyond the park wall.

She closed her eyes and opened them again, blinking in an effort to shake sleep from her eyes, she strained her eyes to see clearly. Yes, there was a figure cloaked in black. She'd seen this a few days before behind the same giant oak tree in the park, but brushed it off.. The tree was diagonally facing her window. She looked again, and became certain now. There was a figure resembling a man there. Its movement now more definite.

In Yoruba mythology there were gods for the spirits of most every living things. But was the myth still alive today? It was, in people like Pa Jibiti, the Babalawo. Someone was watching her, watching the house, watching her window. Perhaps the figure lived in the tree. Some villagers worshipped the god of trees. Auntie Rejoice pondered this for a few seconds. Tree gods were taken seriously and venerated by their devotees. And spirits were supposed to come alive at the bewitching hours before dawn.

Perhaps she should consider speaking to the police. But what good would that do? The voice of Inspector Gberaga rang in her ears. 'Bring me the culprit and I'll take it from there'. She resolved not to go to the police, but would seek the Priests' advice. The threat to her own life was now to be taken seriously indeed.

Before she left the house as a precaution, she decided her maid would stand by the gate and watch until she, Rejoice, reached the T-junction where traffic and people were more visible. If she was attacked before then, the maid was to raise an alarm. No harm would touch the maid since she wasn't the prime target. Deep in her heart, Auntie Rejoice felt Pa Jibiti, the witchdoctor, was at the bottom of this scare tactics. Well he won't succeed. Her body was shivering as she turned away from the window to prepare herself for work. She was sure that the man in the park was Pa Jibiti's second son, a tall, thin colourless man with shrunken watery red eyes.

Suddenly for no apparent reason or even having the intention of saying a prayer, Auntie Rejoice returned to her position at the window and started reciting Psalm 23 'The Lord's my Shepherd' Before reaching the end of the prayer, she saw an amazing spectacle in front of her.

The black clad figure in the park emerged into the dim light, stripping the face cover off first. It was as she suspected, the skeletal face of Pa Jibiti's second son. As he did so, a small spark of flame, as if a match had been struck, appeared at the helm of his black long cloak. In a blink of an eye the cloak suddenly ignited and burst into flames, engulfing the figure. She watched in open- mouth amazement. Then instinct kicked in. She ran down to the maid's quarters and banged on the door shouting, 'Water! Buckets of water! Follow me!' The maid, Misi, groggily opened her door and followed madam to fetch buckets of water from the water-tap in the front garden. Misi glimpsed the dying flames and took in a sharp breath.

They carried the water across the garden to the park opposite. But what met their eyes as they glanced across to the figure was even more terrifying. It stopped them dead in their tracts.

It was as if an invisible vacuum cleaner had swept up the ashes, the figure was vacuumed up completely. All that remained of the black- clad figure were remnants of the black cloak and a few spoons of grey ash, to prove Auntie Rejoice had not been dreaming. Auntie Rejoice gasped in disbelieve, thankful the maid was there to witness. Both maid and madam exchanged glances.

The maid suddenly became conscious to the fact that she'd just witnessed the strangest phenomenon. She let out ear- damaging screams for her mother. The words of Father Mark fleeted through Auntie Rejoice's mind. 'There are things on Earth and the heavens we do not understand. We have open minds about these things.'

TWENTY-FOUR

When Auntie Rejoice arrived at school on the day of the funeral, the Headmaster's car was in the parking lot, but he himself was not in school. He had left her a note to take his first class, French. The trouble with teaching was, thought Rejoice, a teacher had to be prepared to stand- in for colleagues. She herself had not spoken French since she was approached by a French holidaymaker in Spain requesting help with her camera. Well better brushed up the lingo, she whispered to herself. She rummaged through drawers in the Headmaster's office till she found a tape of French conversation. That would have to do. As she entered Mr Jaiye's class, the pupils burst into applause. It was a pleasant start to the day.

"You are very kind all of you" she said cheerfully. One small hand went up in the air.

"Yes Bisi?" said the teacher. Bisi, a pretty little girl with blue ribbon in her plaited hair smiled shyly. "Auntie," Bisi began breathlessly, "Auntie Rejoice, we will like to go to Mama Ayo's funeral too. Can we? Can we please?" Auntie

Rejoice had no doubt the pupils had been discussing the issue at length before they came into class, and chose sweet Bisi as spokesperson. She paused to think before replying.

"I don't think students are going. Maybe one or two. We can't have the whole school there. There will be no room for Ayo's family and friends. Please pray for Ayo, his brothers and the soul of the departed. The fact is we also don't have the permission of your parents. Thank you for asking. I shall tell Ayo of your concern."

A little boy's hand went up. "Auntie Rejoice can we come to the party afterwards?"

The class erupted into laughter. "Trust Yomi! Always thinking of his stomach!" said another. More laughter echoed round the class.

"Now everyone, let's race on with our lesson" the teacher said. At the end of the class, she checked on Mr Jaiye again. He was back sitting at his desk in his office.

"Come in, come in Rejoice!" he said cheerfully. His arms outstretched to embrace. Rejoice wasn't sure whether to walk into them or pretend to not seeing them. The quandary was solved when he rushed forward to embrace her. "Good work, good work Rejoice!" he beamed, adding, "Have you got the poem ready for reading?"

It was common knowledge in the school that Auntie Rejoice was a poet. She'd written many, but too shy to read publicly. Mr Jaiye had requested her to read an appropriate poem at the funeral, to give a feeling of cosiness and class. She wasn't so sure. She would speak with Ayo, see what the boy feels.

"I thought I'll check again on times of Mass and reception, before announcing to the public-" she said.

"Yes, the first school's sponsored funeral is upon us today! I'm sure Ayo would look back on this time as unique if a sad period in his life" The Headmaster concluded as they parted.

Auntie Rejoice cornered Ayo in church. The boys sat in the front pews, looking smart, with their guardians.

"The Headmaster wants me to read a poem at Mass. What do you think?" she said.

The boy looked unconcerned, shrugged his shoulders and spoke.

"I think you will make it more friendly if you read a poem. I can't write one myself but I think it's a nice idea. Me and my brothers will be very grateful if you read your poem." Ayo's smile was wide and warm. It improved Auntie Rejoice's mood.

She had been feeling a little low, the black cloak man, the murder investigation-, The funeral reminded her too much of her own late parents, as funerals always do remind us of our own mortality.

Auntie Rejoice glanced up above Ayo's head, on a stone stand by the wall was a statute of the Holy Mary. The statue seemed to be staring back at Ayo and herself. It reminded Auntie Rejoice of her two week tour of the Vatican in Rome three years previously. It was the Holy Father, the late Pope John Paul the Second's Anniversary of becoming Pope. The school had put a poster up for a pilgrimage to Rome to commemorate the occasion. Father Biodun led the tour group of teachers and parishioners who could afford the trip. During the tour the Italian tour guide stood in front of a marble statue of Our Lady and spoke about the Holy Father. When Pope John Paul the Second was about eight or nine years old, having lost his mother when very young, according to the tour guard, the Pope's father took him to their local church, stood him in front of a statue of the Virgin Mary and said, "Vojtica this is your mother! She'll look after you." It was said, the Pope never forgot this simple instruction and took the Holy Mother literally as his protector. The Pope, so they were told, believed the Blessed Virgin intercepted for him during the attempted assassination on his life.

Now as Auntie Rejoice stood momentarily taken back to Rome in her mind's eye, Ayo's voice interrupted, jolting her from her reverie.

"Auntie Rejoice are you all right?" the boy said.

"Yes, thank you, are you?" the boy nodded his head.

Auntie Rejoice thought, there is just one more thing I must do. Find her killer.

It was half past one and people began trooping into the church, their faces long and suitably funerally sad.

The church filled up quite quickly as it always did at such occasions. Filling pews had never been a problem in Africa. Just before Mass two middle-aged women walked right to the front where the children of the deceased sat. The women peeped into Ayo's face then gazed at the baby in Pa Seyi's arms, shook their heads and burst into loud sobs. "Look at the baby! The poor motherless baby! What will become of him now?" They wept loudly until an usher led them to the back of the church, where they indulged themselves in an orgy of lamentation. Weeping spread like a virus to other women in the church. Father Mark said the Mass assisted by Father Biodun in a sombre and suitably solemn atmosphere.

The children of the deceased looked on as if they were at Sunday school, no more no less.

Auntie Rejoice glanced at the little motherless children in front of her again and wondered what life held in store for them. Without a mother life could be difficult, at least not as easy as for those with mothers. True, there were worthless mothers whose offsprings were better off as orphans. So was the case of Mama Koko.

Married for her beauty, Mama Koko was the third wife of one of the elders in the village. Mama Koko's beauty was the talk of the whole village, which was how Auntie Rejoice heard about her.

She abandoned her eight days old boy, Koko, saying motherhood did not befit her. Koko now roamed the streets of Lagos for food.

Auntie Rejoice glanced at Ayo again. He was crying silently, wiping his eyes with his sleeves. Auntie Rejoice thought he must have suddenly realised the gravity of the occasion, he would never see his mother ever again. But like any small child he soon perked up and became amused by the antics of his brothers.

At the end of the Requiem Mass Father Mark addressed the congregation, then called Auntie Rejoice.

"I call on our excellent, Rejoice Akintola to read out a short poem she had been persuaded to read for this occasion. Rejoice, if you please." The Reverend Father then took his seat at the altar. Auntie Rejoice stood, gave a short cough of nervousness then walked to the front of the congregation, clutching a piece of paper in hand. She fought back tears as she read the poem out in a steady voice.

A poem for the deceased.

'When I'm dead I'm dead. Muscles and bones into the earth from whence they came.

Let the worms and God's creatures come to dine.

Sprinkle me with salt and pepper

A tasty morsel to behold.

When I'm dead I'm dead. Save your tears for times gone by.

When soothing words could have mended my aching heart.

Two slices of bread to feed my hunger

Water to quench my thirst

Solitude was a friend

When I'm dead I'm dead. Untouched by aches and pain

Save your grief for yourselves

Raise your eyes to the sky. Give glory to the Creator

For a life well spent

When I'm dead I'm dead

Gone to a better place

Happy in the bosom of the Prince of peace.

Father Biodun thanked Auntie Rejoice and proceeded to say the concluding rites. A short service of prayer ensued at the burial ground and people dispersed to Mama Ayo's house for entertainment. The school had given money to certain neighbours to shop for food and cook assorted meals for guests. The Headmaster, Mr Jaiye, resplendent in white lace agbada, accompanied by his wife, in white lace iro and buba, had allocated himself the job of barman for the night, serving beer and soft drinks.

He had closed the school for the rest of the day and the next day to give teachers a day of rest.

"What a lovely service! What a poem! I wonder, can we have copies from her" Auntie Rejoice heard someone said after Mass. Requiem Mass was one of her own favourite services. Pity someone had to die first.

TWENTY-FIVE

Prayers at the graveyard lasted only a few minutes after which people, including Ma Taiwo, the dressmaker, proceeded to Mama Ayo's house for the wake party, a special present given to the children by the school and church.

Tables, each with a set of six chairs were arranged round Mama Ayo's front yard for guests. Teachers played hosts as well as being waiters.

In Lagos, parties were never restricted to known guests, strangers always joined in the merriment and served food and drinks. Auntie Rejoice hoped food and drinks would be sufficient for everybody.

Arriving guests sat round in groups with their friends and family. Pa Jibiti, the witchdoctor, made a sudden unexpected appearance and sat at a table with his three wives and nine of his children, dragging additional table and chairs for themselves. Showing their faces without embarrassment was a surprise to everyone, especially after the shameful divination in his house. Pa Jibiti signalled to a young man holding a tray of plates of rice and chicken stew.

"Young man yoo no serve these our tables here with food. We be very hungry, dee service be long one and dee walk to dee cemetery be no joke-" said Pa Jibiti, whom no one saw in church nor at the cemetery.

"Everyone was taken to the burial ground by car. People shared cars. No one walked. How come you are the only one-" the boy was cut short by the witchdoctor's raised tone.

"Yoo riff- raff boy! Yoo dare disagree with me! Do yoo no kno who I am?"

"I know you sir. You are the Babalawo, Pa Jibiti of-" the boy began.

"Don't mind about of where! Bring me and my people good food to eat. What yoo have there? Yoo no get gari?" The boy shook his head denoting the negative.

Pa Jibiti shook his head too but in disgust sighing heavily before speaking.

"What kind wake be dis? Why I fill my stomach with rice,? Rice no be proper food. Gee me something to fill hole in my belly, like eba or pounded yam. OK, geev us the rice but go and bring more chickens and beef. Two chicken legs no fill belly. Also bring us beer, twelve bottles to start!" The boy departed and returned shortly after with rice and four pieces of chicken legs on Pa Jibiti's plate, two pieces each for his wives and children, much to their irritation.

The Headmaster and his staff had calculated and allocated two bottles of beer per person. But Pa Jibiti was a law onto himself. As his wives did not drink alcohol Pa Jibiti was able to consume more than his share, pocketing the rest for home consumption.

It would not have been a party without music especially High Life and Juju music of the Yorubas which now permeated Africa.

The Headmaster, in his wisdom, had brought his own sound system blasting popular music tapes to enliven the occasion. The loud music could be heard half a mile away along Agege Motor road.

Auntie Rejoice, her eyes darting across the road to the bus- stop, stood chatting with an elderly woman Young girls and boys were dancing unashamedly to the music while waiting for their buses to arrive. She knew then that the party was a great success. It would be the talk of the village in years to come. She could almost hear them now. 'Were you at Mama Ayo's wake? No? My o my, what a day! We heard the latest music, people danced in the streets. It was a day to remember!' 'I hope when I'm gone my children would give as good a send off as that, one day. Not now though, I'm not ready to go yet. You know what they say, about being careful for what you wish yourself, in case an angel passes. I repeat, I don't want to die now.

But when that time comes I hope my children saw the good example laid by the church and school."

What Auntie Rejoice hoped was that the children would remember the day they buried their mother. They would remember that the best that could be done was done for their dead mother.

Hours flew by as guests became beer- soaked and ate heartily. Bodies and tongues became loosened and people began to get up from their chairs to the dance floor. Any empty space without chairs or tables became a dancing space, even those possessing two left feet did their best to move to the music.

To no one's surprise Pa Jibiti, wearing a light blue agbada, took the floor with his youngest wife, while his other wives looked on as if the air has been fouled. When the music stopped Pa Jibiti and his young wife took their seats, receiving bad- eye from the two sit- down wives, who felt slighted and would no doubt seek revenge.

The young wife was aware of this also. Being young and foolish she craved attention and liked the showmanship. She expected and thrived on jealousy.

When the rush for food slowed, the young boy helper who had a hard time with Pa Jibiti went to Auntie Rejoice,

"Auntie Rejoice I think I have served all my side of the tables. I think the other helpers too are serving second and third helpings to greedy visito-"

Auntie Rejoice put a finger to the boy's lips "Hush, don't let people hear you say that. All are guests today, let them eat as much as they want. No doubt some people will take food home. Are you sure that everyone had been served food and drinks?" The boy nodded his head. "Yes Auntie, everyone, including those malams by the school who just arrived"

Auntie Rejoice strained her neck to look across the heads of sitting guests to the malams now sitting at a corner of the street eating rice and chicken, their heads covered with long white headscarves. Ayo and his brothers sat together around one table at the edge of the crowd. The children had reserved one extra table and chairs for their teachers who had little use of them. During a lull, several of the teachers including Peter Rotimi sat briefly with the children asking their thoughts on the day. The children on the whole were quite jolly and had accepted the death of their mother as a matter of fact, in the way children often do. Auntie Rejoice reflected on children's ability to take pain and absorb it as quickly as it came. She herself never forgot the horrible way her own parents had been taken from her, long ago.

Auntie Rejoice found Ma Taiwo's table and sat with her and the dressmaker's son.

"This is beyond good. You should be proud of what you've done for the orphans" said Ma Taiwo, chewing a piece of beef.

"Thank you for sewing her dress-" said the teacher.

"Don't thank me, after all, you paid for it." Ma Taiwo replied.

"I see you killed more chickens. What happened to the ones killed the evening of the murder-" Ma Taiwo did not finish her sentence before Auntie Rejoice jumped in.

"You saw chickens killed here, that night?" the teacher said.

"Yes, of course! I saw Pa Seyi and his friends slaughtering and cooking the birds. Pa Jibiti said a prayer. It was like a death ritual, washing away death from their doorsteps. People do that you know!" said the dressmaker. Auntie Rejoice thanked Ma Taiwo and left them to enjoy their meal.

Now she knew. The trail of blood she saw on Mama Ayo's doorstep the evening she returned from the morgue, was not from the murdered woman. One strand of the case closed, she sighed.

It was now several hours into the wake, celebrating Mama Ayo's life. The light of day was fading. In Lagos, the sun's boisterous energy quickly begin to sap by late evening, the night keen to take over by six p. m.

Auntie Rejoice and her fellow teachers had previously decided the celebration would end before darkness fell. As the night drew in, the Headmaster signalled to Auntie Rejoice from his position by the beer barrel beside Pa Seyi's wall. She hurried to him.

"I think we better start clearing up or we'd be here till tomorrow. If you can get the young helpers to start collecting plates and glasses and bottles-"

"What do we do with those still on the dance floor? I don't think they're ready to leave yet!" said Auntie Rejoice smiling. The Headmaster was in no mood to spend more time dishing out booze, now running very low.

"I'm afraid I'm going to turn off the music and announce the end of the party. Anyone who wants can continue after we've packed up our cutlery and plates"

"I'll get the young ones to start clearing up. Don't stop the music Headmaster until it's all done please!"

Auntie Rejoice went round the older school pupils who had volunteered their services and told then, to start clearing up. She returned to Pa Seyi's front room to see what was left of the food. Inside the house, she met a village woman trespassing, who had no right to be in the house. The villager was helping herself to food, wrapping pieces of chicken into a large cotton cloth when Auntie Rejoice appeared.

"Sorry I was looking for the toilet. Then I saw this going to waste-" the woman said, as she disappeared into the crowd with a bagfull of food. Auntie Rejoice ignored her and emptied the rest of the roasted pieces of chicken into a small plate for the children. She glanced out of the window and saw a middle aged man, in a black ill- fitting suit, standing outside in the street, looking in. Auntie Rejoice thought this was odd. The man was not among the congregation in church. He would have stood out, as most people wore native attires, and he was definitely not at the cemetery. He was arriving at the end of the wake. How very odd. What a peculiar behaviour, a disrespect to the dead, an insult to the living. Suddenly the scream of, "Papa! Papa! Papa!" filled the air. The voices of the children were raised in jubilation. Ayo and his brothers were joyful at the return of their father. Auntie Rejoice ran out of the house to take a look and confirm it was the elusive figure. The man in suit had a wide grin on his face as the children crowded round him. He scooped up the two year old from the ground with one hand, hugging him to his chest.

Ayo, holding the baby, ran to his father. Ignoring the baby Pa Ayo dragged Ayo's head to him, whispering "Have I missed you all! Have I missed you!" The children listened to him for a moment, then Ayo became irritated and spoke in a loud angry voice. "If you really missed us why did you run away then?"

A curtain of pain came down on the father's face. He shook his head from side to side before replying. "It's a long story my boy. I will tell you when you are older. For the moment I want you to accept that it wasn't my doing. I was pushed into going away" The children looked up into his face and decided to take him at his word.

"Are you here to stay or are you going away?" Ayo demanded, glancing sideways he noticed Auntie Rejoice and Pa Seyi behind.

"I'm here to stay for ever. To look after you-" Pa Ayo said. Hearing what he wanted to hear, at peace with himself and the whole world now, Ayo turned to his father pointing to Auntie Rejoice. "This is my good teacher Auntie Rejoice from St Mary's" Ayo said.

"Good day Auntie" As Papa Ayo spoke, his eyes caught sight of Pa Seyi, his old neighbour. He turned his attention to Pa Seyi.

"Are you paying for all this? Have you also stolen my position?" Papa Ayo snapped, gazing malevolently at Pa Seyi.

Both Auntie Rejoice and Pa Seyi appeared stunned, unable to believe the figure in front of them, sudden appearance of a fugitive, a murder suspect in all but name.

Pa Seyi comforted himself by cupping his genitals before speaking.

"Of course not! Where would I get the money for entertaining people? You know me-" said Pa Seyi, trying to laugh the accusation off.

"Yes I know you! For all I know, you could have stolen the money to show off the wealth you don't have-" said Papa Ayo mockingly.

"OK fellows, this is not the place nor the time. Settle your differences later. Not now. Go on Papa Ayo, take a few cans of beer!" Auntie Rejoice said, handing him a can of beer.

TWENTY-SIX

The night was drawing in, daylight was fast disappearing. NEPA had done its worse as usual, there was no electricity. The only light came from a collection of candles quickly purchased from hawkers, and oil lamps. The wake ceremony was at an end. The celebration of Mama Ayo's life had surpassed neighbours and teachers' expectations. Most of the guests were now gone except for Pa Jibiti, the jujuman, and his family who continued drinking and eating. All polite hints to send them on their way proved futile so, they were left. Pa Jibiti didn't usually get invited to a lot of parties. It's no wonder he was making the most of it. Auntie Rejoice felt maintaining such a large family on the paltry sum he made from divination must be very difficult. Lately, business had slowed down bringing in little money, following the chicken divination fiasco. Villagers' confidence in him had been shattered.

The gossip round the village was that, Pa Jibiti never had any power to start with. He had fooled them over the years. Villagers themselves realised their gullibility in investing their trust in this man, a self- styled keeper of their forefathers' ancient secrets. Most would take their sick to the Teaching or General Hospitals, but the brick-wall of medicine for cash was almost impenetrable.

Pa Jibiti and his family fed themselves and wrapped up extra food for home consumption in plastic containers they brought with them. The witchdoctor sat rigidly unconcerned, as teachers and helpers gathered and stacked chairs and tables from the floor, until what was left were Pa Jibiti's two tables and chairs. Watching Pa Jibiti from a distance Auntie Rejoice decided she and her colleagues deserved a rest from all the hullabaloo of the last few days. She resolved to challenge Pa Jibiti and send him on his way. She walked slowly to Pa Jibiti's table and heard his slurred speech. The old witchdoctor was blindly drunk. Auntie Rejoice paused to listen. The old man was in his element, talking complete rubbish, as little inadequate men do when drunk. Pity, his senior wife, a woman nearing seventy, couldn't have taken her husband home, saving the witchdoctor the indignity that was about to befall him, Auntie Rejoice thought. But she had to do what she had to do.

She approached Pa Jibiti with a determined stride.

"I think it's time for home now. The party's finished thank you very much for coming." Auntie Rejoice said calmly. Blood- shot eyes startled, as if she'd just slapped him. She looked into his eyeballs and saw red where white should be. At once she felt the heat from the flame of anger oozing out of him.

"Who are you? And where's Mama Ayo, the celebrant?" Pa Jibiti slurred. Auntie Rejoice took a sideways glanced at his senior wife and saw the stamp of embarrassment on her face. "Mama Ayo is dead. We've just buried her and the funeral party has just ended. So, time to go home everyone! We need to take the chairs and tables away now. They were rented and unless you want to pay for extra time for the chairs you can stay- " Hearing the word 'pay' jolted the senior wife into action. She grabbed Pa Jibiti by the arm and hurled him up from his chair, pulling him into standing. "Come on everybody, time to go home! Dee party don end! Don forget the plastic containers" she yelled hooking one hand under her husband's shoulder and dragging him away home.

The chairs and tables were stacked at one corner for the owners to collect. Auntie Rejoice felt one part of her mission had been accomplished. She gave a sigh of joy for a well conducted service and wake. She felt particularly happy that food and drinks were in sufficient quantities for both invited and uninvited guests. The school had calculated well. The Headmaster said his goodbyes and departed, so did other teachers except Auntie Rejoice, and

Peter Rotimi who was busy counting chairs and tables to ensure all was accounted for.

Auntie Rejoice walked towards Mama Ayo's house to say goodbye to the children before she herself called it a day. Glancing toward Pa Seyi's house, she saw him sitting with uncle Bita. Both men were smoking and drinking from cans of beer, smoke bellowing from Pa Seyi's nostrils, like a dragon, while uncle Bita could only manage blowing smoke out of his mouth. It struck Auntie Rejoice that uncle Bita was not really a smoker, but a show- off. Between the two men, Auntie Rejoice's eyes caught a glittering, shinny object on the bench among beer cans. The men had obviously commandeered two cases of beer to themselves. Each case containing twenty four cans. Empty cans lay dangerously scattered on the ground. She took a few steps forward towards the men. Yellow teeth bare themselves into a grin. The men were stone drunk.

"Dee funeral party be good, don yoo tink so?" said Pa Seyi addressing no one in particular. "It was brilliant." answered Auntie Rejoice, keeping a lid on her anger.

Pa Seyi took a swig from a can and opened his mouth to speak, but uncle Bita beat him to it.

"Dee food be reelly good. Yoo go do same for ma funeral, I no ready to go yet. I tink Mama Ayo no wish for better send off! The cheedren be remember what yoo don for em and dey thank yoo and church." The two men were slurring their words as they spoke, their heads rolling up and down like a nodding dog on the dashboard of a car.

"Yoo be gooood womon, the church be gooood church and the school better school in all of dee Africa! Na gooood show! I thank yoo fery much!" said Pa Seyi, swigging from the can again. Auntie Rejoice saw what she wanted to see. The shinning object was the missing silver ashtray. There was just one question now. Which one of the men stole it?

As Auntie Rejoice walked away pondering the question she was approached by Peter Rotimi. "Shall I give you a lift home? The children are in bed, so is their father, fast asleep. The floor is cleared of tables and chairs, and the owner is loading his lorry. The beautiful grass is singing again, back to its former green self! I think our job here is done!" he said with a tired smile, clapping his hands. Auntie Rejoice smiled at him. "Yes our job is done and I am ready to go home. I need a soak in warm water and have a good night's sleep. Thank God tomorrow's free! Yes, please drop me at home, thanks. Before we go I need to talk to uncle Bita" She beckoned uncle Bita to her with a wave of her hand. Uncle Bita staggered forward, wondering what's up? "Yoo forget something?" he slurred when he caught up with her and Peter. "Now that Papa

Ayo is back to look after his children are you going home? Do you want a lift home?" said Auntie Rejoice helpfully.

Uncle Bita gazed through a fog of alcohol fumes at her as if she'd just abused his mother. "Go home? Make I go home?" he shrieked in anger. "I no fit go home now. I don get ma life back! I no fit go home! I happy here!-" uncle Bita slurred.

"Where are you going to stay? You're crowding Ayo's family. They need to be by themselves, to get to know each other again." Auntie Rejoice said.

"No, no. I no stay with Ayo, im family! At all, at all! I no be foolish man yoo know! Now I don find ma friend and bruther again. Hee ask me stay with him. I stay here for some time-" uncle Bita said smiling before Auntie Rejoice interrupted him.

"Some time? What for? You are not looking after the baby!"

"No! But it be nice to near them even if I no get penny for them!" uncle Bita reasoned, beer clouds oozing out of his mouth. Auntie Rejoice took a step backward, unconvinced.

Auntie Rejoice shook her head, knowing uncle Bita was there to freeload. He had no obvious means of making a living. He lived in a ramshackle room with hardly space enough for his possessions. It was an attractive option to stay with Pa Seyi, in his relatively spacious house. Auntie

Rejoice turned her back on him and left. She knew in her heart uncle Bita would never return to his own home unless Pa Seyi threw him out, then he would find an excuse to move in with the children.

When Peter stopped the car at her front gate he decided to ask a question he already knew the answer to. "Can I come in for a night-cap?"

Auntie Rejoice didn't hesitate before replying. "Thank you for the ride and for everything you've done. No you can't come in for a drink. See you back in school-"

A sad smile creased his lips. He was not giving up that easily.

"Can we go out for a meal soon"

Auntie Rejoice contained her irritation. It was only a day or so ago that one of his former girlfriends accosted her and him at a posh hotel. She got out of the car, then stuck her head into the passenger's window before replying.

"You want me to go out with you so I can be attacked again by your girlfriends? No thanks. Goodnight Peter." She walked through the gate to the front door, opened the door and let herself into the house.

To her amazement when Auntie Rejoice stepped into the sitting- room she saw the figure of a stranger, an elderly woman sleeping on her long sofa. The woman wore a blue wrapper with drawings of jungle animals scattered all over it, her blouse and headscarf in the same material. The jangling of keys in the lock brought her maid running into the room, hoping she would get rid of the visitor before her boss opened the door. It was too late, Auntie Rejoice stood beside the stranger wondering who the intruder was. The sound of the stranger's rattling breathing disturbed her. Auntie Rejoice stood there wondering what to do next, call the night-watchman or eject her.

The maid entered and positioned herself behind her madam, shaking like a jelly too worried to speak. Sweat beads began to cascade down her boy- like face. Auntie Rejoice sensed a presence behind her and spoke without turning round.

"Who's this and what's she doing in my house on my sofa?" Auntie Rejoice spoke calmly. The maid remained silent.

"Did you hear what I said or do I have to call the police?" Auntie Rejoice repeated turning round to face her maid who promptly averted her eyes to the floor. After another short pause, the maid found her voice.

"I'm sorry ma. This is my mother. She came to get money from me. She said she can't pay her rent, as I was unable to travel to our town last month to give her the monthly allowance. She arrived very tired-"

"Why can't she stay in your own room? Suppose I brought a guest in with me, what sort of impression would that give?" Auntie Rejoice said, suddenly remembering the stranger now. It's been a few years since Auntie Rejoice met Misi's mother. Since then the woman had put on weight and appeared robust.

"I'm sorry Ma. I truly I am sorry. I asked her to lie there until before you arrive. I didn't know you will arrive so early. Because you went to a party I thought you will not arrive home until after midnight. But you arrive so early-" Misi began.

"So it is my fault for coming back to my home too early before you had time to finish using my home the way you want? Yes?" anger was creeping into Auntie Rejoice's voice, and the maid knew it. If she wasn't careful she and her newly arrived mother would find themselves on the streets of Lagos that night.

"No ma, no Ma! I'm sorry Ma! Only she came saying she was tired-" the maid began but her boss cut her off.

"OK! Wake her up and take her to the visitor's room. Make up the bed there for her"

A smile crumpled the muscles of the maid's face into little gutters. "Oh Ma thank you very much Ma I won't do that again-"

"How long is she staying?" Auntie Rejoice cut in.

"Till tomorrow Ma. She go tomorrow"

"Well, she can have a very good night sleep tonight. I hope you've given her food?"

"Yes Ma she ate when she came!"

"After you put your mother to bed can you pluck some apples from the tree, wash them and put them in the picnic basket. I'm going out early tomorrow"

"Yes Ma, I'll go do that"

"Goodnight then. Give my greetings to your mother when she goes tomorrow" Auntie Rejoice concluded and disappeared into her own room.

TWENTY-SEVEN

Sleep had been an elusive object to catch for Auntie Rejoice in the last few days. The fact that someone wanted her dead didn't help. She decided on a whim to take a few hours and her mind off death and misery and take her old aunt, her father's sister out to the Bar Beach for a picnic. On her way back from the beach she would stop at Aina village to see the children. She felt her mission in that house was incomplete.

By eight in the morning Auntie Rejoice had taken her early morning shower and was on her way to her aunt in Ikoyi, the old colonial area of Lagos. She summoned a taxi from one of the taxi firms she used when fatigue set in, avoiding the unpleasant rituals of jumping on buses. As the taxi entered her aunt's pebble- paved driveway, she saw aunt Rose in the front garden, stretching a hand up to pluck guava fruits. Hearing the taxi, the elderly lady turned her head to see the visitor emerged from the yellow cab. Her face broke into little wrinkles of sunrays, as Rejoice ran into aunt Rose's arms.

"Aunt Rose we are going to the beach-" Rejoice announced cheerfully. Aunt Rose visibly beamed.

"When?" the old lady said.

"Now! I've packed a basket full of food. A few tins of soft drinks and a bottle of your favourite wine and one of medium sweet palmwine. The taxi driver is waiting. So are you ready for the jump or you're too busy?" Rejoice said, knowing the old woman was her's for a glass of her favourite wine.

"For the jump of course! I'm never too busy for a good time at the beach! You know that! I shall go and change from these garden clothes, put something decent on. Come in and make yourself a cup of coffee or get something from the fridge if you're hot. Take the driver a drink."

"He won't drink while driving. I'll give him extra tips. I'm all right for now. There are enough drinks in the basket for me. Come on get dressed let's go enjoy ourselves!"

The excitement in the old lady's voice was infectious. Aunt Rose hurried inside and her niece followed, while the taxi driver sat patiently in his cab. The driver knew Auntie Rejoice well. She was a regular customer and a good tipper. He didn't mind the wait, knowing at the end of it he too would be smiling with satisfaction

Aunt Rose went into the bedroom, while Rejoice, on a guilt trip made herself useful tidying the house for her aunt.

"Why don't you come see me more often? I hardly ever go out unless someone calls for me-" Aunt Rose's voice travelled from the bedroom, protesting about her niece's apparent infrequent visits. Rejoice should be at her beck and call.

"I do visit you often. I brought you a sac of rice last week! Have you forgotten?" Rejoice had wondered if her aunt had the early stages of dementia, because of her forgetfulness of little things.

Rejoice would dearly like to take her aunt to the Teaching Hospital for confirmation, but that won't be easy. In this culture, respect for elders is paramount, suggesting an elder had mental illness was unacceptable. It would be downright rude to tell an elder she needed the services of a shrink.

No matter how often Rejoice visited her aunt, the first question was always 'why don't you visit more often?' It used to rattle the teacher but now with accepted empathy she shrugged it off. She remembered the picnic and her mood lightened. Rejoice had found her groove, the fun, she'd always enjoyed as a kid when her aunt Rose and her then boyfriend, took her to the Bar Beach, had returned. Rejoice walked to the double glass window and glanced out. She saw Mama Ayo's body lying on the pebbles, Ayo was standing over her again, a knife in his small hand. She wasn't sure if this constant image would ever leave her. Her mind seemed to fix itself on Ayo's guilt, she thought. Just then, aunt Rose emerged, she had changed from her garden attire to a light blue buba top and a navy blue and brown strip iro with matching headscarf, a pair of brown leather sling- back sandals graced her feet.

They set off for the beach in excitement but calmly. When the taxi deposited them at Bar Beach, Rejoice disposed of him, requesting him to collect them at four o'clock for the drive home. Bowing his head in respect the driver departed.

The two ladies carried their bags and basket to a shantily built shed, haggled and agreed a price for the covered two deck chairs on either side of a small table.

Gentle breeze lifted Rejoice's skirt and played with aunt Rose's scarf, as they took their seats and unpacked the picnic basket. Rejoice spread a white table cloth, she'd brought with her, on the table and laid out bottles of wine and soft drinks, plastic containers with roast chicken, a sandwich box, a few apples and bananas, varied nuts, finally a box of wet paper napkins. "Meal enough for a queen!" said aunt Rose picking up a paper napkin to wipe her hands. Taking a chicken thigh she bite into it.

"What do you want to drink?" her niece said.

"The white wine, then a soft drink. The palmwine will finish the picnic for me!" aunt Rose beamed

Rejoice opened the white wine and poured two glasses, handed a glass to her aunt and held the second glass up

"Cheers aunt Rose!"

"Cheers! I wish you see me more often! Do this more often! How many more years do I have on Earth? Not many, that's how many! You are such a bringer of joy to an old woman! Thank you Rejoice. Your father would be very proud of you. Now you must find a husband and get married. You've got so much to give a man-"

A gentle breeze ruffled aunt Rose's attire, lifting one side of her wrapper up for the world to see her pretty lace underskirt. She held the glass in one hand and brushed her skirt down with the other hand struggling against the cool breeze. Aunt Rose's conversation was slowly creeping into a place Rejoice hated, preaching an enforced search for a husband.

"It's an unusual woman with such good breeding and education that remained unmarried" aunt Rose continued, sipping wine from her glass in between her sermon. It's more fashionable nowadays to be single, Rejoice thought but kept silent.

"Everyone knows men would be falling over themselves to possess such a woman like you-" Rejoice was not having it and her aunt knew that. Over the years,

Rejoice had perfected an inoffensive way of responding to Aunt Rose.

"Why do you still keep your car in garage? Why don't you sell it? It will rot there you know" The niece knew all she needed do in order to cause distraction was ask another question. Distraction was an easy tool to use now, it never used to be. Pity we all have to go through this stage. Pity no pills for it, one day there will be one. Rejoice thought as she gazed lovingly at her aunt.

"That car's a gem. I can't drive any more because of my bad eyesight but I'm hoping my sight will improve-" said aunt Rose, optimistically.

"Why don't you get a driver to drive you round? I told you that before. After all, you can afford it. What do you want to do with your money than enjoy it? If you're worried about spending money I'll pay for it." Said Rejoice.

"You want me to get a driver? I thought you liked me! A driver? You never know if they will turn up for work and if they do, they'll give you hundred excuses for coming in late. Then they disappear with your car for hours, saying they're going for petrol and use your car as a taxi round Lagos. The next time you see them they'll tell you they were queuing for petrol. Petrol tank was empty, they had to wait for another tanker from the Midwest. They think I was born yesterday! No thank you, no drivers for me.

Now tell me about your work are you happy there, or you want me to speak to the Archbishop?"

"No speaking to the Archbishop please. I'm very happy at school. In fact the school is a very happy place for all of us. At the moment I'm investigating a murder-"

"What did you say? A murder?" Aunt Rose sat upright, depositing her drumstick on the plate. Her glass made a loud banging noise as she stamped it on the table.

"You murder someone or one of the teachers-" she said.

"It's not like that. One of our pupils came to me at school last week, saying he couldn't wake his mother. He found her with a knife in her chest. We buried her yesterday-"

"So I'm a good diversion today!" aunt Rose joked

"No. I wanted a change of atmosphere. I was coming to the beach whether you came or not. The police think the death could be suicide-"

"The police? What do they know?" aunt Rose exclaimed.

"Exactly. Anyway they won't investigate. There were too much evidence pointing to murder. I just couldn't let it go, my conscience won't allow it! I felt something had to be done. I have to prove the police wrong, show them murder of an innocent woman can be solved-"

"She might not be so innocent" Aunt Rose interrupted. Rejoice put down her glass of wine hard on the table almost breaking it.

"Not so innocent? What gave you that idea? The dead woman just had a baby six weeks ago. No one had a bad word to say about the dead woman until now! I'm surprised you said that-"

"The quiet ones are the worse, isn't that how the saying goes? No one speaks ill of the dead you know or no one should speak ill of the dead!" Aunt Rose took a gulp of wine then returned the glass to the table before continuing.

"Her husband killed her-" aunt Rose concluded. The niece interrupted.

"Her husband was not around when she was killed! There goes your theory!" But the aunt wasn't used to defeat. She emptied the rest of the wine in the bottle into her glass and gulped it down.

"Open the palmwine please. The husband might not be around, it doesn't prevent him killing his wife. Has he got an alibi?" Aunt Rose's brain was on high level alert. She was a bright lady before her retirement, as a Consultant Obstetrician at the Teaching Hospital. Though the scars of old age were beginning to show, she was still as sharp as a butcher's knife.

"Well he might. I haven't interviewed any one yet but I bet he has an alibi. As things stand I don't think he killed his wife-" Rejoice persisted.

"Then look for her lover-" said the aunt to the dismay of the niece who almost choked on a piece of cashew-nut.

"Lover? The woman had a baby of s-"

"Six weeks old! I know! I know! It does not mean the baby was the husband's."

"Actually it sounds improbable but you may be right. I planned to go straight to Aina village after dropping you home, to start questioning suspects. In my head I've reached a verdict " said Rejoice.

"You know who killed her?" Aunt Rose refilled her glass with palmwine.

"I do. The killer left footprints behind. I'm setting a trap for whoever the killer is-" said Rejoice contentedly. Aunt Rose didn't like the sound of that.

"You can't do it alone. I don't like that at all. You are playing with fire. I don't want you to get burnt, my love. I worry for you. I'd rather you get married, occupy your mind with house and babies than doing murder investigations-"

"I'm happy doing what I'm doing Aunt Rose. Nothing will happen to me. If I tell you what the Lord has done for me, you won't believe it-" said Rejoice, her mind racing back to that early morning, the combustion of that man in the park. She would not frighten her aunt with the story, she thought.

"I'll believe you all right! You don't have to drop me, I can take a taxi home" said the old lady helpfully.

"No, aunt Rose I'll drop you first, make sure you get home safely otherwise, I'll lie awake thinking you'd been kidnapped-."

"I should be so lucky! Who would want to kidnap an old hag like me!" said aunt Rose jovially.

"You just never know do you? Somewhere there's a man wishing he has someone like you in his life, I'm sure." Rejoice was feeling pleased with herself. The day has turned out exactly the way she hoped and wished for. The sun was a little less hostile to the skin now, and the wind had settled to a pleasant gentle breeze, pleasant and soothing. A lot more people were arriving at the beach, perhaps employees, after a day's work had decided to while away a few hours at the beach before going home for the day. Most people sat on the white sand eating cholera-infested sandwiches or sausage rolls, bought from vendors on the beach. A few people in white robes were preparing to attend prayer meetings at one end of the beach. An older man with long white beard sat on a white painted plastic chair. He seemed to be the leader of a sect. He wore a yellow flowing gown with blue embroidered band with letters across his chest proclaiming 'Doctor Bishop Prophet Reverend Michael.JAH!' A floppy blue hat covered his melon shaped head, a few strands of matted long locks of hair protruded under the hat. He looked well fed and robust but unkempt. About six or seven women of different ages were attending to the prophet, bringing him bowls of water and plates of food which they hacked out of a big plastic food warmer. Rejoice and her aunt watched the proceedings from afar, with interest. These colourful robed people were what Lagosians called the 'Aladuras sect' translated by Rejoice into 'Prayer people' Rejoice had seen and heard of them of course. You couldn't be in Africa and not see them. Some prophets were said to be wealthy beyond anybody's standards. Money donations came from the poorest of the poor as well as the rich but gullible. Someone once whispered into Rejoice's ear that about ninety nine percent were prophesying falsehood. Some were known to visit witchdoctors and others were reputed to be witches themselves. Rejoice believed Faith should be enough to see us through whatever our tribulations.

Rejoice continued to watch the white- robed Aladuras while her aunt dozed on and off, after a sumptuous meal and a share of two bottles of wine.

They watched the antics of the 'prayer people' while waiting for the taxi driver to collect and take aunt Rose home and Rejoice to Aina village to continue her murder investigation.

After his meal, Doctor Bishop Prophet Jah! washed his oily hands into the sand from water poured on by one of the women in his harem. He then washed his face with what appeared to be 'holy' water from a white bottle. His belly full, his thirst quenched, his voice rang out the joy of contentment known only to a Queen Bee. His voice suddenly rose to heaven in praise. 'Alleluha! Aleluha! Aleluha!" he shrieked, as a bell rang out. One of the women started singing and everyone joined in. The service had began, as they clapped, sang and danced, The noise woke aunt Rose who became temporary unsure of her surroundings. She quickly recovered herself and turned to her niece.

"I was dreaming there." She glanced across to the Aladuras and frowned

"These people have started with their noise again. I wish the government would ban them from the beach. It's an eyesore-"

"Where would they go aunt?" the niece replied.

"They can find a church like everyone else. If the government won't do anything about noise nuisance, people will start fighting against noisy people soon. If government fails to act, the result is anarchy! You mark my word!"

"Yes aunt Rose, you are always right. What you say today, comes true tomorrow. I agree with you. Look, here comes the driver, lets pack up our things."

"I have really, really enjoyed myself you know. I wish you will come see me more often Rejoice. Thank you for a wonderful day out" aunt Rose concluded.

TWENTY-EIGHT

When the taxi dropped Rejoice outside Ayo's house she saw the children and their father outside, eating from a communal bowl of rice and meat stew. The children viewed her before their father. They ran to her, abandoning their meal, hugging her with soup and rice coated fingers, the delight in their faces plain to see.

"Auntie Rejoice! Auntie Rejoice welcome!" they shouted with deafening screams. Papa Ayo witnessed the children's enthusiasm then followed suit. He left his food and walked to Auntie Rejoice. "You meet us well" he said licking the soup and grains of rice off his fingers. Auntie Rejoice was uncertain about Papa Ayo's feelings regarding his wife's death. He'd never commented on her or his life with her. Auntie Rejoice had gone along with this. In time she expected he had to speak.

"Thank you, please continue your meal. I'm sorry to disturb you and the children. I've been out all day with my aunt that's why I'm late coming. We went to the Bar

284

Beach. It was brilliant, maybe we can all go one day-" she said.

"Yes, yes, yes please let's go to the beach!" the children chorused. Although they lived only a few miles from the beach, Ayo had said they'd never visited the beach. Everybody in Lagos had grown up hearing stories of mermaids, of good and bad spirits living under the sea. Everyone from the cradle was aware of a world beyond their's. They've also been taught to live with and respect nature.

"One day we will go on a picnic to the beach" Auntie Rejoice promised.

The children yelled with delight.

"Now go and finish your meal while I go say hello to Pa Seyi and uncle Bita next door" she said. The children and their father returned to their meal.

"They are inside the house" Papa Ayo offered helpfully. Auntie Rejoice nodded as she walked across the grass to the next house. As she stretched out a fist to knock on the open doorway, Pa Seyi came out. He smiled nervously, cupping his genitals as if afraid Auntie Rejoice had come to snatch them from him. She overcame her disgust to smile a greeting at him. "How's everything here?" she said, trying to restrain her eyes from straying below his waist. "Very well! We dey fine, we dey well. Thank yoo for dee funeral yesterday. It be a long time away now. How time dey fly" he said, exposing uneven yellow teeth.

Uncle Bita, his hands dripping with water, joined them on the doorway. He was wearing shorts the colour of wet sand, its former white colour long gone due to age. His bulging abdomen hung loosely over the shorts like a pot of bubbling fat on the edge of a cooker. Auntie Rejoice decided to get straight to the point without beating about the bush.

"I didn't know you smoke uncle Bita? Saw you yesterday dragging on that cigarette. I thought to myself, he didn't smoke!" The man took the bate. Uncle Bita smiled then paused before speaking. "I no dey smoke normally, but my friend here, Seyi, geev me cigarette, say we celebrate my sister's life no be her death. I say na deep tin he say. And he speak true, that is reason! We celebrated her life. Dee life she be, not dee death. So I taken the cigarette from 'im. But dee beer better! Cigarette na bad habit. Everything smell and yoo be the last to know yoo dey smell like sheet! No I no smoke. I dey take just the one cigarette!" said uncle Bita, gesticulating with his hands.

"Pa Seyi, of course you smoke. You've always smoked. I like your silver ashtray you know. It was just glittering in the light last night, I was fascinated, couldn't take my eyes off it. It must be really expensive-" said Auntie Rejoice.

"That? It no be my ashtray-" Pa Seyi was cut off by his friend.

"It be for my in-law, my sister's husband. Make Papa Ayo no see it, now he is here for good. I take ashtray from inside dee house. I give it to Seyi for use. He put 'im eyes for it long time you know!"

As Auntie Rejoice understood it, the silver ashtray was taken by uncle Bita not the man she had suspected. She had no doubt that in time, Pa Ayo would get his ashtray back since both men live in such close proximity to each other, they couldn't help but sit together while Pa Seyi smoked and exhibit the other's ashtray. Her thoughts were interrupted by Pa Seyi sudden invitation.

"Make yoo come in for some food-" he said. Uncle Bita parroted him, "Yes, we just cooking supper. Come in for dee bite to eat-"

"I tink dee food no good enough for our teacher! That be so Auntie?" said Pa Seyi showing his crocodile teeth, his right hand went to hug his priced possession, his genitals. They were challenging Auntie Rejoice to share in their meagre super. She accepted the challenge, proving she wasn't too grand for their humble meal.

"I would like to eat with you. Lead the way to the table!" Auntie Rejoice said as she reluctantly followed both men into the house. As Auntie Rejoice entered the house a blanket of dark smoke hit her straight in the face like a slap, followed by a thick pong of kerosene fumes like the hanging, heavy stench of cigarettes after smokers vacated a room. They led her into the kitchen, a dishevelled room. Thank God the baby no longer inhabited a drawer. In one corner, blackened cooking pots were piled on top of one another A pile of unwashed plates and plastic cups filled the small zinc waiting for a liberator to wash them. The cause of the kerosene stench was a small stove at a corner of the kitchen. The stove was burning away, smoke bellowing from it, like a dragon's mouth. It was in need of a cooking pot filled with prepared stew. As she turned to the work- top by the zinc and the water tap with no running water, Auntie Rejoice's heart filled with horror. Her eyes popped open. A cold feeling descended on her. There was something eerie about the place which she couldn't explain. She was temporary lost for words, then she shook off the tingle in her spine.

"Is this the food you invited me in to eat?" she asked. Both men eyed each other then turned their gaze on Auntie Rejoice. A piece of raw meat, about six inches in length sat miserably on a tin plate on the worktop. Uncle Bita was struggling to cut it into small pieces with an old blunt table knife. He wasn't having much luck but was not about to give up. Auntie Rejoice couldn't help but comment on this.

"Why don't you use a sharper knife? That knife will take you forever to cut anything let alone a piece of meat-" she said.

"Seyi no get other knives, only two of this type. We be managing it so far. It dey take time but it dey work!" replied uncle Bita as he continued struggling with the meat. Auntie Rejoice paused for a moment pondering this phenomena of using blunt table knife for kitchen use, then spoke.

"The wooden handle knives are very cheap, sold by hawkers for only a few Naira each. Get one tomorrow, it would make life easier for you in the kitchen" she suggested. They frowned.

"I no get money for buy knife! I no get job! And Seyi be kind to gime room for stay. He too dey managing on little, little money. I tell yoo he no get money! Na true I tell so!" said uncle Bita.

Auntie Rejoice dipped a hand into her handbag to withdraw her wallet for some cash for the men, but then thought better of it. If you give them money today, they would expect money each time they see me, she thought to herself.

The men thought Auntie Rejoice must be feeling disappointed the food was taking so long.

"It go be ready in no time at all!" Pa Seyi said, looking round sheepishly. But Auntie Rejoice had had enough, her watering eyes told her she needed fresh air.

"Not this one and not on that stove. It was nice of you to invite me all the same. I have to go now. I'll pop in again, maybe tomorrow" Before she left there was something she had to do, the real reason for her visit. She had to drop a goat in the midst of hungry lions. She turned her face to the kerosene stove as if watching the boiling stew and made what seemed a casual remark.

"Have you heard-" she began before uncle Bita cuts in. "Heard wot Auntie?" he said. All ears pricked to hear the latest gossip.

"That the police found a piece of evidence in Mama Ayo's room. Something was left, maybe forgotten by the killer. But the police didn't remove it. They said they'll be back for it. You know our police, they are not back yet to remove it-" she said, watching the men's reaction through the corner of her eyes. She thought she glimpsed fear in one of the men's eyes or did she imagine it. It was uncle Bita who spoke first.

"What be the eeedense?"

"What there be again?" Pa Seyi added. "What there be?" he repeated. Auntie Rejoice shrugged her slim shoulders. "Only the police know that and of course the murderer. I have to go now" As she turned round to go, the uneasy tingle she had felt earlier returned. An overwhelming feeling of being watched descended on her. She turned round again to ascertain her conviction. There! In front of her, covered by the faint darkness of an alcove, just beyond the kitchen, was the figure of a man. She recognised the voice when he spoke.

"Goody eevening Auntie Rejoice!" It was Pa Jibiti, the witchdoctor. What could he be doing here? And why was he hiding from her? Auntie Rejoice didn't know the three men were such close friends. You live and learn, she decided

Auntie Rejoice left the two men and their odd guest, to get on with their cooking and ruminated on the bomb she just shelled. If one of them was the killer, he would surely break into Mama Ayo's house one night, perhaps tomorrow, giving them time to digest the news, in search of that evidence, she thought.

All she had to do now was find a hiding place in front of Pa Seyi's house tomorrow and watch the men in action. As she left the men, she heard them arguing about what that evidence was. A sentence by one of the men struck her. They obviously thought she had stepped outside, but she was still within hearing shot.

"She be strange woman, that one! Any woman be glad if man cook for am. No, not she. She be strange woman!"

It was the voice of uncle Bita. The others, she heard, made noises of agreement.

She wondered why neither of them had a woman to call on for help as most useless men would have done. She came to the conclusion that neither Pa Seyi nor uncle Bita enjoyed spending money on any human being but themselves. Both men were the meanest she was ever unfortunate to lay eyes on.

She left the men and walked back to the children and their father. They'd finished their meal and the children were now playing with home made toys while the baby sat in a brother's arm gurgling or doing whatever babies did on full stomachs. Papa Ayo sat on a stool gazing into the distance. When Auntie Rejoice emerged from Pa Seyi's house, he sprang to his feet as soon as he laid eyes on her, and walked towards her. They met midway between the two houses. The children left their toys shrewn all over the road, ran to hug the teacher they had accorded the role of substitute mother, without her consent, a role she delighted in. She felt the discomfort of little hands squeezing her body. "Children! You're squeezing life out of me!" she joked. The children giggled.

"Will I see you in school tomorrow?" Ayo asked excitedly. Auntie Rejoice freed herself from the grip of the others to bend down to Ayo's height, she looked into his little brown eyes, surprised at his question.

"You want to return to school tomorrow?" she asked. The boy nodded his head vigorously. "You don't have to. We give you this week off. Come back on Monday. OK?" The little boy couldn't understood it. He thought that Auntie Rejoice liked him. But why didn't she want him back in school?

"You don't like me any more Auntie Rejoice?" he whined.

Auntie Rejoice felt a cold hand gripping her heart. She meant well but the boy couldn't understood. For children, what was past was past. His mother was gone, though he hadn't forgotten or hurt less, he wanted to get on with life like any child.

"Of course you can come to school if you are sure you want to." She turned to his father standing by her. "Papa Ayo do you mind him returning to school tomorrow?"

"No, as long as he does his share of housework." Said Papa Ayo, shrugging his thin shoulders.

TWENTY-NINE

The following morning Auntie Rejoice arrived at school at her usual time. She noticed the light in Peter Rotimi's office was on. It was unusual for him to arrive before her. A day's holiday had done wonders for him, thought Auntie Rejoice. The Headmaster's car was also in its usual special parking space. The other teachers followed soon after Auntie Rejoice. They all had much to be proud of, the dignified way Mama Ayo's funeral was conducted. In the staff- room a notice was up on the board for a staff meeting that morning. Auntie Rejoice was leafing through her teaching notes when her office door opened following a gentle knock. Peter Rotimi stood there grinning like a cat that just had the best cream of its life.

Auntie Rejoice looked up from her notes and smiled tolerantly at him. He took that as a sign to make himself comfortable in one of the wooden chairs in the room.

"So you are taking a week off work? You dark horse! Why didn't you tell me two days ago at the funeral?" he said.

"What are you talking about? Look it's too early for one of your riddles, I'm quite busy as you can see-" Auntie Rejoice replied, shuffling papers on her desk.

"You don't know that you're taking a week's holiday?" he persisted, taking the hint he got up from the chair and moved slowly towards the door. Holding the door open with one foot in the doorway the other in, the sound of footsteps distracted him. He glanced behind him to see the Headmaster trying to enter Rejoice's office.

"Here he is! He'll tell you all about it! See you. Come see me before you depart!"

Peter said and left the room. The Headmaster entered Auntie Rejoice's room and sat himself down on the same chair Peter just vacated. He sighed heavily as if troubled.

"You still believe that Mama Ayo was murdered?" the Headmaster said.

"I have no doubt about that, Headmaster. She couldn't have stuck a knife that deep in her own chest. What do you think?"

"I try not to think about it. If you believe it, what are you going to do about it? Are you leaving it to the police to solve, I'm sure they will see the error of their way and look again into it-" the Headmaster said.

"No they won't! The case is closed. Inspector Gberaga has concluded it suicide. He said it was post natal blues and the fact that Papa Ayo left her soon after delivery.

No, the police won't investigate. I'll have to do it myself, if only to prove them wrong and avenged the dead." Said Auntie Rejoice quietly.

"You feel quite strongly about this don't you-" said Mr Jaiye, scratching his full head of hair.

"You didn't see her body lying there on the floor, a blood covered baby exhausted from screaming his lungs out lying beside his mother. It's a sight I never ever want to witness again. It's a sight I don't want the police to forget. And it is a sight I want the police take seriously next time it occurs, hopefully never again" It's a sight that gives me nightmares. It hunts my sleep-" her voice trailed off.

"Knowing you feel that strongly about solving the case I have arranged with your colleagues, in fact, I had to visit each one at home yesterday to rearrange the times-tables. I am giving you a week off to solve the murder-" the Headmaster said. Auntie Rejoice sprang up.

"What? That's great sir-" she began. The Headmaster held up a hand to silent her.

"I won't take it from your annual leave but regard it as a sort of compassionate leave. Before you start to thank me, I have a confession to make about the dead woman-"

"Mama Ayo?" Auntie Rejoice volunteered.

"Yes. I met her before she had the baby-" it's confession time for the Headmaster. The shock raced through Auntie Rejoice.

"What? When? Why? I'm Ayo's mentor I don't remember seeing her with you!" Auntie Rejoice burst out.

"No, I saw her in her house. It wasn't deliberate. I took my car to the garage on Lagos Street in Aina village. You know that one by the small village market?" Auntie Rejoice nodded her head.

"Well the mechanic said, no need to go away the car would be ready in fifteen minutes. So I took a walk round the village, finding myself in Ireti road, Ayo's road. To my horror a lady, with heavy makeup, sitting on the stone step of her house beckoned me come forward. It turned out she was Ayo's mother. I didn't recognise her with the crude lipstick and eyeshadow. She invited me into her sitting-room then pulled a chair to sit so close to me, I jumped from my chair into standing-"

"She made a pass at you?" Auntie Rejoice helped with a few chosen words.

"I ran out of the door. I promise you nothing happened-" Mr Jaiye said, casting his eyes down.

"Why haven't you told me this before?" said Auntie Rejoice.

"Because there's nothing to tell. I don't want anyone else in the village telling you the Headmaster was Mama Ayo's lover or any erroneous tales. That's why I'm telling you now and I know you're basically honest yourself. So go on your way to investigate the murder. God be with you" Mr Jaiye turned round and walked out of the room, without waiting for Auntie Rejoice's verdict.

On her way home Auntie Rejoice's mind was already calculating the names of Mama Ayo's murder suspects. She was incredibly sad now that one more name had to be added to that list of names. The name was that of the Headmaster's, Mr Jaiye.

Thirty

After Auntie Rejoice had her shower and supper that night she dismissed her maid and retired into her bedroom. She sat at the brown oak desk that used to belong to her late father, passed on to her by aunt Rose. She had inherited many personal possessions from her parents but this desk was one of the things she cherished. She opened a drawer and withdrew a white A-4 writing pad, and from the carved wood pen- holder on the desk she took out a pen. Tearing off a sheet of paper she placed it on top of the desk. Drawing a circle in the middle of the paper, she wrote Mama Ayo's name in the centre of the circle, from where arrows shot out. Names of murder suspects were scribbled on the point of each arrow, among them, 'Jaiye' with a question mark after it. She had known Mr Jaiye for many years now and they were always honest with each other. Rejoice was brought up to be honest and so was Mr Jaiye. The school was a close knitted family, in which pupils and teachers unite to make it such a joyful place to study and work.

Was Mama Ayo that stupid to make a sexual pass at the Headmaster of her son's school? Was that wise? What mother would embarrass her own child in this way? Auntie Rejoice asked herself a second time. There was certainly much to think about. Mama Ayo's death was looking more and more mysterious. How could she, a simple school teacher, unravel something so complicated?

In her heart of heart Auntie Rejoice could not make herself believe in Mr Jaiye's guilt. But then she reasoned, most victims were killed by close relatives or people known and trusted by them.

Mr Jaiye might looked and acted like a harmless kindly human being but who's to say what else he was capable? At the back of her mind she still felt the Headmaster was beyond reproach, a man of infinite benevolence who would not harm a single hair on a human head.

Why did he go to see Mama Ayo at her house and kept that fact a secret?

He hinted Mama Ayo made a sexual pass at him. Surely all the more reason to bring this to the attention of Auntie Rejoice and other teachers who cared for the boy? And why was he making life more complicated for her now, by revealing this secret? Auntie Rejoice ruminated on the names on a piece of paper before coming to a conclusion. She sat and thought long and hard before taking off her dressing gown and rolling into bed. By the time sleep came she'd already made up her mind. She was certain, now more than ever, she knew Mama Ayo's killer. Tomorrow the long search for evidence beyond doubt continued, the murderer would be nailed, as sure as she knew the sun would rise in the morning.

THIRTY-ONE

Though she'd been given a week of compassionate leave Auntie Rejoice left home early morning as usual. She was going to waylaid those she suspected knew a lot more about Mama Ayo's death. Early call would be unexpected and caught them unaware at home. Her first call was to Pa Seyi in Aina village. When she arrived at the house the doors were locked and bolted on the inside but the wooden windows were wide open. Auntie Rejoice stuck her nose through a window and saw uncle Bita stretched out, fast asleep snoring on a mattress on the stone ground. His big abdomen lopping slightly to one side.

No obvious sign of Pa Seyi. She guessed he must be in an inner room off the corridor, away from her prying eyes.

She decided to wake the house, and tapped gently on the window with her right fist. Uncle Bita made some gurgling noises, rolled his left ankle from side to side then settled on his back. She knocked harder on the window. Uncle Bita opened both eyes looked around then closed them again. More knocks, this time harder. Uncle Bita sat bolt upright. His eyes followed the sound on the window and saw Auntie Rejoice. It shocked his eyes into opening wide. He rubbed them to rid himself of over- powering sleep. "Hello! Open the door!" Auntie Rejoice said quietly. As by command, uncle Bita rose from the floor like an overdue pregnant whale, walked to the door, unbolted the locks and opened it.

"Good morning Auntie. Yoo be early bird yoo be? We sleep late last night. We dey drink till late. Seyi be in bed. Yoo want make I wake im or yoo come see my pretty face?" he said, chuckling. As Auntie Rejoice stepped into the house the smell of tobacco mingled with the odour of sweat and beer, hit her hard. She quickly stepped outside again. "Come in!" uncle Bita said holding her by the elbow.

"I need the early breeze to wake me up proper. Go call Pa Seyi but before you go answer this. Has he said anything to you about the death of Mama Ayo?" said Auntie Rejoice, trying to show the cheer she didn't feel.

Uncle Bita stood still for a moment thinking about what Pa Seyi might or might not have said to him, since the renewal of their week- long friendship began. He shook his head from side to side, followed by the sound of 'hmm, hmm, hmm' eventually he put into words what he was thinking.

"Yoo know, he no talk about dee woman. He be say she be one hot baby. I no ask im 'bout what he say. He know Mama Ayo be my sister, I tink he no fit say anything bad 'bout her. He talking 'bout my sister's kindness. Everybody dey say so!

I go wake im up now." He walked back into the house and disappeared, only to return a few seconds later with Pa Seyi still rubbing his drowsy eyes. Pa Seyi joined her outside. He wore his typically long flowing formerly white now light brown robe, yawning loudly without covering his mouth, letting out a small spay of spit into the air. Auntie Rejoice took a diplomatic step backwards to avoid the squirt on her clothes. Pa Seyi smiled, Auntie Rejoice averted her eyes as Pa Seyi's hand travelled to his crotch. She fixed her eyes on his blackberry eyes, coloured red where white should be.

"Yoo be welcome Auntie Rejoice. Yoo be early my God! Yoo be every time early! Yoo no like yoor bed at all at all! I just dey go off to sleep when ma friend come wake me. I no happy Auntie-" said Pa Seyi, with another loud yawn.

"Well sorry about that. There's nothing like an early start, those who work will tell you that. Can I speak to you alone, for a moment? I need some honest answers"

"Course. Yoo want come into house, I-" he said.

"No! Let's sit on the bench here"

Uncle Bita disappeared into the house. A few minutes later they heard him snoring like a constipated goat. Pa Seyi sat down on the bench, she remain standing.

"I want to ask you a few questions about Mama Ayo's death and I will appreciate truthful answers-" Auntie Rejoice began but was interrupted.

"I tink everything settle now that she buried? Why yoo drag eeverything up again? Dee children dey happy and-" Pa Seyi and his lodger seemed upset at the mention of her investigation but Auntie Rejoice was ready for them.

"Excuse me! Are you saying you don't want me to find Mama Ayo's killer? Do you have anything to hide? Are you afraid of something or someone?" she said

"'Course not! 'Course not! I dey want killer be punish! But I dey sorry for the chindrens. I go geev yoo all the help yoo dey want. I go efen elp yoo find killer!" Pa Seyi said pleadingly with genuine sympathy.

"Great! At the moment I just want you to answer some questions. Tell me about your relationship with Mama Ayo please" said Auntie Rejoice as Pa Seyi shifted uncomfortably in his seat. Auntie Rejoice knew nothing of the relationship between him and the dead woman, but knew there was one. Only he can enlightened her.

"We dey be good friends. When she dey for life. She be really kind woman. She dey bring me food. I never cook any more, until we dey fall out-"

"You fell out with her? Why?" Auntie Rejoice cut in, almost before Pa Seyi realised the meaning of what he just said.

"I no meen it in bad way. We get small argument-" he corrected himself.

Auntie Rejoice felt she had uncovered a dent in his earlier story and she wasn't going to let it slip by now. "What was the argument about?" she repeated. Pa Seyi looked as uncomfortable as he felt.

"I dey tell her too much men friends no good. She no listin" He said then stopped talking.

"What men friends?" Auntie Rejoice prodded.

"Mama Ayo dey get lot of men come to her, when her husband no dey around. She dey be bad sumtime, very bad, wild. I no like am-"

"Was she selling herself for money?" Auntie Rejoice said bluntly.

"She dey sell hersef to anyone. She no get money for feed dem children. That time I get money, I get tenant. I give her money. The tenant don go, I no get money. The woman na curse, believe me Auntie!" Pa Seyi sighed heavily.

"Did you see anyone with her the night of her death?" the teacher said.

"I see two men in out of dee house. I never see dem before" He smiled as his hand weighed up his drooping genitals. Auntie Rejoice thought it was time to leave him and his dirty habit.

"Is that all you can tell me about your late neighbour?" she threw one last question at him. He raised his eyes upwards to the sky as if seeking inspiration.

"God be my witnes. That be all I know" he said. She thanked him and turned away.

Auntie Rejoice walked across the wet grass to knock on Papa Ayo's door. It was Ayo who opened the door. He was already in his school uniform, looking smart. When he saw Auntie Rejoice he beamed brightly.

"Auntie Rejoice come to take me to school" he shouted across the house so everyone could hear. His brothers came rushing to the door. Their father appeared from the back of the house. "Let your teacher into the house! What a rude boy! Keeping your teacher waiting on the doorstep. Come in Auntie Rejoice please. I was just getting the brood ready for school and lesson" said Papa Ayo light-heartedly.

"Good morning Pa Ayo. I thought I'd start early before everybody go to work-" said Auntie Rejoice, smiling.

"I'm not working yet but I have an offer to help the charity Oxfam, and other charities combining their effort to change the European Agricultural Policy, Fairtrade and all that-" Papa Ayo said.

"There's little publicity or understanding of the Agricultural Policy here, perhaps-"

"I'll explain when these lot go out in a minute. You're not taking Ayo to school are you? He knows his way"

"No. I'm here for something else." Said Auntie Rejoice taking a seat in one of the single chairs at a corner of the room.

"I thought so. You must have better things to do than coming to take Ayo to school" the father said with cheerful disposition.

"He's too big now to be accompanied, are you not, Ayo?" the teacher joked.

"Yes Auntie!" replied Ayo gratefully. It brought joy to the child's heart to be considered old. It was a declaration of adulthood by adults, a certificate of grown- upship. What he didn't realised was in next to no time at all, the children too would wonder where the years had gone. Auntie Rejoice thought.

When the children were pushed out of the house and the baby put in his crib Papa Ayo sat opposite his guest. "So you've found another job? That's great! You were saying it's for a charity-" said Auntie Rejoice quietly.

The house seemed too quiet, almost like a morgue once the noisy children vacated.

"I have a friend who work full time for Oxfam charity. All the charities are combining to gain justice for our farmers. The whitemen, Americans and Europeans who run the World Bank lend us money only if African governments stop aiding our farmers, did you know that?" Papa Ayo said.

"I heard about it but not many people know that. So these wicked white men buy agricultural produce from their own farmers and sell them by force to Africa.

How's that for justice in the world? Anyway I'm helping my friend three days a week"

"That's something. Keeps you occupied till you find a paying job. I'm trying to find out who killed your wife. Do you mind?" Auntie Rejoice watched Papa Ayo's reaction to her question. His expression remains the same as she first saw him few minutes before.

"Why should I. I heard the Police refuse to investigate her death saying it was suicide. Blaming me for leaving which is a lot of bulls. I'm glad you or somebody is investigating. We live in an unsafe country. According to the UN Chatter we all are suppose to have rights to a safe world. I don't know what the UN is doing about the violation of our safety rights by the government! Thank you for the investigation" he said.

"How did you hear about your wife's death?"

"I saw it in the newspapers! I tell you I was shocked to my bones. I came home to look after the children including that one" He said, nodding in the baby's direction.

"You and your wife were not in good terms I heard. The last night you left home you slapped her hard. Why was that?" said Auntie Rejoice. Papa Ayo looked startled, wondering how she found out but, he soon regained his composure.

"I've never hit a woman in my life but my dead wife could test the patience of a saint. She was becoming impossible to live with."

"What exactly did she do to deserve such treatment? It is low to hit a woman. Most women are defenceless against the power of men. I'm not talking about those women built like King Kong who can floor any man easily- " said Auntie Rejoice.

"That baby is not mine! Is that low enough for you? That rascal next door was also having it off with my wife" Papa Ayo blurted out as if he'd been looking for a sympathetic ear for a long time. He wasn't letting this chance escape him. Auntie Rejoice was shocked into silence. She was dumbfounded into silence, hearing it from him, but maintained a calm exterior. She finally spoke.

"What?" she said, rising from the chair, "I will be back later today. I need to go out for now. Is that all right with you?"

Papa Ayo nodded his head and replied "I'm going nowhere today. I shall be around when you come back Auntie"

She thanked him and walked out of the house still reeling from his revelation.

Thirty-Two

When Auntie Rejoice left Papa Ayo's house, questions were buzzing round her head like a swam of bees. She felt she needed to discuss with someone else. An exchange of ideas and views was called for. Returning to school was out of the question since she had been given a week's compassionate leave to solve Mama Ayo's murder by the Headmaster, who was himself now under suspicion with his secret rendezvous with Mama Ayo.

Auntie Rejoice stood pensively at Agege Motor road waiting patiently for a taxi. The yellow and black striped cab stopped almost immediately she flagged one down. Taxi drivers in Lagos seemed to have a nose for educated ladies regarded as easy game for inflated fares. She was too much in a swirling frame of mind to pay attention to his exhobitant charge for the one and a half mile ride back to her house.

Traffic was mild, she got home within ten minutes. She paid her fare and the taxi sped off. As Auntie Rejoice turned the key in the lock to enter her house, she heard a male voice whispering sweet nothings to her maid. It was the voice of a neighbour's male servant, Joseph. By the sound of him, it was obvious they were up to no good in her sitting- room. They were deaf to the jangling sound of keys in the lock. Her maid, Misi, obviously wasn't expecting Auntie Rejoice back home at that particular time. Misi erroneously assumed her boss was at school and so would not be home till late as usual. The two lovers laughed and joked . The couple continued to whisper sweet nothings to each other, as Auntie Rejoice entered and stood for a few seconds at the foot of the sofa they laid on. The realisation that someone was in the room suddenly hit one of them.

Joseph noticed her first and remained frozen in position, his hand on her breasts. Auntie Rejoice stood staring at the couple. Joseph's shirt and trousers were on the floor. He had on an immaculate white Y-Front, which he probably borrowed from his master's wardrobe. Misi was naked from the waist up, her back to the door. She was at first unaware anything was amiss and surprised at Joseph's frozen pose.

"Go on, what are you doing? I have to go to market for our food, soon-" Joseph's stare and inaction suddenly alerted Misi to the fact, there was a presence in the room. Misi raised herself on an elbow to look up. She hastily pushed Joseph away so hard that he landed at

Auntie Rejoice's feet. He quickly scrambled out of the house grabbing his clothes and using them to cover his prominent essentials. Misi hurriedly put her blouse back on and went down on her knees to her wronged boss.

"Please Auntie, I beg, forgive me. Please Ma it was him. It was his fault. He made me do it. I was minding my own business, doing my housework when he just enter the house like that. I didn't invite him. This is true, Madam, I no lie. Please forgive me Auntie!" Misi wailed. Auntie Rejoice looked at her with scorn. She would like to sack her there and then but her mind went back to the reason the maid was employed in the first place, so wealth would cascaded downwards.

It was eight years previously, Auntie Rejoice was on her way home from a teachers' conference at St. Mathias Catholic school in Lafiaji when she saw a crowd gathered near the Sangross market. The large crowd was gazing at something she couldn't see well at a distance. She decided to go and take a proper look at whatever was attracting the crowd's interest. As she neared the crowd she saw a pair of legs stretched out on the sandy ground. A child of about eight or nine years old sat beside what appeared to be a sleeping woman. Auntie Rejoice went nearer the sleeping woman and asked a male spectator what it all meant. The man made a hissing sound of sadness before speaking in pidgin English.

"Na dat woman. The chid dey cry say him mama don die! No one to take the mama to hopital now!" Apparently the sleeping woman had been begging for alms in that area of Lagos for many years. No one knew who fathered the crying child. Both mother and child grew up in full public glare. Auntie Rejoice called a taxi, took child and mother to the General Hospital and ended up taking the child, named Misi, home. On admission, Misi's mother begged Auntie Rejoice to employ the child.

The story of Misi now reminded her of Mama Ayo's death but Misi's mother didn't die. The woman was only unconscious and was suffering from pneumonia. She slowly recovered in hospital and begged Auntie Rejoice to employ the child as her maid. The woman fully recovered and returned to her hometown in Ife, leaving her child with Auntie Rejoice. The child was one of the lucky ones. She was registered at St. Mary's by Auntie Rejoice. After completion of primary schooling the girl declined higher education, and was enrolled into a two- day a week typing school, which she still attended, paid for by Auntie Rejoice. Misi's mother had grown fat and healthy unrecognisable even to Auntie Rejoice.

At least Mama Misi's story had a happy ending. She was alive to see her child grew and prospered.

Now staring at Misi all Auntie Rejoice could see was that little girl screaming her head off that day at Sangross market in Lafiaji. Then her mind turned to betrayal. This was how that pathetic little girl was repaying her for giving her shelter and a bank account. The consolation was Misi said she was an unwilling actor in this boy- girl drama, but hard to believe. She turned her back to Misi as she spoke.

"Get out of my sight! I'm expecting a visitor shortly, open the gate for him"

Misi hurried out of the room, frantically adjusting her attire. Auntie Rejoice crossed the room to the small table, withdrew her cell phone from its cradle and punched numbers into it. The reply was instant. Peter Rotimi came on the phone as if he'd been expecting her call all day.

"Great to hear from you! What's up?" he spoke enthusiastically into the mouth piece, expecting good news, a dinner out or an outing with the unrequited love of his life. Auntie Rejoice smiled knowingly.

"Listen Peter, I want you to come round at lunch time. I have something to discuss with you" she said, then remembering that Peter's imagination might be working overtime and getting the wrong end of her sentence she added, "It's about Mama Ayo's death" She could hear a sigh of disappointment in his voice. Well, there was no need giving him wrong impression about her feeling. But she did need someone to chew over the shock statements she just heard from both Papa Ayo and Pa Seyi.

"I'm on my way now. I have no class until later this afternoon. Is that all right with you?" he said.

"Yes, that's great. If you're good, I'll get Misi to prepare lunch for you"

"Haven't I always been good? Good is my middle name! I'm on my way" He made good his word and was knocking on her door soon enough.

Gulping down half a glass of ice cold beer that Misi served him, Peter made himself comfortable in an armchair opposite Auntie Rejoice. He listened to her, relating what she'd heard at Aina village. To her pleasure, Peter was as shocked as she was, to hear tales of Mama Ayo's lifestyle as told by the men who knew her best.

"What?" said Peter, sitting bolt upright almost knocking the glass of beer off the coffee table with his knees. "Exactly what I said when I heard it" Auntie Rejoice said quietly.

"But the woman was painted a saint! At least that's what I understood by the eulogy of her friends and neighbours! Are you sure? Of course you are! What 'am I saying. I don't doubt it's the truth. My goodness! How wrong can you be about people! But the school and church spent so much money and time on a prostitu-" Peter was cut off by his host.

"Let him who have no sin cast the first stone Peter!" In one sentence she reminded him of his own murky life of sin. His eyes settled on his glass. He picked it up and drained the remaining liquid. "Misi! Bring Peter another bottle of beer" Auntie Rejoice shouted across the room to the kitchen where Misi was busy preparing dodo and fish stew for Peter and herself. Misi appeared as if by magic carrying a bottle of beer and a clean glass. She opened the beer, poured it into the clean glass and disappeared with the empty bottle. As soon as she left the room the two continued their conversation with an eye on the wall clock for Peter's classes.

"I feel the husband killed her, knowing about her illicit activities and the baby she was carrying! It's enough to drive any man to murder! Don't you think so?" Peter said after sipping the beer and replacing the glass on the table. Auntie Rejoice paused for a few seconds before answering him.

"The husband is certainly a suspect but, so is Pa Seyi, so is Pa Doyin, So is Pa Jibiti. Lots of suspects. Even uncle Bita is not excluded. Each and everyone around her is a suspect, capable of killing her-"

"Bita? But he wasn't around Aina village when Mama Ayo snuffed it. He's also the deceased's brother! What can he gain by killing his own sister?" Peter exclaimed

"Uncle Bita would sell his own mother for a few pennies. From what I've seen of him he would kill any one who debarred him getting to a source of money or gets in his way, sister or no sister." Said Auntie Rejoice sadly.

"But why would he want to kill his own sister? For what reason?" Peter still couldn't believe anyone would kill a family member for pennies. Auntie Rejoice was reluctant to repeat tales told her by Mama Ayo's neighbours. Unsubstantiated tales of attempted incest and brutish domestic violence at the sister's rejection. She couldn't relate that. No, it's too murky. Let the dead carried what little dignity she possessed to the grave.

"I don't know but I mean to find out. I was told there's a secret between sister and brother, each refusing to divulged to outsiders, exposing it could have led to one killing the other. Who knows if it's true? Believe me there's lots of hidden secrets within the cosy but sometimes thorny blanket called family-" she was interrupted just then by the appearance of Misi in the room.

The meal is ready Madam" Misi said. Auntie Rejoice usually preferred her own cooking. She always joked that she preferred to know what went into her cooking pot. She had seen the very unhygienic way many cooks prepared meals for their masters. She was even told once of a cook who always spat into his master's meals before presenting it to the master. The servant would watch his master eats the servant's spit, with much glee. She didn't want that to happen to her. Besides, she enjoyed cooking her own meals. Misi sometimes did the cutting up. But today, she'd lost the will to eat or prepare food.

"Come go eat, you haven't got long till your class." Said Auntie Rejoice, leading the way to the dinning table, at the other end of the room.

"Can I have one more bottle of beer please?" Peter said, raising his right hand to retreating Misi. She glanced back over her shoulder with, "Yes sir." Auntie Rejoice frowned, looking quizzically at Peter. She spoke quietly so it didn't sound like an admonishment. "Will you not fall asleep at the wheel or in class?" Peter shook his head vigorously as if shaking water off just- washed hair. "No. I'm used to drinking at lunch time. In this heat a cool beer takes the edge off the heat. I'll be all right." Peter replied with confidence.

"A lot of Mama Ayo's neighbours are under suspicion, including Pa Jibiti-" Auntie Rejoice repeated.

"Pa Jibiti? The jujuman? The Babalawo? He should be the first suspect in line! Ahead of the queue! Did you hear about the case involving him two years ago, or was it last year?"

Auntie Rejoice paused for thought as she took her seat and uncovered the food dishes. Peter took his seat opposite her. "The death at the riverbank? That's another!" he said, his eyes darting from one plate of food to the other.

"OK! The one about the woman found dead in her home after drinking the potion Jibiti gave her?" said Auntie Rejoice, handing Peter the serving spoon. He took it and ladled a heap of fish stew and dodo onto his plate.

"Yes! Jibiti and his son, Jayle, were seen hurrying out of her house-" Peter added but was interrupted by his host. "They were arrested, locked up for a day or so to placate angry protesters, then, released by that timid coward, Inspector Gberaga of our City Police. He's so slimily timid. He could slide himself under a bus! I don't think the Inspector has done a day's work in his life! He just goes round telling victims of crime not to bother him-" said Peter, stuffing dodo into his mouth.

"He is despicable. No matter how hard I tried to make him see that Mama Ayo's death was murder he just would not buy it. I mean you can see it, the Headmaster can see it. Everyone can see it but not Inspector Gberaga! He's not only blind but dumb. Let's forget him and get on with what's at hand-" Auntie Rejoice had not touched her food, but unnoticed by Peter. She stabbed a piece of dodo with her fork and took a tiny bite.

"So what's your next step?" Peter said. Auntie Rejoice chewed and swallowed a tiny mouthful of food before replying.

"I'm going back this afternoon to interrogate, no, to chat to the neighbours again. I told them I'd be back.

I wanted to give them time to think about what had happened, hoping giving them time to digest it would jolt their memories even more"

"Please call me, as soon as you find out the secret between Mama Ayo and her brother, I'm just so intrigued!" said Peter as he departed. "My lips are sealed!" Auntie Rejoice shouted after him.

Thirty-Three

When Peter got back to school he made straight to the Headmaster's office. Mr Jaiye was having his lunch. A white paper napkin was spread over the centre of his desk on which were his usual small flask of coffee, its cover containing small quantity of the liquid. Beside the flask was an open foil wrap with half his lunch. In Mr Jaiye's right hand was a bacon sandwich with bite marks in it. The Headmaster was about to take another bite when he heard a knock on his door. He held the white bread in mid- air, "Come!" he snorted, looking suspiciously at the door.

Everyone in school knew the Headmaster hated being disturbed at meal times, except for emergency reasons. But then Mr Jaiye's meal times sometimes varied when classes over- ran or meetings rambled on for too long. The Headmaster gave allowances at such times. This wasn't one of them. The door gently opened and Peter Rotimi entered the room. "Sorry Headmaster, didn't know you're still at lunch" Peter said, retracing his steps backwards, hoping Mr Jaiye would call him back.

"Come in. You meet me well. Have some food, it's far too much for me. I've told my wife, several times, to give me small portions, that I'm watching my figure. She insists if I don't put on weight people would accuse her of starving me to death!" The Head was in good humour, Peter thought. The two men laughed. "I just ate with Rejoice" said Peter.

Mr Jaiye waved a hand ushering one of his best teachers to enter. Peter moved forward then closed the door gently behind him. The Headmaster signalled him to a chair opposite his own. "Lucky you! How's she keeping?"

Peter's infatuation with Auntie Rejoice hadn't escaped the Headmaster's attention, nor other teachers'

"It's about Mama Ayo's investigation. She told me some surprising things about the case, I thought I should see you at once-" said Peter.

"What happened? Don't tell me Rejoice is in trouble?"

"No Headmaster! Rejoice went first thing this morning to Aina village to investigate. Horror of horrors! Mama Ayo's baby belonged not to Papa Ayo but someone else-"

"Does Papa Ayo know that?" the Headmaster interrupted. Peter frowned.

"Yes! Papa Ayo told Rejoice this secret himself! And that's not all! Pa Seyi, the neighbour, was Mama Ayo's lover! Papa Ayo said so himself! He knew everything Mama Ayo was up to, and that was up to no good! On his part, in a separate interview Pa Seyi told Auntie Rejoice that Mama Ayo was a prostitute, selling her body to anyone and everyone for money!" Peter blurted.

"Looks can deceive. I know she was up to no good, a few weeks before her death. As I told Rejoice, I might as well tell you, Mama Ayo made sexual pass at me. I took my car to be serviced and strolled pass her house. But I don't want to make a big thing out of it-" said the Headmaster, looking sheepish.

Peter Rotimi's jaw dropped momentarily into silence. A shocking new information from the Headmaster. It seemed everybody had a secret except him and Rejoice. How much more could he take in one day?

"I'm shocked! Rejoice didn't tell me that-" Peter said when he regained his voice.

"Well, keep it to yourself. I don't want to speak ill of the dead. I'll appreciate it if you don't even discuss it with Rejoice." Said the Headmaster, placing his sandwich on the napkin, his appetite gone.

"No I won't say a word to anyone unless Rejoice bring it up first. So Mama Ayo must really be up for it. I can't get over it" Peter mumbled.

"How is Rejoice taking all the shocks?" Mr Jaiye asked in concern.

"To tell you the truth Headmaster, I think it's a bit much for her. That's why she called me. I think she needed someone to chat with. It's so obvious to me, the husband, Papa Ayo killed his wife. He has a good reason to do so. I'm sure he'll be let off by the courts" Peter said, warming to his own voice.

"When you see her again tell Rejoice I'm always here for her-. In fact, is she at home now?" the Headmaster hesitated then leapt up from his chair, leaving his food on the desk. "I left her at home. I think she said she's going back to Aina village this afternoon to clarify some points" Peter watched as the Headmaster gathered his car keys and wallet from an adjoining table by the wall. "I'll go and see her now. Tell anyone who wants me I'll be back in thirty minutes" With this Mr Jaiye drove his car out of the school compound and headed for Auntie Rejoice's house on at number One, Luggard Crescent, a stone's throw away.

A journey that should have taken two or three minutes' drive maximum, even in Lagos traffic, took him more than an hour. Near the junction of trees- lined Luggard and Agege Motor road, an old pine tree sat majestically under which a family of beggars congregated begging for alms during lunch- hours. Their clothes torn and dark with dirt. The men wore on their heads small skullcaps, their long flowing robes dragging the ground as they walked.

As Mr Jaiye came close to the junction he looked ahead to the small vehicle in front of him. He brought his car to a stop and waited for the car in front to join the line of traffic along Agege Motor road, when the road was clear enough to do so. He saw the beggars at a distance dancing and playing, with their five young children, the eldest no older than six years old. The adult beggars, four female and two elderly males were clapping their hands in rhythm.

Suddenly the six year old danced her way into the bumper of the car in front of the Headmaster's car, as it turned to join the main road.

The car screeched to a stop. The sound of bone crashing on metal rang out. Yells from beggars and other pedestrians filled the air. Within seconds a crowd had gathered muttering under their breaths, "Is the child dead? It's not the driver's fault but he could have slowed down a little!"

Mr Jaiye applied his hand break, opened the car door and came out of the car.

"Is the child all right?" he said to the crashed car driver. Both men hurried to the young girl, now lying in the middle of the road. Before they could lift her up from the hot cement, the child had jumped up badly shaken but unhurt. Mr Jaiye persuaded the child's mother, now by her child's side, to follow him to the Priests House for a thorough check up. Both priests were First Aiders. It was the housekeeper who answered the doorbell.

"Father Mark de say Mass. I tell Father Biodun you here. Father Biodun took them indoors and pronounced the girl fit. Mother and child accepted thirst- quenching iced lemonade drinks and were soon back where they started, on the street. By the time the Headmaster rang Auntie Rejoice's doorbell, she had already left the house to hail a cab for Aina village.

When Auntie Rejoice left her house an hour after Peter Rotimi, she walked down to the T- junction of Lugard and Agege Motor road, heard the commotion about the accident but the crowd had been too tick to penetrate if not, she would have seen the Headmaster comforting the beggar girl.

While waiting for a taxi, her mind wandered off to the discovery of the heart she recovered from the sacrificial clay pot two days previously. Her heart sank as she remembered what her pathologist friend said.

"The specimen is human but it's too degraded. It's impossible to be certain what happened to the host-" Pa Jibiti had won again, she thought.

When Auntie Rejoice got to Aina village she went straight to see Papa Ayo. The children were still at school. The father was on his own with the baby sleeping in his cot, the father bought since his arrival. It crossed her mind, that this middle-aged man had a right to neglect or hate the sight of this helpless baby. No one would blame the father if he found the child an irritation, a reminder of what went wrong in his own life and the circumstances of his birth.

Papa Ayo sat outside his door chewing boiled peanuts bought from a hawker few minutes before. He rose to his feet when he laid eyes on Auntie Rejoice and walked towards her extending a hand in greetings. She took it, as if they hadn't met that same morning. The welcome was warm and friendly more than she expected. She was beginning to feel more like a nuisance to them. She felt her confidence boosted ready to carry on her interviewing. "Shall we sit here or you want us to enter the house?" said Papa Ayo, his hand sweeping the expanse of green grass in front of his house. She felt it was better to retain his good-naturedness and remained in the front yard. "Here is good, fresh air" she said.

"I'll bring you a chair" He ran into the house and returned with two wooden chairs which he placed facing each other. They both sat down before he asked her,

"Can I bring you soft drink?"

"No, thank you. In fact I just had lunch and I don't usually have a full meal during the day. But today I did, so I'm quite full up! Thank you. Shall we progress to talk about what happened to your wife?" she said to him. Papa Ayo nodded his head without saying a word, his countenance changed to sadness. His pain visible to see. When he failed to speak, Auntie Rejoice goaded him on.

"As you know I'm only trying to find your wife's killer. No one who saw her lying on that mat with a knife through her heart would leave the case in the air. No one who saw her could forget the agony on that face, I can't forget it ever! I still have nightmares about it. I must try and get to the bottom of it unless you don't want it-"

"My heart asks the question, how could I not want it? Is she not the mother of my children before she became corrupted? Of course my heart wants you to find whoever killed her! It's not right to kill a woman or man. It's wrong to kill what you can't create, is it not? If she annoys you, then a slap or two! But not to kill her outright! My head really wants you to leave everything as it is. Let us learn to live with our misery and in time our aching hearts will learn to put it in the backs of our minds, I need to know what happened." Papa Ayo said. Auntie Rejoice occasionally nodded her head in acknowledgement. Whatever he said she had made up her mind to continue her murder investigation anyway. She paused for a few seconds to let his words sink into his own mind before she spoke.

"When did you find out that your wife was unfaithful? Is it before or after the baby was conceived?" said Auntie Rejoice.

"Before the baby. Much before the baby. One night I came back from work earlier than my normal shift. I did extra late shifts so I could put more food on the table. But it was never enough. I had put in more hours than I should, hoping my employer would pay me overtime! Instead they gave me time off in lieu. I was furious! I left work in anger, wishing to get home and have a drink or two and play with the children, I met the children outside when they should have been in bed. They said their mother chucked them out to play at that time of night. She didn't even have the decency to lock the door to the house. I suppose she had the children as gatekeepers. I found this man on top of her. I beat both of them senseless. Since then I never touched her. That was about six months before she became pregnant. That's why I knew the baby was not mine, see!" He said, shaking his head. Auntie Rejoice thought there was nothing sadder than seeing a broken man in the throes of misery.

"Who was the man? And do you know other men who visited her?"

Papa Ayo paused for what seemed like an eternity then put the rest of the wrapped up peanuts bag on top of one of the stone steps into the house before speaking.

"As I said Seyi was one of her lovers, so were a few of the men in the village. I won't be surprised if one of them stabbed her. Some men are very jealous you know-" he said almost in a whisper.

"You are not?" Auntie Rejoice put in. Papa Ayo didn't like the inference. The skin on his forehead rolled into a hundred folds to become a frown.

"I will not kill anyone, even if I'm jealous Auntie!"he snapped. That was the first time he appeared to show a flicker of emotion, hot temper in Auntie Rejoice's presence. She'd always thought his son, Ayo, had inherited his father's calm unflappable temperament, now Auntie Rejoice was not so sure.

"No, of course not." She said, in an effort to make up for irritating him, then added,

"How did you know Seyi was your wife's lover?"

"It was obvious for all to see. After I told her I wasn't interested in her, she taunted me with 'if you don't want me Seyi will' I knew anyway, that they were lovers long before that. She used to make soup and little errands for him thinking I didn't notice. One day I challenged Seyi himself. He confessed to sleeping with my wife but said half the village was doing the same thing, so why was

I fussing over little him! The cheek of the man. He has mouth but nothing else, no money, no gut, no shame-" Papa Ayo's chest rose and fell with each word.

In an attempt to calm him, Auntie Rejoice cut into his flow. "Can you think of anyone who could possibly want your wife dead?"

"I really can't! Husband's and wives fight but not to death. Sometimes you wish-" Papa Ayo stopped in mid sentence, realising that he might incriminate himself. His visitor knew exactly what he was about to say and completed the sentence for him.

"Sometimes you wish your wife dead so you can bring into the house that younger model, that beautiful thin girl who had more sense than you?" The host remain silent. Auntie Rejoice detected a rising hostility towards herself bubbling inside Pa Ayo and decided to let him be for now.

"Is your neighbour, Pa Seyi at home?" she said.

"I don't know, I'm not his keeper. But he has nowhere to go. He's abandoned his relatives since his brother's death. He should be at home" said Papa Ayo grudgingly.

"Are you on speaking terms with him?"

"We greet each other, if that's what you mean. Women are not worth fighting over. Most men with brains know that, if she did this to me there's a likelihood she'd do the same to you some time, some day! We speak now"

"I'll go see him then come say goodbye before I leave" As she approached Pa Seyi's house she heard the voice of the witchdoctor, Pa Jibiti. She had no doubt something was brewing in that house. Retracing her steps she decided tonight was the night to catch the killer in her net.

Though it was ten o'clock, the night was blacker than midnight. Daylight had long gone to its resting place. Rejoice took great trouble to dress herself in a dark long-sleeved blouse and black trousers. She wore a turned down hat that covered her pretty face. She was ready for a stake out at Pa Seyi's house. The three men, Pa Jibiti, uncle Bita and the host, Pa Seyi were in league. Did the three had liaison with Mama Ayo? Were they, right now, joking and comparing notes on how good or bad she was in bed? Were they united in planning Mama Ayo's murder or was it solely the work of one man? Auntie Rejoice had to find out. And tonight was the right night. She had dropped them a bombshell. A special evidence, she told the men, was left in Mama Ayo's house by the killer. An evidence the police failed to remove. She was convinced this would lead the killer to break into Mama Ayo's house for the evidence. She hadn't realised Pa Jibiti, the witchdoctor, stayed over at Pa Seyi's house. That the three men were so intimate had been a surprise but not a shock.

Auntie Rejoice decided to walk to Aina village to avoid eyewitnesses for what she was about to do.

When she got to the side of the road opposite Pa Seyi's house, she hid herself behind a mango tree directly facing his house. At that time of night there were hardly anyone in the streets. It wouldn't have mattered if there were, because with her dark clothes, she merged well into her surroundings. Auntie Rejoice was prepared for a long wait but didn't have long to wait. She watched as lights were turned off in one room then another. Pa Seyi's house was now in complete darkness, like its neighbours. Everyone was supposed to be in bed. People slept early for an early rise in Aina village.

She watched and waited, hoping the killer would take the bait and break through an open window into Ayo's house, to recoup the bloody school shirt. She hoped the shirt would not be located. She stood, her heart thumping her chest like a talking drum. Nothing happened. Time past. The quiet hiss of every day life that no one ever noticed suddenly went silent. NEPA had done its worse, the electricity was gone again. Now her heart was really beating a danger signal. A lady alone in the dark world of killers and witches. If she were to tell herself the truth, a feeling of terror was creeping into her body. She fingered the rosary beads in the pocket of her blouse then recited the Hail Mary to steady her nerves. A feeling of calm washed through her. She sighed. She was on the verge of returning home when Pa Seyi's door slowly creaked opened and a figure, looking round as if afraid he might be seen, crept out of the house. In the darkness, she strained her eyes to gain recognition. No good, it was too dark. She knew if she tried harder, recognition would come. She watched as the figure tip toed to the open window of the house next door. The house too was in darkness, suggesting Papa Ayo and the children were asleep. Auntie Rejoice strained her eyes again. Suddenly NEPA was back, the streets aglow with lights again. Recognition slowly crept into her brain. Is that not Pa -, She thought jubilantly.

Suddenly a foul smell of strange hospital- like gas filled the air. The smell grew stronger around her. She began to wonder where it was coming from. She was too immersed in her watch to give a second thought to her own safety.

The figure climbed into Mama Ayo's bedroom window and disappeared inside. Now the identity of the murderer was no longer a puzzle. She was definite. A confirmation of her suspicion. There was no need to wait until he emerged from Mama Ayo's house before she herself returned home. She was about to turn round and head for home when a beer- laden voice whispered in her ears.

"You don see too much! You don see yoor last. Yoo be food for dee gods!" A cold iron hand gripped her on the shoulder and turned her round to face her worse fear. The blood in her body turned into ice chips. A wet cloth, smelling of hospital went over her face. That was the last thing she remembered. She didn't feel the dragging of her feet behind her into a dark blue Toyota, nor the dirty wrapper used to conceal and roll her whole body into a ball. She had always prayed for a quiet but quick death in old age, just like everyone else. But to die in the hands of Godless savages, to be used as a sacrificial lamb to paper gods? Surely, that's not what her God would want for her?

THIRTY-FOUR

Peter Rotimi left work at five thirty and by five forty five he was ringing the doorbell at Auntie Rejoice's front door. The maid, Misi came hurrying to the door.

"Aunty Rejoice is not in. She didn't come home last night-" said Misi.

Peter could hardly believe what the maid was saying Auntie Rejoice had not returned home since leaving after their lunch together. He was a little concerned but tried not to let his anxiety show. Maybe Auntie Rejoice went on a visit to her second living relative, Aunt Emilia who lived in Victoria Island.

"OK. When she returns tell her I'll be here first thing in the morning on my way to school. I want to know how she got on with the villagers in Aina" Peter said to the maid who nodded her head in reply. He drove home thinking his anxiety was misplaced. The fact was Auntie Rejoice had said she only had one errand that afternoon, and that was the interview with Papa Ayo and his enemy Pa Seyi. It wouldn't take the whole afternoon and part of the evening to do what should have taken an hour to perform.

True to his word Peter called on Auntie Rejoice at six o'clock the next morning. It was not unusual for early morning visits in Lagos. It meant the rest of the day was free to do whatever job was in hand. The horrific state of public transport in the country meant people were forced to leave home very early for work to arrive in time. Misi opened the door to Peter, this time, the concern in her voice told him all he needed to know that something dreadful had happened to the beloved Auntie Rejoice.

"She never came home sir! I didn't know why she never come back sir! I worry too much for her! I don't know what to do sir. Because you say you be here this morning I wait for you sir. I don't know what to do sir-" the maid ranted on until Peter laid a hand on her shoulder and led her back into the house, sitting her down at the dining table.

"Do something for me yes?" he said, looking into Misi's pleading eyes.

"Yes sir." Replied Misi, wiping a tear with the helm of her skirt.

"You calm down. Nothing has happened to Auntie Rejoice. We need to be calm for when she returns. You don't want to alarm her do you? You don't want her to think you've been thinking ill of her?" Peter said. The maid's eyes opened wide. She couldn't be the carrier of evil omen, perish the thought.

"Oh no sir! No oga!" the maid replied. His statement seemed to cheer her up. Giving an impression you think evil of others, especially those who fed and clothed you, was an act of betrayal. One might be regarded a witch who wanted no good for no one.

Peter left the maid and returned to school to relate the unhappy news of Auntie Rejoice's disappearance to the Headmaster. Soon the whole school was buzzing with the news of the school's favourite teacher's imminent death, from the hands of unknown persons. The Headmaster instigated a search party which included Peter and Mr Jaiye himself. As many school staff as two cars could take trooped into Mr Jaiye's and Peter's cars.

The search party went back to Auntie Rejoice's house and interviewed the maid again, to ascertain Auntie Rejoice movements. When they were satisfied that Auntie Rejoice's disappearance started and ended in the same area, they headed for Aina village. They decided to keep the police out of it until they'd failed in their quest to trace their teacher.

Their first call was Papa Ayo's house.

The Headmaster knocked and Ayo's father came to the door. He could see beyond Papa Ayo's shoulders that, the children were getting ready for school or lesson. Ayo wasn't' visible however.

"Headmaster! To what do I owe this early visit. Hope every-" Papa Ayo began.

The Headmaster wasn't in the mood for pleasantries, he went straight to the focus of their visit. "One of my teachers, Rejoice, came to see you yesterday afternoon. Is she still here?"

"What? Since yesterday? Of course she's not here! Why?" Papa Ayo said sympathetically.

"She's disappeared! The only place she came was here, to see people at Aina village, we're looking for her. Did you see her?" Peter but in.

"She came to see me then went across to Seyi. Then she said she was coming back to see me but I waited she never came back. I don't know what happened to her after that." Papa Ayo said with a tinge of surprise in his voice.

"You won't mind us looking round the house then?" Mr Jaiye said. The group of seven, all the four men in the school and three women teachers, brushed pass Papa Ayo to troop into his house. They searched the rooms, backyard and hidden crevices for the lost teacher. Nothing. Satisfied that Papa Ayo might be innocent of abduction they left him standing on his doorway as they descended on Pa Seyi's house. Another search revealed no Auntie Rejoice. The Headmaster and his staff stood in the front yard of both houses talking about their next move. While the two friends continued gazing at their departing backs in disbelieve.

Thirty-Five

The Headmaster concluded that the next step was return to school and called the police. A shiver ran through him at the thought of calling Inspector Gberaga, the uncaring police officer- in- charge, a great disciple of Pa Jibiti, the witchdoctor.

Auntie Rejoice had now been missing for almost twenty four hours, an unknown phenomenon. She never left home without informing someone of her destination and in this instance she told her maid and her lunch partner, Peter. They both heard from her lips, that she was off to Aina village. It was time to bring in the law if only to frightened whoever held her into releasing her. It was a long shot but worth trying. The teachers argued. The Headmaster had given the class of senior students, study period in exchange for double class that afternoon. Now Mr Jaiye insisted on handing it to the police.

Peter retuned to the classroom to make up for lost time. The Headmaster telephoned City Police and was at once redirected to Inspector Gberaga, who promised to visit the school as soon as he was free to do so.

Inspector Gberaga duly burst into the Headmaster's office with his pompous stance and attitude accompanied by two underfed young police constables, who could easily model for an Oxfam poster.

"What's this I hear about one of your teachers going missing?" said Inspector Gberaga without any niceties. The Headmaster felt if that was the way the Inspector wanted to play it then he too would be direct and acidic.

"One of my best teachers is missing. She left home yesterday to visit Aina village and has never been seen or heard of-" the Headmaster began.

"Only yesterday? People disappear for two, three weeks without word then reappear again without harm! This is nothing new you know!" said the Inspector laughing. The Headmaster didn't think it was a laughing matter, he remained tight-lipped.

"Not so with Rejoice. She-" Mr Jaiye began but was again interrupted.

"That name rings a bell in my ears!" the Inspector said with a frown.

"I'm sure you've met her. She was the one who called you in to investigate the death of Mama Ayo in Aina village-"

"Now I remember! The big mouth teacher who was telling me how to do my job! Ha-" the laughter lines in his face turned into a baby- hating snare.

"She was no big mouth. She just pointed out that Mama Ayo's death was suspicious and should be investigated. I see nothing wrong in that" The Headmaster defended Rejoice.

"I say the same thing I told her then, you are too soft with your women staff Headmaster! Women like strong men! Believe me Headmaster, they don't care for wishy, washy men! I know! I'm a man of experience." said the Inspector, tapping his shoulder with the leather whip he always carried.

"That maybe so but I get results. Will you get your men to look for her? I'm sure whoever is holding her, she's still in Aina village-" said Mr Jaiye.

"Listen oga. This is Nigeria, people go and come. There is no good telephone system to call people and say I'm not coming home tonight. Me, myself, sometimes I don't go home for two three days! My wife knows not to search for me. I'm my own master! I come into the world alone, I go alone where I like! End of story! People have to go on the road to talk to anyone, pity, but true. People do what they have to do then reappear. People come, people go, come go, come go, same difference!. No harm done! Twenty four hours on the run is nothing in this country!

Give her another couple of days then start worrying! If she's not back in a couple of days let my office know then we take it from there" said Inspector Gberaga as he bade farewell to the Headmaster without glancing backwards. It was exactly the inaction expected from the Inspector, no one was surprised.

The following morning the Headmaster rose even earlier than usual. He decided to pay a visit to Auntie Rejoice's house in the unlikely event that she had slipped back home without anyone noticing. Unknown to the Headmaster Peter Rotimi had the same idea. It was no surprise they collided on Auntie Rejoice's doorstep. "Mine O mine! Great minds think alike!" The Headmaster exclaimed. Peter threw his hands up in the air and smiled. "We're both very worried about Rejoice. I'll ring the bell" he pressed the doorbell a couple of times with no response from within. Suddenly a voice across the road shouted "You have to bang the garage door hard!" it was the voice of the owner of the house few yards away from Auntie Rejoice. He was cleaning the windscreen of his posh car with a dry yellow duster. Seeing the teachers he paused, gazed then strolled over to them.

"Good-morning gentlemen. The maid, Misi, slept in her room at the back. She has a little self-contained apartment. If you knock on the garage door it will be nearer her room. Sorry I'm Leye, that's my house. I'll leave you to it-" The neighbour turned to go but paused at the voice of the Headmaster.

"Morning. Have you seen Rejoice in the past two days?" Mr Jaiye said.

"No sir" the neighbour said "She's gone missing? It's difficult to think of a grown woman being abducted. I don't know what the world is coming to. Rejoice was such a good neighbour I can't-"

"Thank you Mr Leye, thank you" the Headmaster cut him off, irritated at the use of past tense. Leye walked back to his car. They watched him picked up the yellow duster from the bonnet, entered the car and drove off to work.

"Did you hear what he said? Addressing Rejoice as 'was' does he know something we don't?" Peter fumed. The Headmaster ignored the question, walked a few paces to the garage door and banged his fist on it. Within seconds Misi appeared in the main door entrance rubbing her eyes. She peeped through half closed eyes to see the teachers on the doorstep.

"Good morning sir!" Misi said, adjusting her wrapper.

"Is your madam back yet?" the Headmaster snapped. The girl jumped back at his sharp tone, her eyes wide awake now. "No sir. She's not here sir. She never come back since two days since"

Mr Jaiye turned away from the maid and spoke to Peter Rotimi.

"I think the next sensible step would be to go see Rejoice's aunt in Ikoyi. What do you think?" They began to walk back towards their separate cars, then stopped.

"I feel we should have done that yesterday. I never even thought about her aunt-" Peter replied, scratching his low cut hair.

"She has one more aunt and a lot of forgotten cousins who never cared about her after her parents' death. They thought Rejoice would never amounted to anything. Now of course it's a different story. By the time she graduated and got a teaching job she'd moved on from family get-togethers, to family regrets! They've missed another money making factory!" said Peter.

"I know! My relatives are like that too. They ignore you when you're nothing! But as soon as they see you having a regular salary, no worry if the salary is not enough for you to live on, they're banging on your door, ready to suck off the peanuts in your pocket! Shall we go now? We can take my car. You collect yours later." The Headmaster shook his head from side to side.

"No, let's go back to school first. I'm sure a couple of the teachers will be there by now" The Headmaster glanced at his wristwatch then continued. "We'll rearrange our classes then-" he was interrupted by Peter before he'd finished talking.

"I have free periods this morning. My next class is at one thirty. I'm free to roam!"

"Even then, we'll go back to school and see the others, tell them of our plan. Besides I do have a class to teach at eleven. But just in case we return late, we shouldn't, I'll let everyone, including the pupils, know our movement. On second thoughts bring your car. You can drive, I'll leave my car in school"

Thirty-Six

Aunt Rose heard banging on her front door and looked out of the window of her parlour. She was surprised to see two grown men neatly attired in what she called smart get-ons. She recognised none of the men. She never usually gets visitors at that time of day unless her niece was taking her out for the day. She ignored the visitors, but continued to gaze at then through thick black rimed glasses, a bright red patterned scarf covering her hair. They knocked again but silence reigned. The Headmaster back off from the doorway and let his eyes roamed round the L-shaped house and its servants' quarters. His eyes settled on the figure peering out of the middle window of what she thought was her bedroom. He smiled and waved a hand at aunt Rose. She ignored him but continued to stare unsmiling.

"Good morning Ma. Can we speak to you?" said Mr Jaiye pleasantly.

Aunt Rose shifted her gaze to look at Peter. "Are you burglars? Have you come to rob me? If so you'll be wasting your time. I don't keep anything valuable in the house you know! No money to speak of, all valuables are in the bank you know. I'm not one of those old fogies who keep huge money under the bed! My niece goes to the bank and do my shopping for me-" The old lady rattled on, to the amusement of the men.

The two teachers listened patiently, smiling wryly to the elderly aunt who they've met once or twice at the school's annual Christmas parties. She had forgotten their faces but they still remembered her. The Headmaster interrupted her ranting.

"Ma, we're here because of your niece-"

"Why didn't you say so before? Letting me waste my saliva!" Aunt Rose said, She left her position at the window and came to the door to let in her unexpected visitors. They entered a large sitting- room which seemed large enough to hold a New Year's Ball. The room was sparsely bur elegantly decorated. The teachers took seats opposite aunt Rose's well worn comfortable armchair. No sooner did Aunt Rose sat down than she got up again, walked to a huge fridge at the corner of the room, opened it in full view of the visitors, withdrew two bottles of cold beer and brought them to the teachers. She handed the bottles to them and sat down again.

"There's opener on the table and glasses in that glass cupboard" she said, pointing a well-manicured finger.

The visitors were overwhelmed with her generosity but declined the offer. It was the Headmaster who spoke for them.

"We can't drink now I'm afraid. It's too early, thank you Ma. Very kind of you. We are here because we want to see your niece-" the Headmaster tried to be gentle. He searched for appropriate words to describe the abduction of her niece. He would like to save the elderly woman the heartache of telling her that her lovable niece was actually missing, missing for a couple of days now.

Aunt Rose looked puzzled. She paused to consider the Headmaster's statement before speaking.

"Who? Who is that? Who? What are you muttering about?" a question mark contorted the muscles of her fine face.

"Your niece. Can we see your niece?" Mr Jaiye repeated.

"I don't know what you're muttering about young man! Speak up!"

"Can we see Rejoice please?" Peter shouted, to the annoyance of their host.

"You don't have to shout young man! It is rude to shout! I'm not deaf, you know! If you want to see Rejoice you should go to her house or school! Where are you from anyway?" she gazed at them suspiciously through her glasses, then took off the glasses to peer even more closely at her visitors, her eyes becoming two narrow slits.

"We're from St Mary's. I'm the Headmaster. I-"

"You are the Headmaster, did you say? You can't be very good if you keep misplacing your staff, can you? Or if you keep losing your staff. You'll find her in her own house in Lugard Avenue. Now if there is nothing more I can do for you, you don't want the drink-" she said, returning the spectacles to her face. She'd had enough of a careless Headmaster.

"No, thank you very much. We better be going. Thanks again" The teachers got up without narrating the real reason of their visit, and walked to the wooden door through which they came in. The elderly lady's voice stopped them in their track.

"Are you not suppose to be in school teaching? Why are you wandering the streets at this time of day?" aunt Rose admonished.

The Headmaster kept his cool and spoke with controlled politeness,

"We're on a special mission to visit people in aid of the school. Thank you again."

They returned to school empty-handed again.

THIRTY-SEVEN

Peter was leaving the classroom when he suddenly remembered that during lunch with Auntie Rejoice, the name of Pa Jibiti had cropped up, he mentioned this to the Headmaster.

"Right, that's our next search. If this fail I don't know what else to do. We have to involve the police again if only to publicise the fact of her missing. Agreed?" Everyone agreed.

The mud and straw house was about twenty minutes drive from their starting point. At Aina, women recognised their children's Head teacher and greeted him enthusiastically as he passed their houses.

Pa Jibiti was sitting on a mat outside his house surrounded by his wives and a couple of his children, chanting over a black clay pot filled with black potion. When he saw the Headmaster and his party, Pa Jibiti shouted to one of his sons to carry the pot into the house. The pot was not for outsiders' eyes. He rose from the mat to greet the Headmaster, as one of his sons attended St. Mary's.

"Headmaster, yoo be most welcome! Dis must be great, great day yoo set foot in ma house! We never-" Pa Jibiti began but was cut off by Mr Jaiye.

"We're here on business. One of your son's teachers is missing, I'm sure you've met her, Auntie Rejoice-" said the Headmaster.

"Auntie Rejoice? 'Course I kno am. She be good at Mama Ayo's funeral. I meeet her one time during sports day for school, one year since. Very nice woman, very nice. Yoo sure she missing? Maybe she go to see her boyfriend, yoo know what young women are nowadays-" Pa Jibiti said.

"If she went to see a boyfriend she would have told her maid or someone from the school who saw her the afternoon of her disappearance-" said the Headmaster.

"Maybe the one who see her dat afternoon take her? Yoo consider that one?" Pa Jibiti interrupted.

When Peter kicked a large plastic container with anger, Pa Jibiti added,

"No do that! Yoo go spill the kerosene and set the place on fire, yoo fool!" the jujuman snapped at Peter.

"Have you heard of the word 'bullshit'?" Peter asked in all seriousness.

"Dat na Americain bad word for cow shit" the Babalawo replied, wondering if the young man had gone bonkers.

"Well, it's coming out of your mouth in bucket- load." Peter said angrily. The witchdoctor's eyes blazed with fury. "I go get yoo!" he said.

"What rubbish you talk! No one from the school abducted her" Peter raged, invisible smoke oozing out of his nostrils.

"Yoo come here to insult old man?" Pa Jibiti said

"No one is insulting you. You brainless fool! Besides, you may look decrepit but the Headmaster's about the same age as you and that's not an insult either. You didn't see her yesterday or today?" said Peter, restraining himself from hitting the witchdoctor.

"Definitely no! Why I want to see her? The woman is trouble! The woman be odd!" Pa Jibiti spat.

"You won't mind if we go in to look round for ourselves" the Headmaster said, leading his team into the house.

Pa Jibiti, fearful of their discovery, followed suit, yelling,

'No yoo can't! The gods forbid it!'

The house was dark and dingy inside with hardly any light, except for a narrow beam of daylight streaming into the hallway then defusing into the rooms. Reflection of oil lamps coming from a room off the hall, merged with the shadow of daylight to give the house a mystic, cave-like glow. All round the walls were tiny black or grey cloth bags, the tops of which were tied up into knots, which obviously contain black magic objects or powders. Skeletons of animal heads or tails lay beside each bag for potency. In some places the tiny bags were replaced with whole skeletons of rats or monkeys or other animals the teachers couldn't fathomed.

They entered and searched the live-in rooms in the compound. In a little room at the back of the house, they saw oil lamps burning. Idols in the shapes of little wooden male and female figures stood on high little round wooden tables. Under a square table the Headmaster noticed a pile of junk, in shape of a parcel wrapped in black linen.

An almost inaudible whimpering sound, like a constipated cat, emanated from the direction of the parcel. Pa Jibiti hoped none of the teachers heard the whimpering sound. It was coming from the muffled voice of Auntie Rejoice, tied and bound into a kneeling position and kept under the table that bear the figure of the god of clay.

The Headmaster's ears pricked. He could definitely hear the sound of a cat. Mr Jaiye turned to Pa Jibiti behind him.

"Do you have a cat?" he asked. The witchdoctor smiled nervously, exposing black rotting teeth. "Yeees sir! We get plenty cats. Two cats. They be always hungry! Cry all dee time. They eat, eat, eat too much! Yeeees sir, plenty cats! You hear 'em now crying, meao, meao, meaow!"

Rejoice heard voices other than her captors'. She whimpered louder, trying to make herself heard. She was awake but still groggy. She didn't want to die and she knew death was nearer than she could imagine. She decided to scream and scratched her way out of the wrappings. She screamed but only a strange sound came out.

Her throat and mouth were numbed, as if there was an iron hand on her vocal cord.

Her feet seemed stuck to the ground. The feeling of helplessness washed over her. It was no good. The gag round her mouth was too tight and painful.

The Headmaster and his staff turned and dejectedly made their way out of the house. Rejoice heard footsteps and knew time was running out for her. This was her last chance to escape. She decided to put on the greatest fight of her life. Suddenly a rush of power surged through her. "Let me out!" she whimpered, but the school party were already on the way out to their cars. Jayle, Pa Jibiti's son, heard the raised voice and rushed to Auntie Rejoice. "Yoo be dead meat tonight! Yoo shut up! Tonight yoo be gone! Another sacrifice to the gods! The gods want fresh blood, yoor blood!" he said angrily, kicking the bundle that was Auntie Rejoice. She screamed silently, then lurched herself in the direction of the voice, knocking him to the ground.

The sound of him falling gave her increased impetus. He squealed as his head hit the hard stone floor. His father, Pa Jibiti, hurried to his son's side. "Dis witch wan kill my son!" he said, kicking the teacher. The father grabbed Auntie Rejoice by her hooded neck. She felt his crushing grip, as blood began to drain from her brain. With one huge effort, she struggled free.

Jayle jumped on her and they both rolled on the floor, while the father looked on, shrieking!Kill her now! Kill her now!" Auntie Rejoice rolled this way then that, knowing the big man would soon tire and loosen his grip.

She wriggled and kicked until she tumbled from the wrappings and strings holding her in a kneeling position. When she freed herself, her eyes were not accustomed to light, however dim. She blinked several times before seeing her surroundings.

Auntie Rejoice looked up to see Pa Jibiti and his son, Jayle standing in front of her.

"I like feisty ladies!" said Jayle. "Where yoo tink yoo dey go? Yoo be doom. Yoor teachers don come and go. They no go come back again. They don search dis house. They don satisfy. Yoo are for dee gods tonight! Tonight, tonight be dee night!" he said gleefully.

As he spoke Auntie Rejoice gave the loudest scream in the universe. The sound brought the Headmaster and her other colleagues crashing into the room.

"Rejoice it's the Headmaster! Are you all right?" said Mr Jaiye, robbing her shoulders. "She's in shock, she's been doped!" Peter said.

"Let's take her home then call doctor Bose to examine her" The Headmaster said, straightening up from bending over her. Slowly Auntie Rejoice opened her eyes wide and smiled at the gathering of her colleagues coming to her rescue.

"I think we should call the police to-" the Headmaster began to a slow murmuring, "No, no, no" from Auntie Rejoice.

"No we shouldn't call the police?" the Headmaster said, adding, "Let's take her home and get the doctor"

"OK. There's one thing I have to do first. Can you lead her to the car. I'll be with you in one minute-" Peter said, but the group stayed with him. He grabbed a wrapper from the pile on the floor and spread the cloth out. He went round the rooms gathering idols of human and animal skeletons, black magic bags and bottles of potions into the wrapper. The teachers followed and watched him with dismay. Pa Jibiti and his family watched with alarm, screaming "Yoo no fit touch the gods! It no done! I, Jibiti alone I'm dee priest to handle dee gods, the gods of our forefathers! No one cain touch! Stop! Yoo hear me? Stop I say stop!"

The Headmaster butt in, "Peter what are you going to do with these things? You're not taking them to school are you?"

Peter was determined to reek revenge on Pa Jibiti for all the unhappiness he'd put everyone through.

"I have to show this Godless, brainless, imbecile that there's only one and true God!" Peter said, carrying the heavily laden cloth and its contents outside. He poured a gallon of kerosene on it. He found a matchbox by a clay oven and set fire to the bundle.

Pa Jibiti's wives cried bitterly, throwing themselves onto the ground, while Pa Jibiti looked on helplessly, saying "You caint do dis! It's no lawful!"

The party of rescuers and the rescued Auntie Rejoice drove back to Lugard Crescent to the joyous welcome of the maid and her few neighbours.

"I suggest you go to bed and we'll try and put some food together-" Mr Jaiye said but Auntie Rejoice was her normal self again.

"I'll have a long soak in hot water first. I've been without food for three days I'm not hungry" The party eyed her as if she'd just swore at them. The Headmaster expressed their feeling. "You must eat something. I know I'm no good cook but I know someone who is" he said smiling at Peter and Auntie Therese. They in turn nodded their heads and turned in the direction of the kitchen to prepare her a meal.

Auntie Rejoice spent no time at all in the bath before emerging, in a clean dress, looking more like her old self if a little thinner.

"You look much more like the Rejoice we knew!" Auntie Therese said as she came into the sitting- room from the kitchen.

"I'll be all right if you want to return to school-" Auntie Rejoice offered but the others turned down her request. They had made enough provision for their classes, there was no need to rush back, they reassured her. Turning to Auntie Rejoice, it was Auntie Therese who broached the subject of her kidnapping again.

"I still can't understand why Jibiti, the wizard, wanted to do away with you. Do you think he wanted to kill you? Why? What for?"

"The jujuman hates my gut. Remember that first morning I escorted Ayo back to his house to check on his dead mother?" Everyone nodded agreement. She leaned forward in the armchair.

"Jibiti got very angry, accusing me of usurping his power. I should have chosen him to lead the investigation. He was the leading elder, the one everyone bow homage to. He should have been the one I brought Ayo to. Instead of going into Mama Ayo's house I should have brought the boy straight to him. I mean, that would have happened in the bad old days, whether the leader was good or bad. Anyway, we have good Oba Aina. This is the millennium, not eighteen century! As I walked out of Ayo's house that morning he promised to 'get me'. I must say I didn't take his warning seriously-" said Auntie Rejoice.

"How did he get you?" Peter said.

"He waylaid me as I stood outside Pa Seyi's house. Fumes of something in my nose knocked me out. I turned to face Jayle. I was carried by what seemed like four men, a wet cloth covering my nose and mouth. I felt being dragged across the streets to a car-" said Auntie Rejoice, determined not to reveal what she was doing outside Pa Seyi's house, why and what time it was.

"No one intervened?" said the Headmaster in bewilderment.

"No one! It was late. Not many people about, of course few cars drove past. Most people know to keep away from the Jibiti family. Anyway, I'm back and I have you lot to thank for my life" said Auntie Rejoice.

"No, you liberated yourself! It was incredible! You fought like a tiger! Well done!" The Headmaster said, the others joined in to sing her praise.

"What is the next move Rejoice? You can't continue the murder investigation now?" Auntie Therese said bringing in a plate of food on a tray.

"No, that place is a no- go area for you until further notice-" Mr Jaiye agreed. Auntie Rejoice shook her head from side to side. "I have to go back. Nothing will happen to me now" she said

"And why not?" Peter asked, puzzled about her certainty.

"Don't you see, now everyone will be afraid to harm a hair on my head because of what we did. The villagers would think burning down their houses is not worth the prize for touching me. If you can burn down gods then you are more powerful than any jujuman. The villagers already think I'm a powerful witch! I said, yes, I'm a witch for Jesus! I have to go find out more from Papa Ayo-"

"Papa Ayo? What has he done?" said Peter anxiously.

"We know he killed his wife, that much is obvious" said the Headmaster

"That apart I can't help thinking Papa Ayo has a secret. That he's hiding something from me. It's in his eyes when he speaks or looks at me, it's in the words he says to me. Something is missing, something's not connecting. Do you understand what I'm saying!" said Rejoice.

The whole party said in unison, "No!"

"I'll tell you tomorrow, after a good night's sleep!" she said. Peter shifted uncomfortably in his seat. "Be careful and seek help when necessary" he said

"Of course" Auntie Therese and the others helped themselves to drinks and left.

THIRTY-EIGHT

Her resolution to continue the search for Mama Ayo's killer had driven Auntie Rejoice to rise even earlier, the sound of the doorbell was an indication the day would not go according to plan.

On the doorstep was Mukai, one of Aunt Rose's maids. Seeing the maid, Aunt Rejoice instantly knew her favourite relative must be ill. Aunt Rose had led a fruitful and enjoyable life. She was recognised as one of the pillars of the medical world in the country and in her church, so she was never short of adoring well- wishers.

"What has happened to aunt Rose, Mukai?" Auntie Rejoice said, her chest heaving with panic.

"I come to tell you say your aunt is sick in hospital-" the maid began but the teacher cut in.

"What? Come let me get my keys! Which hospital? When did she go to hospital? Why didn't you use the telephone instead of jumping on the bus? It's quicker" said Auntie Rejoice.

"My mistress phone no good again Ma. The phone na ordinary Nigerian telephone Ma. She keep the mobile inside her bag Ma-"

As they spoke Auntie Rejoice's maid, Misi, brought her a cup of coffee on a tray but was waved away, "I'm going to aunt Rose. She's sick in hospital" The teacher explained to the maid. "Oh, sorry Madam." Said Misi, as she disappeared into the kitchen again..

Auntie Rejoice took Mukai in a taxi to the Teaching Hospital in Surulere where they were directed to Ward F. They found aunt Rose lying on a naked plastic mattress with no bed linen, in a small self contained side room. Aunt Rose was in a long colourful silk dress, which Auntie Rejoice recognised as a gift to her aunt many years before. On aunt Rose's head was a plain white scarf tie in a knot in front of her head. The old lady seemed dazed and confused unable to recognise her brother's daughter. Auntie Rejoice moved closer to her aunt and cradled the old lady's head in her palms.

"Aunt Rose what happened to you? It's your niece. Can you hear me?" the niece's shouts did the trick. Aunt Rose opened her eyes as recognition seeped into her eyes. "Hello Rejoice! What are you doing here?" said aunt Rose cheerfully. She explained her predicament. She had fallen while pruning her roses though badly bruised and shaken, no broken bones. She was discharged two days later.

Thirty-Nine

A good night's sleep had condemned memory of her abduction to the back of her mind, but when Auntie Rejoice arrived just before eight in the morning in Aina village, bad memory of her kidnapping came flooding back.

She doubted the man she was visiting would give her the warm open- arm greetings he'd given her over the past week. Auntie Rejoice guessed that Papa Ayo's feeling of gratitude was now turning to ingratitude and perhaps apprehension of what she might discover. She was expecting him to be unco-operative, perhaps slam the door in her face, tell her he preferred the Police to handle his wife's murder investigation. She had given a lot of thought to this investigation, done a lot of work and almost got killed in the process. She was certain of the murderer now. But until she collected all the facts she was keeping her own counsel.

When she knocked on his door and Papa Ayo emerged in the doorway, the expression of oh- not- you- again was what she expected and got.

"I suppose you want to come in" he said grudgingly and led her into the house.

After they were seated, Auntie Rejoice apologised for troubling him yet again

"It's your wife's murder, I'm sure you want to know who killed her" she added hoping this would jerk his memory. He smiled wryly as if remembering, before speaking.

"We heard what you did to Pa Jibiti, the jujuman. He certainly deserves it. The whole village is in awe of you, that is to say they respect you. The way you fought your way out! The way the whole school came out to fight for you! We've never seen anything like it before! Word reached us that, you and the school contributed bricks and cement to help rebuilt Pa Jibiti's partly burnt house. That was too generous of you, I couldn't do that! This man kidnapped you and was going to-. Never mind me, I'm an old fool. Pa Jibiti's children are rebuilding his house right now with material you gave him. He couldn't go to the police, of course! I think if you didn't escape he and his evil family would have sacrificed you to their gods. I heard you destroyed all his deities! Fantastic! But then, if the gods revenge-" his eyes widened.

"I'm here to talk about your dead wife." Auntie Rejoice cut him off. He stretched out his legs from under him almost reaching under Auntie Rejoice's chair.

Papa Ayo did not offer Auntie Rejoice a customary drink or meal. That, she thought, confirmed his anger. "What now?" he said calmly.

"I believe very strongly that you're keeping something from me. I wish-" she began before being interrupted.

"What are you talking about woman? I thought you're trying to find the murderer not poking your nose into my affairs?" Papa Ayo snapped.

"True. I repeat, you have not told me the whole truth. Do you want to do so now? The dead woman we call Mama Ayo was not really Ayo's mother was she?" Auntie Rejoice suggested, fumbling in the dark, pretending to know more than she actually did.

"Ayo's mother and me divorced when Ayo was about three years old." He revealed, looking at his feet.

"Where is the real Mama Ayo?" Auntie Rejoice said.

"She went to live in Ghana. As far as everyone is concerned she's dead also. The child never talked about his mother anymore. I beat it out of him. How did you find out? Ayo told you? Wait till he comes back from school, I'll show him how to keep his mouth shut!" Pa Ayo sulked.

"Don't do that please. Ayo is the best chum you could have. No, he didn't tell me. I saw two different dress sizes in the wardrobe when I came in with Ayo. From my deductions, one size fitted the dead woman's measurements. The other size I couldn't work out, until I figured it out. I came to the conclusion there must have been two women sharing this house one time or the other. And the whole atmosphere around you gave me the impression the dead woman wasn't your first love-" Auntie Rejoice said.

"You are a very cleaver woman. It is a pity no man had grabbed you and married you. You will make a good clever wife one day for somebody who is not afraid of clever women, mind my word!" said Papa Ayo, smiling for the first time.

"Thank you, I accept that as a compliment. Now let's speak another truth. Mama Ayo can't be in Ghana, otherwise Ayo would have mentioned it to me. All this time no one mentioned a mother living in another country. Don't you think that is strange?" Auntie Rejoice was looking into the man's eyes, reading his thoughts.

Papa Ayo looked to the ceiling as if searching for inspiration on what to say. He had said Ghana to arrest Auntie Rejoice nosing into his family business. He was expecting her to take him at his word and leave him alone. She did no such thing. The less he said the more she wanted to know. The baby would soon need feeding, and he'd rather do it in the solitude of his home than have a nosy- packer standing over him, perhaps, criticising the temperature of the baby's milk. As soon as Auntie Rejoice delved into his past he immediately realised he should have been straight with her from the beginning, he thought. It was a long time habit of his, saying whatever came into his head when reluctant to discuss a truth. He'd promised himself over and over again to stop this childish behaviour but he always fell into the same pit but full of regrets later.

"You are right. I thought it won't matter, after all, you are a woman. Women are not given to deep thinking like men. Or so I thought. I thought you would pranced around, got tired and go home, forget about any investigation. I just told you what came into my head. I should have known you'd see through me. Ayo's birth mother is no longer with us. She died when Ayo was three years old-" Papa Ayo said quietly

"I even heard that you used to fight, physically fought with her. She was tiny. I saw her picture behind the wardrobe. You must have done her some damage?" Auntie Rejoice cut in. Papa Ayo looked pensive as if wishing away the past. He sighed heavily, rubbed his eyes then spoke in a quiet tone.

"Yes, I was guilty of physically abusing her. I confess it added to her death. I feel bad. I know what you are thinking and you are wrong, very wrong. I did not kill my last wife. She saw fit to have affairs with various men as it emerged now. I knew of her affair with Seyi and one other man. Surely if I wanted to kill her I could have done that with my hands not a knife. That was too obvious. In any case I was away when she died. I was far, far away." He pulled his legs under his chair again.

"In the arms of some woman, no doubt, while the mother of your children got knifed in the chest-" Auntie Rejoice snapped, the other remained silent.

Auntie Rejoice's anger had slowly crawled out of her skin until she couldn't remain polite and sympathetic any more. She felt the man siting in front of her should, at least, shouldered some degree of responsibility for his wife's death. To her, he appeared arrogant and basking in his own importance. As she expected, he had ready excuses at hand.

Pa Ayo stood up, walked away from the chair to open the door and stood at the entrance looking out into the street. A woman passed, looked at his direction and waved. He waved back but continued to talk to Auntie Rejoice.

"You think you know everything but you don't! You have no idea what agony women put me through. I am a kind person and I've known and seen the way other men, my friends treat women and get away with what I think is cruel. Women love evil men! That I can never and will never understand-" he said, his voice full of pain. Auntie Rejoice pondered if she'd misjudged him.

"You should just love them, preferably one at a time. It will save you a lot of heartache. Are you going to tell me the truth about what really happened to the real Mama Ayo? Or do I find out from other sources? I will find out you know that?" Auntie Rejoice was like a dog with a sweet bone in its mouth, she wouldn't let go.

"You know she's dead anyway. She did go away with a Ghanaian man, a trader, who bought goods here and take to Ghana to sell. Three months later I was called to her bedside. She was full of bruises and fractures. She died a few days later. Ayo was too small to understand. I just told him my new wife was his new mother. Children are gullible at that age."

"He still doesn't know?" Auntie Rejoice said in surprise.

"No. By the time he was four, he'd forgotten his mother's face. He still thinks the dead woman was his mother!"

"I think that's quite cruel! If you were the boy would you like to assume the wrong woman as your real mother? If not, then you should find time to tell him. Show him a few pictures of his real mother. Ayo is a lovely boy. It's because of him I got into this mess in the first place. And I'm going to see it through no matter what anyone says" Auntie Rejoice said as she left.

FORTY

Auntie Rejoice burst into the Headmaster's office with enthusiasm.

"I need to speak to you immediately sir." Auntie Rejoice said to the Headmaster, Mr Jaiye, MA, BSc (Hon.), "Can it wait? I have a fifteen minutes break before I'm due for another meeting" he said.

"It's about Mama Ayo's death sir. I know who killed Mama Ayo. In fact I know for certain now who murdered Mama Ayo-" Auntie Rejoice enthused.

Tension was bubbling inside the Headmaster's stomach, waiting was out of the question. He didn't wait for Auntie Rejoice to complete her sentence.

"Who killed her? Who? Tell me please-" he yelled.

"The killer, the wicked murderer is- No, I must whisper it in your ears. Just in case someone is right now listening through the wall to our conversation!" Auntie Rejoice moved closer to the Headmaster and whispered in his ears. He sprang back as if some electric volts just surged through his body. His eyes sprang wide open unbelieving. Opened and closed his mouth then paused for breath. His Adam's apple jolted up and down as he swallowed involuntarily. He had not expected the name whispered in his ears.

"What? No! Impossible! Are you forgetting how much help he'd given you?" the Headmaster said in awe.

"No I haven't forgotten. But we must call a spade a spade. He is the killer, no doubt in my mind." Auntie Rejoice insisted.

"How do you prove that? Where is the motive?" The Headmaster's astonished voice reached a high pitch of excitement.

"I set a trap and he fell into it like a rat chasing a piece of cheese! There is a motive. And I know it. It will all be clear in a day or so." Auntie Rejoice said confidently.

"Rejoice Akintola, be careful. Those men are dangerous. You've heard the rumours going round about him. Whether true or not you don't want to be the one to find out"

"I will be careful. I talk only to you, Headmaster" she concluded

FORTY-ONE

Auntie Rejoice was boiling with rage and didn't care on whose foot she stepped. Having patched up her quarrel with Pa Jibiti with gifts of building materials, she had asked the village's self appointed leader, the jujuman to call a meeting of all villagers in her name Pa Jibiti had asked the reason why.

"Because the killer of Mama Ayo is going to be exposed today. I think everybody would want to be there, to see and hear what the murderer has to say-" she replied.

"Do you know who the murderer is?" asked Pa Jibiti suspiciously,

Auntie Rejoice stopped to think weighing up her words carefully before speaking. She wondered why he wanted to know if he wasn't involved or knew the killer.

"It will all become clear in a few hours. Let's say eleven o'clock this morning?" said Auntie Rejoice.

"I suppose it has to be" Pa Jibiti grunted unhappily

What Auntie Rejoice failed to tell the witchdoctor was that she had invited the police as well as the Headmaster and staff of St Mary's. The hope was that Inspector Gberaga would be in attendance to apprehend the killer if he had the gut, and prevent any lynching by the mob.

Everyone, excluding none was at the Akintola Memorial Hall waiting patiently before the allotted time. A platform had been erected with six plastic chairs along a narrow square table. Pa Jibiti sat at the head of the table and allocating himself the important role of chairman, awaiting the arrival of Auntie Rejoice and other school staff. The Hall was large, with a capacity for five hundred people, but now held double that, with standing room only. The chairs were arranged in a semicircle round the hall with a narrow pathway in the centre of the large space. A picture of the President of the Republic gazed down over the head of Pa Jibiti.

Pa Seyi, uncle Bita, Papa Ayo and their neighbours sat in front just below the podium. For some reason, Papa Ayo decided to leave the children at home. Ayo was capable of taking care of his brothers. He's been doing it since he was old enough to bath a baby when he was only five years old.

Auntie Rejoice breezed in accompanied by the Headmaster, Peter Rotimi and a host of other school colleagues who knew Ayo well and had been on the case with Auntie Rejoice for the last eleven days. In her left hand was the old blood- soaked mat recovered from under the body of Mama Ayo that she'd hidden. Auntie Rejoice gazed round the room. Her eyes settled on Pa Jibiti on the raised platform and ignored him. She hoped he was stewing with the blood of his past victims. She spoke to the crowd and her colleagues.

"We will sit among the people-" As she uttered these words, a cry of "Good! we love you Auntie Rejoice!" rented the air, as they clapped. Raised voices went round the room extolling her bravery. Auntie Rejoice gave a wide smile. Seeing the reception Auntie Rejoice received, Pa Jibiti slowly stood up from the raised podium, and descended the platform to sit in the front row beside the Headmaster and Peter Rotimi. Auntie Rejoice took a sideways glance at him and smiled, then she continued her short speech.

"The Headmaster will begin the session now. Headmaster?" A loud clap greeted Mr Jaiye as he rose to his feet that surprised him. He knew Auntie Rejoice was a very popular person in both the school and the village, he never for once considered himself in the same league as her. The warm welcome was like a cool breeze in that hot hall. He was not a resident of Aina, living in a house ten minutes drive from the village. He, like his staff, was hardly in contact with any of the villagers, except they were summon to school for parents' meetings.

"Ladies and gentlemen of this great village I salute you all. Before we begin can we stand up and pray silently, for the soul of the lady we all called Mama Ayo. A minute silence please" said the Headmaster as everyone stood with their eyes closed. Mr Jaiye said a short prayer then asked they be seated, before continuing his speech.

"As you know the incident of Mama Ayo's death started the investigation by yours and my honourable friend, Rejoice Akintola, one of the best teachers any school could produce. It all began when that young boy, Ayo- I can't see him in the hall. He should be here!" the Headmaster's eyes searched the hall. Someone shouted.

"He's at home minding the baby!"

Everyone glanced in the direction of the voice coming from the front of the hall. It was Papa Ayo's, sitting between Pa Seyi and uncle Bita in the front row. The Headmaster turned to him, and continued. "I thank you for that. That boy is a treasure to you if I may say so. Ayo came to school that horrible morning, the morning of his mother's death, just over a week ago now. Our kind sister, Rejoice Akintola, took it upon herself to help the little motherless boy." The Headmaster's speech was interrupted with a chorus of 'Hmmm' as people shook their heads in sorrow. Mr Jaiye paused for a few seconds for effect, before resuming his speech.

"Rejoice and the school gave Mama Ayo a good send off-"

"It was more than good it was the best funeral the village has seen!" a man at the back of the hall shouted again. As it was not a law court Mr Jaiye decided that he had to make room for interruptions so as not to appear dictatorial.

"We thank God that everything went well and Ayo and his brothers are now back with their father, as it should be. That now leads me to the main reason we are all gathered here. We will now like to hear the result of her investigation into Mama Ayo's death. And indeed I'm glad to say here is the verdict. I give you Rejoice or Auntie Rejoice as her pupils call her." The Headmaster sat down as Auntie Rejoice stood to a thunderous applause. Her eyes scan the hall and saw reporters jostling for a better view of her. She was surprised to see cameras with big letters proclaiming 'BBC World Service' Cameras began snapping her. This was most embarrassing for a solitude-loving lady. She ignored them and concentrated her mind on the present.

The whole hall exploded into the sounds of 'God bless you Auntie!' 'Hooray for justice!' She waved her hands for silence and a hush descended on the hall. Then she began unwrapping the mystery of Mama Ayo's murder.

"Thank you Headmaster. Thank you sir, thank you everybody for coming. Thanks to all the teachers. Now to Mama Ayo's death. My involvement started with Ayo running to me crying his eyes out. He couldn't wake his mother, he cried. The Headmaster kindly sent me off to investigate and report back to him while other teachers did my work and I thank them again for it-" A clap rang out from the audience in appreciation. Auntie Rejoice waited until the clapping died down before resuming.

"When I arrived at the house with Ayo I asked the child to wait outside, while I entered the house. I saw the body of Mama Ayo on the mat, her baby by her side whimpering, obviously very tired from crying-" another interruption.

Two women at the back could be heard weeping loudly. Auntie Rejoice cast an eye in their direction but swiftly continued.

"The body of a woman laid on the floor with her baby by her side as I said. I picked up the baby, wrapped it up and took it out to Ayo, then went back to school to call the police-" More interruptions.

"Waste of time!" a man in the middle of the hall yelled. He stood up to emphasise his point. "Yes, I know the Inspector is present. But what can the police do for us except to direct traffic where there is none! They're all growing big tummies while we're getting thinner, the

Inspector's carrying the whole weight of the village in his stomach!" The whole hall erupted into laughter. The Inspector sat stiffly right at the back of the hall as if on guard duty, staring at his boots coyly.

"I will now continue. Inspector Gberaga wasn't interested in dead bodies. He proclaimed it as suicide. He had decided that Mama Ayo killed herself because her husband left her to cope with a new baby. He called it baby blues. She got the blues, that is, she was depressed. True she could have been depressed, a lot of women would be in that situation. But it was impossible for a depressed woman to plunge a long knife into herself, that deep and that powerfully. Any sensible person could see that. I saw it and couldn't believe that Mama Ayo killed herself. That goaded me to investigate. I thought if the dead woman was my relative, would I just sit back and said her death didn't concern me, and just go about my business? No, I felt we all should be our brother's keepers. I set about finding the killer with the support of my fellow teachers and the Priests. And I think I know who killed Mama Ayo-" Gasps of disbelieve went round the hall, as if a shot just rang out, interrupting Auntie Rejoice's flow. She waited a few seconds before resuming. ^Before I go into disclosing the killer let me give pointers to my conclusion. No one-"

Someone interrupted her again. This time it was uncle Bita. He had his hand stretched up to the sky like a school kid, waiting to be excused for a toilet break. Auntie Rejoice couldn't understand the working of uncle Bita's mind. He was never overwhelmingly upset about his sister's death, nor showed that he cared about her pointless murder.

She thought an offer of help would have shown Bita wanted the killer caught. He stood up after a nod of the head from Auntie Rejoice.

"Why is it up to you to find the killer? Why don't we leave it to the police?" he said. Auntie Rejoice looked at him. Bita had put on weight since his arrival in Aina village. His cheeks were now rounded and glowing like the backside of a monkey. A feeling of triumph washed over her. She felt she must be on the right track if he's upset. Perhaps this man knew what she was about to reveal. This was an attempt to put a stop to her revelation.

"Because she's more nosy than everyone else!" someone else answered. The hall reeked with the sound of laughter. Auntie Rejoice strained her neck to see who that someone was. It was non other than Pa Seyi. She ignored him and continued her speech.

"I want to tell you that the one who killed Mama Ayo is in this room, sitting next to someone-" A collective gasp of disbelieve rented the air. Fear was in the faces of women. A screaming voice from the right side of the hall interrupted Auntie Rejoice.

"Can we go home, I don't want to be killed in this place!" Pa Jibiti was on his feet waving his arms frantically for attention, Murmurs went round the room until one of Pa Jibiti's three wives spoke.

"Listen to Pa Jibiti! Listen to the words of the wise!" she said looking up adoringly, at her husband's face. He adjusted his white wrapper and cleared his throat. He made it obvious that, he had an important announcement to make.

"I wan dis meeting to be put forward. 'am an old man and caint take too much excitement. Dis is getting too much for us. Let us break and continue, if yoo must, another day. Do yoo not agree teacher Rejoice?" The teacher took a quick glance at the Headmaster. He nodded in agreement to the old man's plea. But before she could reply someone else cut in.

"If we are tired we are tired there is anyone do, is there? Auntie Rejoice has youth on her side. In any case she, like the rest of we, will get old in time, if she watch herself" Pa Seyi said, his right hand on its way to between his legs as he spoke.

"It is true I am younger than some of you here. But I, like all young people in our country, respect the elders. It is also true that anyone, if only a day older than us, must be given due respect. As most of you know I was brought up in a good home, most of you knew my parents, so I respect Pa Jibiti's suggestion of postponing this meeting. The murderer had nowhere else to run. Besides, a real man will not run away from his punishment so, the murderer, I'm sure will face his crime We postpone till tomorrow lunchtime if the Headmaster has no objection-" said Auntie Rejoice. The Headmaster interrupted. "Till tomorrow"

Auntie Rejoice took a quick glance at the old wizard and thought she recognised a triumphant smile on Pa Jibiti's age- sabotaged face. From the corner of her eyes she could see the Headmaster walking towards her. She turned to face him as he approached on her left side. He smiled and touched her shoulder, as if to say 'I'm with you'

"I think you should stay with me and my wife tonight until this matter is settled-" he said, his voice full of concern.

"Why?" Auntie Rejoice replied, her eyes wide in astonishment. It was not that she didn't like the Headmaster and his family, she liked the couple very much. It was that she couldn't understand the sudden invitation and she loved her own home comforts. The Headmaster read her mind and smiled again. "I'll explain. I'm afraid for your safety. These men are very wicked and the fact that you have more or less told them you know the killer, they might, just might come after you tonight. You'll be safe with us. I know you have a security guard but we have four security guards and we'll be around. You shouldn't be alone with just a maid-"

"I appreciate your kindness, Headmaster. I really do. I know I can rely on you. But I can defend myself. I took up judo you know. I can defend myself very well. It won't be the same as the kidnap by Pa Jibiri and his family. I will hurt someone. Thank you for your concern Headmaster. I'm grateful" Auntie Rejoice replied, full of thankfulness. The Headmaster seemed reassured by her confidence.

"I didn't know you were doing judo. When did you learn it?" the Headmaster said.

"After I was kidnapped I promised myself that something like that would never happened to me again. You know the large billboard overlooking Agege Motor road in big letters proclaiming, 'Keep fit. Learn to help yourself!' The Headmaster nodded. He'd seen it every time he drove past. Almost every teacher at St Mary's had to drive pass the signpost.

"After being freed from the shackles of that wicked old man, I went in the next day and registered for an intensive course. A little expensive but worth it!" she said

"I'm glad. Let me know if you need any help. I better be on my way too"

As they turned to go the hall erupted into chaos. Villagers began arguing among themselves. Majority of the crowd disagreed with the closure of the meeting. They wanted the name of the killer. The tension of waiting was boiling over. Shouts of 'Justice now!' 'Tell us the killer's name!' 'Justice delayed-!' 'We need the name!' 'We will not go home!' rented the air.

Auntie Rejoice consulted with the Headmaster. The school staff decided the only way out was to conclude the deliberation there and then.

"Return to your seats ladies and gentlemen please!" the Headmaster shouted above the din. The crowd obeyed.

FORTY-TWO

Everyone, including Pa Jibiti, the jujuman, returned to their seats in the community hall. It seemed the hall was more packed with people than earlier. People with no seats, stood round the room behind the rows of chairs.

The crowd had hardly taken their seats before someone said, in a stage whisper, "Where's the murderer, the old wizard?"

"Pa Jibiti is one of the suspects here, one of the celebrants!" a voice said, laughing inappropriately.

"Do you think he did it, killed Mama Ayo I mean?" said another voice behind the laughter. Several voices began debating the evil deeds of Pa Jibitii, and the coming verdict

"Well, he's got all the means to do it and if pushed he'll give a good explanation for his deadly act" "He's met his superior in Auntie Rejoice!" said another.

"Pa Jibiti is evil, everyone knows that! But to kill a breastfeeding woman- make a baby motherless, when you know the father is useless. To kill a woman like that-"

"Evil has no boundary, don't you know that? He is here in front. In any case Pa Jibiti thinks he's untouchable! No one would be brave enough to point a finger at him. That's what he is counting on and has been counting on, all these years."

"If he's the murderer, nothing would happen to him! The Inspector will see to that!"

"The monster! One of these days his retribution will come." Said another voice. It seemed the majority in the hall agreed on Pa Jibiti's guilt. But who was brave enough to give out his punishment?

Auntie Rejoice returned to her position in front of the hall to a thunderous applauds, followed by the Headmaster, Peter Rotimi and some of the school staff.

Auntie Rejoice said, "Should I continue Headmaster? The hall is full and hot. And we all have other things to do. Is that all right Headmaster?" Waving her hands round the hall, she added, "They want justice!"

The Headmaster grinned. "Of course! It's your show! We are all as anxious to hear who done it and why did it, as everyone else in this room.

Auntie Rejoice cleared her throat loudly for attention. The hall fell silent. The tension of excitement could be cut with a knife. Everyone was anxiously waiting to see if their own verdict matched the true verdict from the teacher.

"Mama Ayo was killed in a jealous rage by one of the wickedest men in this beautiful village. A man who mistook lust for love. That man is among us now-" Auntie Rejoice was cut off again by a huge wave of 'ha aaa' 'among us?' 'I will leave here but not alone!' 'a killer among us!' God save us ' When the hall was hush again, Auntie Rejoice continued her deliberation.

"My suspicion was aroused when I came back from the General Hospital where I deposited Mama Ayo's body" another loud wave of sympathy went round the hall.

"I saw the children peeling potatoes with tablespoons. I asked myself where was the kitchen knife. Something started to germinate in me. I won't go into the whole detail. I also noticed Papa Ayo's silver ashtray had been used the night of the murder. The murderer tried to wipe it clean. But signs of ashes remained. The important thing is to say that the killer left bloody footprints on this mat." She held the mat up to the crowd, who went wild with shock. Some women were screaming, others were weeping uncontrollably. When everything subsided Auntie Rejoice continued.

"I saw the murderer with my own eyes. I told three men who are present here now, that the Police failed to remove this bloody shirt used to wipe hands or cleaned feet, I don't know which. Knowing the murderer would break into Ayo's house, I watched the house from across the road. True enough. The killer climbed Ayo's window and entered the house. Pa Ayo and the children were sleeping. They weren't expecting someone to climb into their house-" Auntie Rejoice was interrupted again.

"No, not at all. No!" said a woman's voice from the front of the hall. The teacher continued when the voice stopped.

"The killer went into Ayo's house to retrieve a shirt, a blood- soaked shirt he left behind" A wailing voice shouted Mama Ayo's name. A few women began weeping silently. They wept for the dead and wept harder for the living dead.

"I had the shirt well hidden so no one could get at it. I knew the killer would never think to look in the place I hid it." Auntie Rejoice was stopped again.

"Give us the killer's name!" "Yes, who's the killer?" "Let's deal with him"

When voices quietened down again, Auntie Rejoice resumed her talk.

"You will know the killer in no time. If he doesn't show his face. If he is such a coward not to voice his own sin, the evidence will name him. Listen everyone." She scan the room for attention which she got.

"I have Mama Ayo's mat here" she pointed to the mat resting against a wall on the podium. Gasps echoed round the room. Pointing to the mat, she continued.

"That mat is my core evidence. This mat has footprints of the killer. I want each one of you to come up and press your foot on each print on the mat. The foot that matches the prints belonged to the killer. Let's start from-" A voice, interrupting Auntie Rejoice shrieked out.

"OK! I kill im! She no good woman! I kill am again if she here now! Wot yoo wan do to me? I get powerful friends here. Dee Inspector na my friend, the witch-" As Mama Ayo's neighbour, Pa Seyi, spoke he took steps backwards until he got to the entrance of the hall. Suddenly a male voice rang out. "Stop him! Stop the murderer! Don't let him get away! Stop him!"

Auntie Rejoice glanced across the doorway and saw Ayo with two of his brothers jumping up and down shouting enthusiastically,

"Auntie Rejoice found the killer! Auntie Rejoice found him!" He was beaming. She had never seen him so openly joyful, not in a crowd. All the doubts she ever had melted away.

Pa Seyi ran off, chased by the crowd. They caught up with him and lynched him to a second of his life.

Auntie Rejoice momentarily stopped at the door to pat Ayo's head as she, the Headmaster, and other school staff chased after the chasers, shouting as they ran, "Don't kill him! Please don't kill him! Leave him for the Police-"

When Auntie Rejoice got to Pa Seyi his breathing was shallow and very faint. She took his hand to feel his pulse. It had stopped.

He was dead.

Auntie Rejoice crossed herself and recited the Hail Mary.

Author's Note.

Born in Nigeria she was educated in England. She gained a degree in Social Anthropology from the University of London but has been working mainly as a Chartered Physiotherapist. One Step to Murder is her first novel. She lives in London.

Printed in the United Kingdom
by Lightning Source UK Ltd.
110254UKS00001B/11